PERFECT VISION

L.M. HALLORAN

COPYRIGHT

Copyright © 2018 by L.M. Halloran

All rights reserved.

This is a work of fiction. Names, characters, places, and incidents are either the product of the author's imagination or are used fictitiously, and any resemblance to actual persons, living or dead, events, or locales is entirely coincidental.

No part of this book may be reproduced in any form or by any electronic or mechanical means, including information storage and retrieval systems, without written permission from the author, except for the use of brief quotations in a book review.

Cover photography from Shutterstock.com

Editing by Lawrence Editing

Paperback ISBN: 979-8-9864180-5-6

lmhalloran.com

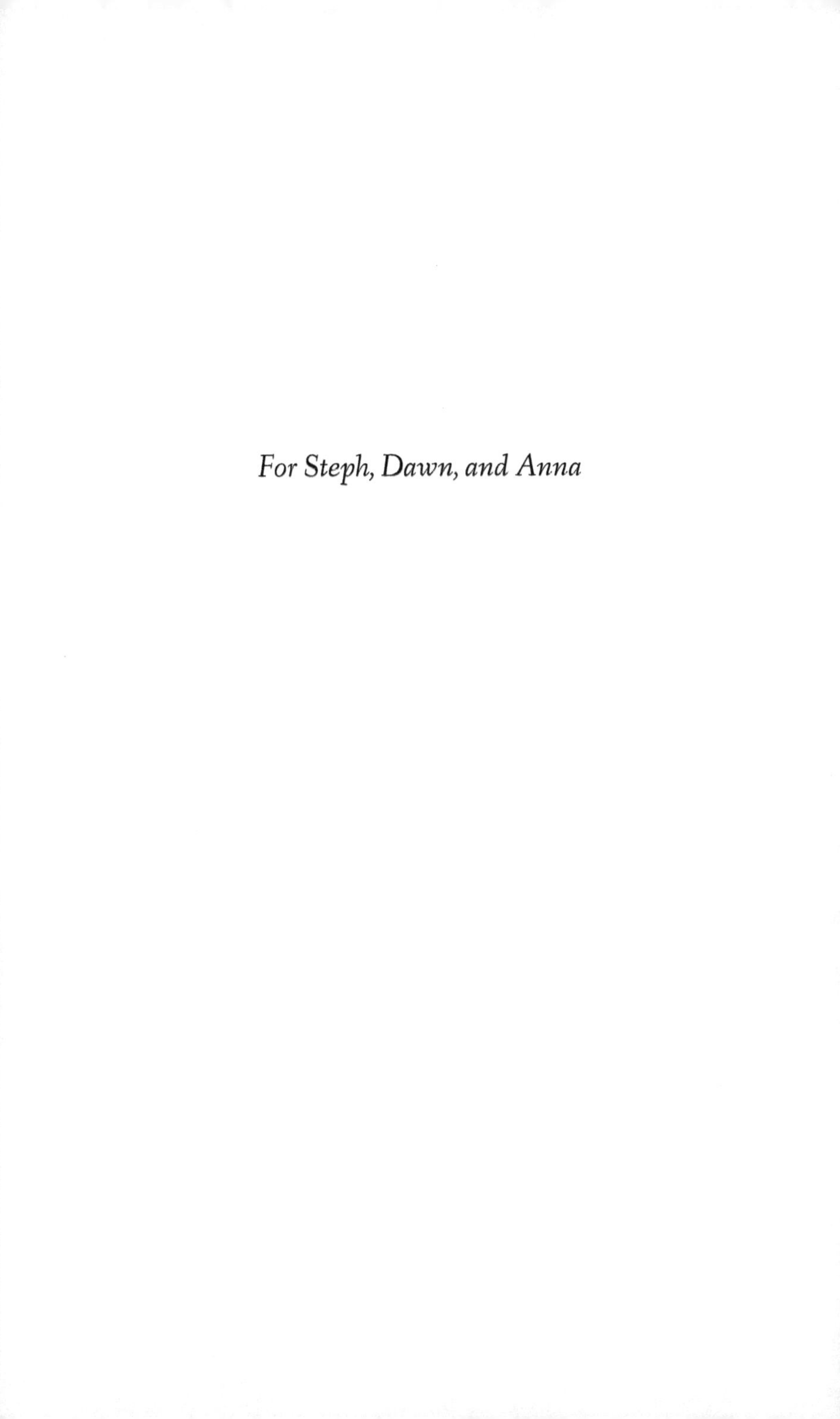

For Steph, Dawn, and Anna

Wherever you go, there you are.

UNKNOWN

1

NOW

It's one of those moments. The kind people talk about always remembering perfectly no matter how much time has passed. Flash-freeze of surroundings. Colors and smells. Like how my parents remember exactly where they were, what they were doing—down to what they were wearing—when a man first walked on the moon, and when JFK died.

Frozen memories latch to human extremes. We never hang on to the mundane—those experiences are the thinnest threads between beads of trauma or exultation. They make us real, give us life, but rarely do they define us.

We each have our own string of beads, different colors and shapes that build over the course of our lives. But every once in a while, beads are shared among many. Almost exact duplicates, save slight differences in texture or tone. Binding us together despite our best efforts to remain apart. *Do you remember where you were? What you were doing?* And everyone remembers.

I wonder if he will remember, like I will. I wonder if we'll share the same bead on our timeline-threads. If we do share this moment, its bead of space and time, mine is matte black and pitted. His is white and sparkling, lit by fires of righteous rage.

But regardless of color, they're the same shape. And their cores will hold the same sensory memories, if not the same emotional ones.

The floor, sticky yet slippery. The smell, a mixture of gas fumes, wet copper, and unwashed bodies. The sounds of women screaming, sobbing, and the click of the lighter in his hand.

As chains rattle and bladders release in terror, I'm one of the quiet ones. An empty body-shell. I watch him, and he watches me.

"This is your fault," he says.

I nod, wet my lips and rasp, "I know."

Am I horrified at my end? Afraid of pain?

Not quite.

Honestly, I'm relieved.

2

THEN

A FEW OF my mental screws are loose. Why else would I be sitting on a bench in brightly-lit hallway beside two women doing sexed-up Edward Scissorhands impressions? Halloween was four months ago.

Their black latex bodysuits have cutouts around the shoulders and waist, highlighting their toned, tanned bodies. I can't even imagine the crotch-sweat happening right now. What if they have to pee? Is there a zipper down there?

Defying logic, they don't look uncomfortable as they chat and laugh quietly. In fact, they look like they're exactly where they're supposed to be. Like they belong here. I'm clearly missing a big piece of the puzzle. Did I overlook some fine print in the email? Was there a specified dress code?

Here to interview for a bartending position, I'm wearing skin-hugging black pants, my comfiest ankle boots, and a tight black t-shirt—a nice one, flattering and new. Black on black, but actual, practical clothing. I look good. Sleek and professional, my dark blond hair pulled back and my makeup perfect thanks to YouTube tutorials.

What I saw of the newly constructed nightclub on my walk through was modern and on trend. White walls. Discreet lighting. Various seating areas—tables, couches, chaises—that in my former life I wouldn't mind enjoying on a night out. A huge, sleek bar that I can definitely see myself behind. Zero indication that the intended clientele are people with latex fetishes.

The online job advertisement had been oddly obscure, the description of the club vague and heavy on words like *exclusive* and *private*. God willing, the club's exclusivity doesn't translate to obligatory background checks for employees. Either way, the gamble is one I have to take. Despite working part time at two other bars, I have fourteen dollars in my bank account. Living alone in Los Angeles is *not* cheap.

The fluorescent lights overhead are giving me a headache, and the presence of four closed doors in the hallway feels increasingly ominous. Clearly television has rotted my brain, because for several minutes I entertain the possibility I'm in a horror movie. Any second one of the doors will open and a clown with a chainsaw will jump out.

To distract myself, I stare at the tantalizing glow of the Exit sign at the end of the hallway and fantasize about running away. Far, far away where no one knows my name. Maybe I should have left the country when I had the chance, before my savings disappeared into the pockets of impotent lawyers.

Among other things—like grief and rage—what stopped me then was one of my mom's favorite catchphrases. *No matter where you go, there you are.* In our childhood home, a sign with the words hung in the entryway where it couldn't be missed. And it's true.

There's no running from the past—it comes with you. Nearly three-thousand miles between me and the past, and it's with me all the goddamn time.

"I'm sorry, we're being so rude! We don't mean to ignore you, we're just super excited."

Grateful for the reprieve from my chaotic thoughts, I

turn toward the voice. The latex-women are smiling at me. Besides the dominatrix gear, they look... normal. Gorgeous, polished Los Angeles women. *In latex.*

"I'm Maggie, and this is Beatrix," says the woman closest to me.

I force a smile. "I'm London, nice to meet you."

"You too," gushes Maggie. "What are you interviewing for?"

"Bartender," I reply, but it comes out like a question. "Is that, uh, what you guys are here for, too?"

They giggle like schoolgirls. "Oh no," says Maggie. "We're auditioning."

Auditioning?

As I open my mouth to ask for what, the door just past our bench opens. A smooth, deep voice says, "Maggie and Beatrix, come in."

Their immediate nervousness is palpable. I have a feeling—a bad feeling—about what they're auditioning for. They stand up, smoothing nonexistent wrinkles in their latex, and turn toward the open door.

My desperation for this job takes an immediate step to the back shelf. I blurt, "You don't have to do this."

Hair flies as the women's heads whip around. Instead of the embarrassment or affront I expected, they wear twinned expressions of anger.

"Honey," snaps Beatrix, "you have no idea what you're talking about."

"That's enough," says the man, still unseen in the room beyond. "Come in ladies." When they hesitate, he says calmly, "Now."

His tone holds no edge, no emotion, but the power of it echoes down my spine.

"Yes, sir," the women say in unison.

They slip into the room and the door closes.

3

"I THINK THERE'S BEEN A MISTAKE," I tell the first person I see, who happens to be the man who answered the door of the club.

Seated alone at the bar, he swivels on a stool to face me and blinks placid blue eyes. He looks barely-legal, with an angelic face and long, white-blond hair.

"Did you or did you not apply online for a bartending position?" His voice is smooth and bored.

"Yes, but... I'm not—that is..." I trail off, my cheeks hot with discomfort.

Understanding dawns on his face, humor brimming in his eyes. "You didn't know we were a BDSMM club," he guesses.

Well, that certainly explains the latex.

My short laugh tapers into a groan. "Nope. Definitely not."

The man chuckles, suddenly looking his age. Mid-twenties or thereabouts. "Why don't you have a seat?" he asks, nodding at the chrome and leather stool beside his. "Charlie is late as usual. She's the one interviewing you."

My brain hits the pause button on my body. Frozen, I stare at him without blinking. *Is this seriously what my life has come to? Interviewing for a job at a sex club? I'm out of my goddamn mind.*

Old, stale despair crackles in my belly. I'm so used to the feeling, I just accept what it signifies—I'm a complete and utter failure destined for suffering.

The man's focus narrows; I quickly school my expression.

"What's your name again?" he asks softly. "I'm Nathan, but most people call me Nate. The Doms call me Nathan, of course. They know I hate it."

"London Limerick," I say, my voice tripping over my Kirkland name. I'm still not used to it, having been London Kirkland for four years.

"Hi, London Limerick." He smiles broadly. "Cool name. Ever had any interest in kink?"

His grin is authentic and contagious, soothing my anxiety and bringing me back to the present. *I can do this.*

Playing the game his teasing eyes demand, I tap my chin pensively. "Thinking... thinking... yeah, no."

Nate laughs again. It's a good sound, and I'm glad I could make it happen. Something tells me he doesn't smile often. We have that in common.

"Probably a good thing," he says easily. "You don't seem very squeamish, though. I've already had two potential hires run out."

I shrug, glancing toward the back hallway again. Despite my inner chaos, the vibrations of the invisible man's voice are still with me, a residue in my bones. The power in it was like nothing I've heard before, like his voice owned the very air it traveled through.

I clear my throat and turn back to Nate. "I have a high threshold for weird. Why didn't the job posting mention this little—*important*—detail?"

"Consider the surprise as sort of like a pre-interview. The bosses don't want bartenders to be a part of the aesthetic. Doms don't take orders well and subs can get squirrelly when a Dom asks for a drink. But you also can't be freaked out. Just sit, sugarplum. You're putting a crick in my neck."

The thought of going home right now and facing my empty, barely furnished apartment has me plopping down on the stool next to Nate. The padding is so plush my hipbones sigh in relief. I bounce a little in sheer appreciation.

"Pretty comfy huh?"

I can't help smiling. "What are they stuffed with, magic?"

He laughs. "Wait till you get behind the bar. You'll never have sore feet again."

I resist the urge to lean up and peer over the gleaming white counter. "The website said the club opens in a few weeks?" I ask, and he nods. "What are you doing here? And by that I mean, what do you *do* here?"

He laughs again, and I give myself another mental high-five. Something about Nate's presence puts me oddly at ease, a feeling I haven't had in a long time. Since before... everything.

"What I'm doing here is a long-ass story," he answers cheekily. "If you score the job and stick around, someday you can get me drunk and I'll tell you about it."

I smile a little, not sure I actually want to know. I'm about to point out that he still hasn't said what his actual job is when he continues, "Go ahead and ask the million-dollar question."

I clear my throat and take the bait. "What kind of stuff is going to happen here? Like, *visible* stuff."

Nate smirks. "It won't be as bad as you think.

Nudity and some light play are allowed, but no hardcore kink in the public space." He nods toward a shadowed hallway on the opposite side of the club. "Private rooms are thatta-way."

Behind us, a woman laughs. "Nathan, stop scaring her."

As I turn toward the voice, he mutters, "Told you they won't call me Nate."

The woman walking toward us brings to mind Mediterranean beaches, tropical breezes, and sex. A whole lot of sweaty, gasping sex. No latex on her. Not even much skin on display. But her lush body *owns* a pair of casual linen pants and a flowy white blouse.

"Scram, sweet one," she purrs at Nate.

I blink in surprise as Nate blushes, his chin dropping and his long hair sliding forward to shadow his face. Without another glance or word for me, he slips grace-fully from the stool and walks toward the front room.

"It's a bit odd, isn't it?" asks the woman as she reaches the bar. Moving between two stools, she leans an elbow on the counter and regards me from lustrous dark eyes. Shiny black hair cascades over one shoulder as she tilts her head.

More intimidated than I've been in a long-ass time, I meet her gaze with effort. "You must be Charlie."

Full, carmine lips curve. "That's me. Charlene

Rhodes. And you're London Limerick. I must say, I was hoping you'd be less attractive."

My eyes widen. "What?"

She waves a hand laconically. "Forgive me. I certainly won't discriminate based on your looks. Nor am I going to ask you why a woman with your professional background is looking for a bartending job. We all have pasts, do we not?"

I have no idea if she's referring to my education or if the statement means she Googled my name. Feeling like an idiot, I nod and flounder for words. "I'm sorry—this is a little..."

"Unexpected?" she asks lightly. "Yes, well, before you decide to run away screaming, let me give you an idea of what we expect from our bartenders."

Wilting with relief, I nod. "Okay, great."

"Rule number one: no fraternizing with the clients. Rule number two: no fraternizing with the clients. Can you guess what rule number three is?"

"Yes," I say wryly. "Nate said you don't want your bartenders to be 'a part of the aesthetic.' I can definitely say I'm not into, uh..."

"Bondage, discipline, sadism, or masochism," she supplies, her smile widening and suddenly predatory.

A hot blush floods my face. "Right. That."

She laughs—an airy, beautiful sound that's also

somehow frightening. "You're going to have to get used to the idea of it if you want a place here at Crossroads."

I look down at the gleaming bar-top.

How desperate am I?

Seriously fucking desperate.

I suck in a deep breath and meet Charlie's steady gaze. "Nate didn't give me details. Can you tell me what type of things I'm going to see?"

She nods. "Good question. The lifestyle certainly isn't for everyone, and we don't want employees who are morally repelled by the choices we make. This is a safe space—if you can't respect the choices of our clientele, then you can't be here."

My brows lift. "I have no problem with sex or people's private choices. And that wasn't an answer."

She laughs delightedly. "Phase two of your interview begins in fifteen minutes. We're having a small, private party and you'll be serving drinks. Take a few minutes to acquaint yourself with the bar—that is, if you'd like to stay?"

The challenge in her eyes is unmistakable. I wonder if she knows that being underestimated is nothing new to me. In fact, it's my Ace in the Hole.

I stand and toss my low ponytail over my shoulder. "What terms of address do I use?"

Another small, private smile crosses her lips. "Sir or madam."

"And people like Nate?"

"Call them whatever you want."

4

"CLUB SODA, PLEASE," whispers the woman opposite me. All I can see of her is the top of her head, as her eyes are trained on the floor.

"Coming right up," I tell her, injecting cheer into my voice.

The last twenty minutes have stacked mindfuck on top of mindfuck. Not five minutes ago, I saw the same woman before me being fingered to an orgasm by a man holding her leash.

At this point, my face feels sunburned from a permanent blush. But by the same token, I understand why this is a necessary part of the interview. Charlie needs to see if I can handle being exposed to live kink. Little does she know I grew up in a family where building teepees for the purpose of full-moon orgies wasn't uncommon.

Probably the only belief of my hippie-parents that rubbed off on me is a lack of shame about sex. That, and an understanding of the vast range of human sexual proclivities. Once, my sister and I came home from school to find a neighborhood couple experimenting with Pony Play in the backyard while our parents cheered them on. We'd merely rolled our eyes and started on homework.

But knowing about different kinks doesn't mean I'm unaffected by seeing them in person. A web search on *bondage* doesn't really compare to seeing a living, breathing man walking around in nipple clamps, a ball-gag, and ass-less chaps. At least what I told Nate is true —I have a high threshold for weird.

Handing the woman her club soda, I glance across the club at Nate. Fully clothed but blindfolded, he's kneeling, unmoving, next to Charlie's legs. She doesn't seem to be aware of him as she sips red wine and chats with a man whose face I can't see.

Apparently mine isn't the only interview with phases—nearby, Maggie and Beatrix are sprawled to either side of a petite redhead who's smoking a cigar like a boss. At the women's feet sit two men, naked but for black briefs. As I watch, a short whip flies and cracks against one of the men's backs.

I flinch.

"You'll have to do better than that."

I freeze at the sound of *that* voice. Slow and smooth. Richly textured and faintly amused. My eyes close, and in the millisecond of darkness, I hope against hope that he's short, fat, and balding.

Opening my eyes, I turn toward the stretch of bar on my right. My newest patron occupies the middle stool, and of course, he's built like a Greek God. Thick dark hair and glorious olive skin, wearing a black button-up shirt with the sleeves rolled up over powerful forearms. Full lips. High, exotic cheekbones. Almond-shaped brown eyes and a jaw I'd be happy to sit on. Repeatedly.

The thought startles me, freezes me in place. Beneath the surprise, there's relief mixed with guilt. *Underneath everything, I'm still a woman. Still alive.* But even though my husband has been gone over a year, it still feels a bit like betrayal.

When the man's brows lift, I realize I've been staring at him far past the point of propriety. At least my cheeks can't get any redder.

I plaster a smile on my face. "What can I get you?"

"Whiskey Sour."

I make the drink, doing my best to ignore the weight of his gaze following my movements. When I place the cocktail in front of him, he doesn't smile or say thank you before lifting it to his lips and taking a sip. A moment later, he sets the glass down.

"Not the best I've tasted."

Ew. What a dick.

"Would you like me to make another?"

"No. I'd like you to get a job somewhere else."

My jaw drops; my thoughts stall. "Excuse me?" I gasp.

"I don't think you're hard of hearing, kitten. If you can't handle watching a love tap from a whip, there's no way you'll be able to handle working here."

Kitten? Really?

His demeaning moniker jumpstarts an ego I didn't know still existed inside me. There was a time when I didn't take shit from anyone, when I was respected in high circles, when *no one* would have spoken to me like this.

My smile sharp and humorless now, I step forward until my hips meet the lower counter. "You have no idea what I can and can't handle," I say through my teeth. "I don't know who you are, or what your problem is, but I flinched because I was surprised. That's it."

His features twitch, dark eyes glinting dangerously. "Not repulsed?"

"Nope."

"Ah." His gaze flickers to my lower half, concealed

by the bar between us. When he looks up, a brow is cocked knowingly. "You're wet, aren't you, kitten?"

My brain short-circuits. Three seconds later, his empty cocktail glass is in my hand, whiskey dripping down his astonished face.

The thick, sudden silence in the club is broken by Charlie's unrestrained laughter. She lifts her wine glass in my direction.

"London, my dear, you're hired!"

Horrified and embarrassed—and dementedly satisfied by his reaction—I grab a nearby hand towel and toss it on the bar. Mr. Tight Ass snatches it and wipes his face. Then, propping his elbows on the counter, he fixes me with a stare that would wither a lesser woman. Or man. Or anyone who isn't fueled by crazy, like I am.

Churning with unfamiliar, frenetic energy, I smile in the way I know brings out my dimples. "Can I get you another drink?"

Charlie slides onto the stool beside his, grinning as she swipes a finger down his cheek. "Aw, poor baby is in a bad mood today. Want me to take care of you?"

Tight Ass glances at her. For a second, his expression alters. Becomes real. Human. Tired and stressed. And methinks Charlie might have hit the nail on the head— I'm no expert, having slept with one man in my life, but he seems wound up. In need of a release. Maybe Margot and Beatrix's audition didn't have a happy ending, after all.

Feeling like a voyeur in their private moment, I turn and meander to the other end of the bar. I don't have any customers at the moment, so I wipe down the already sparkling counters.

"I meant it, London," calls Charlie. "The job is yours if you want it."

Turning around, I glance between her sensual smile and the man's tight-lipped frown. Dragging my gaze to his midnight eyes, I ask, "Are we going to have a problem?"

To my shock, he smiles. Just a little curve of his mouth, but my stomach tingles alarmingly.

"Undoubtedly."

5

CHARLIE SLAPS HIS ARM. "NO FRATERNIZING."

As his eyes veer away from my face, I can't repress a shiver. *Man, he's intense.* I can just as easily see him commanding a boardroom as negotiating hostage situations. Basically doing anything that includes telling people what to do.

"Not tempted," he says mildly.

Ouch, asshole.

He reaches out and drags his thumb over Charlie's lower lip. "You, on the other hand... feel like being topped tonight?"

The ballsy Charlie blinks out like a light. Her chin lowers, her posture softening until she radiates compliance. I stare raptly at them, the towel forgotten in my hand.

"I do, sir," she whispers.

He hums in satisfaction, the vibration tightening my nipples. And Charlie's, I notice.

"Good. Let's christen Room Three. I'll be with you shortly."

She nods and slips off the stool, then walks swiftly across the club toward the hallway Nate pointed out earlier. She disappears inside. The party goes on, the fifteen or so people drinking, chatting, and laughing. I should really see if anyone needs another drink, but my feet are glued to the floor.

"What's your name?" asks the *voice*.

He's left his stool and walked around the bar to where I'm standing. I can now see the rest of him, which looks just as perfect as his upper half.

I clear my throat. "London Limerick."

He blinks in surprise—most people do. I stopped keeping track years ago of the number of times people have asked me if I'm a stripper. I can't tell what Tight Ass is thinking, but it isn't what I look like spinning on a pole.

"I still don't want you working here."

I nod. "Duly noted. Too bad it's not up to you."

Another snarly half-smile. This time, the tingles are

a lot lower than my stomach. Almost, I wish I was Charlie.

Almost.

I'm actually grateful he's a dickhead.

"Ah, but that's where you're wrong," he murmurs. "Since you're the first person to *ever* throw a drink in my face, I'll give you my name for free. Dominic Cross."

It takes a second to sink in.

Dominic *Cross*—Charlie *Rhodes*.

Crossroads.

Damn.

Given that he was auditioning the Latex Twins, I figured he was an entertainment manager or something. Plus, Charlie made it seem like his authority didn't extend to me.

That's what I get for assuming anything.

I swallow hard. "You're one of the owners."

"I am." He raps knuckles on the counter between us. "Your sixty-day probation starts now. If you fuck up, you're fired."

Without waiting for a response, he turns and walks away.

"Are you at least going to tell me what defines a fuck-up?" I call after him.

The smile he throws over his shoulder is nothing short of lethal. "No. I'll enjoy watching you squirm."

Double Damn.

I watch his broad back as he weaves through the tables toward the far door. Even after it closes behind him, I still feel the electric current of his presence. If Charlie is sex on legs, Dominic is sexual napalm. Thinking of what they're about to engage in, my already warm face goes supernova.

Nate appears at the bar, sans blindfold. Correctly interpreting my expression, he says brightly, "Sorry, but Mr. Cross doesn't do vanilla."

I don't bother with denial; pretty sure he caught me staring at Dominic Cross' ass and drooling. Frankly, I could kiss the bastard just for that. For the reminder that I'm still kicking.

"What *does* he do?" I ask curiously.

"He's a strictly hetero dominant, so I haven't had the pleasure—sadly. He keeps his rep on the down-low, but bondage is his thing."

"Like handcuffs and stuff?"

Nate laughs. "You are so cute. Bring me a Gin and Tonic and I'll corrupt your mind."

I laugh—surprisingly easily—and start his drink. "A little late for that, but I'm all ears."

As I serve him, I notice the club emptying into the distant hallway. Nate notices my stare. "Showtime."

I put two and two together. "Test drives for the rooms in back, huh?"

He grins. "Exactly."

As he sips his cocktail, I study his calm face. "Are you bummed you're not back there?"

His eyes widen briefly, then he barks a laugh. "We're going to be great friends, sugarplum. You say what you think. Charlie and Dominic need someone like you around."

I roll my eyes to disguise the swell of relief his words bring. *I did it. I got the job.* "I'm what—one of ten bartenders they plan to hire?"

He shrugs. "I saw your resume. Sure, the bosses are smart, but they don't have masters degrees. Sooner or later they're going to angle for free advice. Pro tip: make them pay."

I chuckle to hide my wince. My Masters in Journalism might as well be used to roll the mother of all joints. And I highly doubt Charlie or Dominic need advice on how to spin a story or write an exposé.

Ignoring Nate's narrowed gaze, I begin stacking tumblers and tossing used lemon wedges. "You dodged my question, *Nathan.*"

He makes a sour face. "If you never call me that again, I'll tell you."

I grin. "Deal."

He passes me his empty glass. "I'm not bummed, no. I'm a bottom who likes being topped by both men and women, but I don't have a commitment to a single dom. Charlie and I mess around occasionally." He shrugs. "I wasn't really in the mood tonight, anyway. Pour yourself a drink, London. You're off the clock."

The club is empty. Even the Latex Twins are gone, engaging in whatever fun is being had in the private rooms. With a mental shrug, I make myself a Jack and Coke with a splash of lime, then lean a hip on the counter.

"So why did Dominic hate me on sight?"

Nate messes with his hair, winding it in a knot and securing it with a band from his wrist. From his sudden fidgeting and shuttered expression, I realize the answer to my question isn't a simple one.

"Does he have some weird prejudice against people not into BDSM?"

Nate finally lowers his hands to the bar and meets my gaze. "First, don't call him Dominic, only *sir*, Mr. Cross, Cross, or Master Dominic. Second, there's a reason he doesn't like you but I can't talk about it. Just know that it's not about you, exactly." He waves a hand toward my face. "It's all... that. The green eyes and blonde hair thing."

I laugh a little. "Ignoring the ridiculousness of his

approved monikers, what are you saying? Do I look like one of his exes or something?" When he just stares at me unblinking, I groan. "Fabulous. No offense, Nate, but if I didn't need this job, I'd never tolerate that asshole."

"Seems to me you didn't tolerate him," he says with a smirk. "Even though I was blindfolded when you doused him, it's already my number one favorite moment of our friendship."

Chuckling, I finish my drink, toss the ice, and load the glass with the other used ones. "Okay, new friend, why don't you help me clean up the mess out there and tell me how the hell I'm supposed to know when to come back, seeing as how my bosses have disappeared for some freaky sex."

Nate smiles and grabs the empty tray I've propped on the bar. "I'll handle clean-up tonight. Why don't you go grab your purse and meet me in the front room? I'll pull up the training schedule and figure out when you're back."

"Training?" I echo at his back.

"Oh yes," he says drolly. "You were thrown in the water tonight to see if you could swim. Now that they know you can, they're going to release the sharks."

"Holy metaphor, batman," I mutter.

"I heard that!"

6

HALFWAY INTO MY DRIVE HOME, loneliness hits. As strange and shocking as my evening was, it was wholly consuming. For brief moments, I'd felt *seen*. A part of my own life. Now, the truth rises up to swallow me. This is my reality—solitude no longer a choice but a necessity.

Work to pay bills and eat.

Sleep and survive the nightmares.

My recent glimpse of color only magnifies the empty, ashen landscape in which I exist. It hurts like a limb waking up from sleep. Sharp and fiery. The reminder that I used to be free to feel whatever I wanted, express my truth, and follow my heart. Although I'm alive, I'm not free, bound forever in my prison of sorrow and guilt.

The echoes of my laughter with Nate tonight find and clash with younger, freer sounds of my childhood. I think of my sister, Paris, and the hellions we were as teenagers. The late-night, whispered conversations. Sneaking out to parties—not because our parents would care, necessarily, but because of the thrill. That elusive, seducing feel of danger.

Floating in memories that for once aren't painful, I use my car's bluetooth to dial my sister.

It's close to one in the morning, but she answers anyway. Just like she always does.

"London? What's wrong?"

"Relax, sis. Nothing's on fire." I hear soft music in the background, but still ask, "Did I wake you?"

"I wish."

"Damning the Man is hard work, huh?"

She chuckles. "Something like that."

Paris only sleeps a few hours a night when she's working on a case. A defense attorney with a firm back East, she specializes in class action and civil liberties lawsuits. If memory serves, right now she's defending several rural families whose well-water was contaminated by a nearby factory. The suits at the factory, of course, are denying culpability.

The fact that horrible shit happens to people all the time—and is mostly ignored—is why Paris pursued Law.

She's lucky enough to work for a firm that believes in her. Or rather, they believe in her track record of winning insane settlement amounts. But I'm terminally cynical.

A kettle whistles on her end. We don't speak as she prepares a cup of tea. As I listen and envision my sister, warmth and gratitude spread through me. We've had our challenges, but she's the one sane thing in my world.

"I'm worried about you," Paris says finally, her voice thin and whispery. I imagine her words flattened and eroded by the space between us. There are 2797 miles between Los Angeles and New York.

I clench my teeth, focus on taking a deep breath. The kind that expands the bottom of your rib cage like wings. For a few seconds, my body soars in its very own oxygen sky. This particular technique is the only useful tool my former therapist gave me.

I clear my throat. Choke on the emptiness there. What possible words can I offer? Nothing will reassure her, because she's right to worry. Even I don't know who I am anymore, what I'm doing, how I'm living and breathing.

"I'm okay," I finally say.

"Did you find a therapist yet?" asks Paris.

"Still looking," I lie, then change the subject. "How's Suzie?"

"She's great. Yesterday she said *fuck* in her kinder-garten class and came home with a nice note from the teacher. We're so proud."

I laugh so hard I almost pee my pants, and Paris makes it her mission to keep me laughing until I reach the tiny apartment I'm renting in Culver City.

When I pull into my parking spot and cut the engine, she yawns loudly. I follow suit, and she chuckles. When we were kids, she used to fake yawn all the time just to laugh at my inability to control the reflex.

"Home safe?" she asks.

"Yeah." I grab my purse from the passenger seat, then pause, closing my eyes and letting my head hit the headrest. "You know why I had to leave, right?"

She's quiet a long moment. "I do. I just wish... things had been different."

I snort with wry humor. "Me too."

"Are you sure you won't talk to Josh? He could—"

I cut her off. "He can't do anything. You know it, I know it. We went down that road two years ago, remem-ber?" I'm struggling to keep the bitterness from my voice. "No one believed me. The DA wouldn't take my case. The press crucified me. I know Josh means well, but let's be real—there's no way he'll get clearance to reopen the case."

"London..." whispers Paris. "Please, I'm just scared

for you. Mom and dad want so bad for you to come home."

Home.

I don't have one.

Not anymore.

LOSING everything isn't something anyone wants. Even those who deserve it—deserve to have their life go up in flames—don't want it. But it happens. And like a hurricane or earthquake, there can be little warning. One day, your world is full of color and light and sound, and the next it's monochrome, silent, and cold.

Once upon a time, I had a life. A husband, a house, a six-year-old Lab named Felix we adopted as a puppy. Paul and I loved that dog. Not yet ready for kids, Felix was our surrogate child. Our family.

I don't know why I think about the dog most. Like the way he drank water from his bowl—the slurping sound, how his tongue seemed to splash more water onto the kitchen tile than into his mouth. Sometimes when I wake up in the morning, in the moments before I remember, I imagine the sound of Felix's doggy snores. For brief, happy seconds, the pillow jammed against my leg is a canine body.

But Felix is gone now. So is Paul, but I don't think about him as often these days. Not because the loss of my dog was worse than the loss of my husband. Not even close. Maybe it's simply easier to give my pain to Felix. He had no part in what happened. My feelings about Paul are more complex.

He did have a part—though he was only doing his job. I occasionally wonder if things would have gone differently had I known his job would kill him. Would I have been so supportive when he brought up wanting to enroll in the Police Academy all those years ago, when we were young and idealistic and in love? Sometimes I think I would be. Other times I don't.

Hindsight isn't always 20/20. It can also be like looking through wax, hazy and distorted. People who say it is haven't lost what I lost. Didn't watch their spouse vanish in a fireball right before their eyes. Didn't see their own career crumble shortly thereafter.

Guilty people escape justice.

The world isn't fair.

And sometimes, when you think you're doing the right thing, there's a grinning devil on your shoulder waiting for the perfect moment to say, "Joke's on you!"

7

NOW

The girl next to me is one of the silent ones. She can't be more than fourteen or fifteen. Empty eyes, arms too loose around the body of a sobbing toddler. Maybe her sister. Maybe her daughter.

I don't smell the gas fumes anymore. Either I'm used to them, or enough time has passed that most of it has evaporated. He wasn't actually going to light the warehouse on fire—I knew it, even if he didn't. Even if the madness in his eyes told me there was a 50/50 chance of death.

I know men like him. I understand them. He thrives off asserting power over others. Making them weak, enslaved to fear. They love it when women tremble before their might.

But they're also surprisingly simple creatures. Greed dominates their list of motives. And killing us would mean losing an investment in the millions. Maybe billions.

I've met his kind before.

I'm not afraid of him.

He can't kill me, can't hurt me.

I'm already dead.

8

THEN

OVER THE NEXT two weeks of training at Crossroads, the exhibitionism steadily increases. The private parties grow bigger, louder, and kinkier. After a series of mild shocks—two words, *cattle prod*—I grow mostly immune. I no longer blink when an ass or other body part is slapped, whipped, or paddled. I do, however, have to occasionally remind myself consent has been given.

Now, as I'm getting ready to head home from my last shift before the grand opening, I'm feeling pretty confident I can keep my wits while working here. The remainder of them, anyway. I don't think about tomorrow, or tomorrow's tomorrow. Just the present.

One foot in front of the other, I keep moving.

A walking dead-woman.

Waving goodbye to the two other bartenders on duty, I skirt around a few patrons and head into the now-familiar administrative hallway. Sometime in the last weeks, the fluorescents have been replaced with mellower lighting, and the carpet is now plush instead of industrial.

The walls are still white and bare, though, and the second door on the left still ominous. Unfortunately, that's where I'm headed—at Charlie's instruction—to pick up my first paycheck. As I approach the door, I hear the low tones of his voice.

Cross.

My physical attraction to him hasn't dimmed, which is disappointing, but thankfully I don't see much of him. If Crossroads was a circus, Charlie would be its ringleader and Cross the behind-the-scenes talent scout. He rarely partakes in the festivities. When he does appear, it's for a Whiskey Sour and silent, brooding appraisal. Not of me, though. He's barely glanced at me since that first night.

When he stops talking, I wait a few moments to

make sure he's off the phone. Then I knock lightly on the door.

"Come in."

Goosebumps ripple down my exposed arms. Ignoring the urge to bolt, I open the door and step inside. For some fucking reason, I can't bring myself to look at him. I stare at the floor in front of his desk instead.

"Charlie told me to come see you for my paycheck." I risk a glance up, barely registering his face, before looking back down. "Hopefully not my last one?"

He doesn't speak for long enough that my armpits prickle. To my horror, my panties are damp. *What the hell is wrong with me?*

"You have a Masters in Journalism from NYU?" he asks abruptly.

Startled, my head jerks up. "Yes, but—"

"Close the door."

"Uhh—"

He huffs. "I'm not going to bite. Get in here and sit down. And stop acting like you're a submissive. It's not earning you any points."

At long last, I remember what a douche he is. "Are the words *please* and *thank you* even in your vocabulary?"

His expression turns positively flinty. "Yes, thank you for asking. Now, please, London."

My jaw drops. "Did you just make a joke?"

"For the love of—"

"Fine, fine."

I take another step inside and shut the door. Cross sits behind a sleek mahogany desk to my right. Hands clasped behind his head. Bitchy look on his face. Opposite the desk is a small coffee table and couch. Presumably the location of *auditions*.

Other than the laptop and the mess of paperwork on the surface of his desk, the space is utilitarian and utterly devoid of personality. Not really surprising, given that the man occupying the office has the personality of wet plaster.

Making an effort to wipe my previous, inex-fucking-plicable passivity from both our memories, I settle on the dark leather couch and lean back. Crossing my legs and shifting, I try not to think about whether the surface beneath me has been cleaned recently.

When His Majesty doesn't say anything, merely continues staring at me with an unreadable expression, I clear my throat.

"So, boss, why are you asking about my degree?"

His right eyelid twitches. I suppress a smile of pure, wicked glee.

Instead of answering the question, he says, "I Googled you."

I have to be imagining the undertone of embarrassment in the words. What I'm *not* imagining is the instant sinking in my stomach.

Fuck.

"Don't believe everything you read on the internet," I reply with forced levity.

"I don't," he says shortly, "but I do have a question for you."

The muscles in my shoulders coil with tension. "What's that?"

Please don't ask—

"Did you do it?"

—that.

Fighting for calm, I stare him in the eye. "Why does it matter?"

"Because I don't want a criminal working here."

Anger unfurls in my gut. I uncross my legs and straighten. "No charges were filed because the accusations were bullshit."

His hard expression doesn't waver. "And the photographs of you and Andre Romanov?"

"I was *interviewing* him," I snarl through my teeth.

With the last of my dignity, I stand and walk to the desk. Even sitting, he radiates danger—a wild predator pretending to nap while his prey stupidly saunters close.

At least my guiding emotion right now is fury—despair will come later.

I hold out my hand, hoping he can't see it shaking. "Since I'm about to go postal on you, why don't you hand me my final check and we can forget we ever crossed paths."

His brows lift. "I've offended you."

I shake my head in bafflement. "You can't possibly be that stupid. Of course you've offended me. You insulted my credibility and my character."

Dark eyes scan mine. "It's hard, isn't it? Wanting something so badly and knowing you'll never have it?" He doesn't wait for me to decipher the loaded question. "Sit down, London. I believe you."

Beyond confused, I blurt, "Why?"

In a rare show of humanness, he drags a hand through his hair. "Your reaction. You wear every emotion on your face."

My hand finally falls to my side. Staring at him, unable to look away, I have the oddest sensation of falling. Not the scary part of it, either—the freedom. With the sensation, a bit of of his Tight-Ass-mystique fades. He becomes more real.

And infinitely more threatening.

"Do you play a lot of poker, Mr. Cross?"

A hand swipes lazily across his jaw. My gaze follows

the movement and gets stuck on his mouth. *Shit, stop staring at his mouth.* A smirk tells me that my flush doesn't go unnoticed.

"No, I don't," he replies. "Are you trying to intimidate me by standing while I'm sitting?"

I consider the question, this dangerous dance we're performing. I don't want to be enjoying myself, but I am. My sister was the one inexplicably attracted to assholes when we were younger. Not me. But can I really blame myself? This man sighs and women think about his cock moving. And I'm ninety-nine percent sure it's a huge cock. Like the ones you read about but never see except in porn.

Horrified by the direction of my thoughts, I snap, "Maybe. Is it working?"

When he looks up through his eyelashes, my knees go liquid. And I have my answer. There's nothing remotely soft or weak about this man. He is decisive, exacting, and uncompromising. The idea that I intimidate him is laughable. My defiance intrigues him much as a mouse intrigues a cat.

Both scenarios end the same way—being eaten.

"What do you think?" he murmurs.

I take a step back. "I think that's enough of your eyeball-voodoo." I keep backing up, not watching where I'm going, until I smack into the wall beside the door.

The bastard laughs. Keeps laughing as he grabs an envelope from the desk and stands, then crosses the space between us. The smile on his face is short-circuiting my brain, but not enough to prevent me from grabbing my check as his hand rises.

"Thanks," I wheeze.

Cross tilts his head, smile falling, and that predatory darkness spreads once more through his eyes. With a final cataloguing of my features, he turns toward the desk. I grip the doorknob and ready my escape.

"You're still on probation, London, and for the record, I still don't want you working here."

My idiot mouth blurts, "Seriously? What have I done wrong?"

He doesn't look at me. "Another thing you can't have, kitten, is the answer to that question. Goodnight."

I'm dismissed.

9

IN THE CRAMPED employee dressing room at Crossroads the following evening, I look from the fabric in my hands to Nate's grinning face.

"Absolutely not," I say for the tenth time.

Nearby, a fellow bartender—aptly named Jack—chuckles. "At least you don't look like an extra for Magic Mike."

Beyond him, several other men I've come to know over the last two weeks give commiserating nods. Only one of them seems happy about the painted-on-pants-and-no-shirt situation, but Gary is probably more at home in a speedo than trunks.

Despite the men's grumbling, I'm not remotely sympathetic. "Can it, you guys. Every one of you is built like a fitness-magazine reject." I return my attention to Nate. "Charlie said I wouldn't hate the outfit. She lied."

Nate chuckles. "What did you expect? We're a sex club, London. Did you really think you could wear jeans and a t-shirt to work?"

Groaning, I hold up the bodysuit—if it can even be called that. At least it's black. The halter top portion is connected to the boy-short bottoms by tens of tiny, braided ropes.

"How do I even get in this thing?" I muse, lifting it to stare at Nate through the middle. "Look, your head is in prison. Like I'm about to be. Good lord, who makes this stuff? Costume shops?"

Nate crosses his legs, smirking as he leans back on the couch. "You babble when you're nervous. It's cute."

"Fuck you."

His grin widens. "Say the word, sugarplum."

I roll my eyes. "You're basically jailbait."

In a final effort to avoid the inevitable, I point at Steph, a saucy, tattooed beauty in her thirties and the only other female bartender working tonight.

Ignoring the fact that I can see her nipples through her barely-there top, I demand, "How come she gets to wear pants?"

"Because my legs aren't four-miles long," answers Steph sweetly.

"Bullshit. Who did you bribe?"

She just laughs. "Take it up with management, London. Bossman dressed us."

I flush hot, then cold.

Nate's eyes narrow, but I wave him off before he can give me any snark. "Fine. But only because I can't wait to tell *management* that I have rope burns on my hips."

Nate quickly shakes his head—I belatedly realize why. "I'm kidding! Kidding." I wheeze a laugh. "No telling bondage fans about rope burns. Check."

Oh fuck, I'm in so far over my head I can't see the sky anymore. What the hell am I doing here?

Charlie pokes her head in the room, gaze narrowing immediately on me—the one bartender not dressed. She gives me her standard angry-domme face, but I'm impervious to it by now. Everyone else, however, goes eerily quiet.

"London? We open in ten."

I nod. "Got it."

With a final glare, she disappears. Sighing, I look across the room at Steph. We communicate silently—as women do—and she jumps up.

"Boys, you look fabulous. Now get out."

Moaning and groaning, the testosterone files from the room. Nate is the last to go, leaving with a parting wink. I give Steph the bodysuit and shuck off my leggings and t-shirt.

"Underwear?" I ask hopefully.

She holds up the bottoms. "Not likely. Did you shave today?"

I swallow hard. "Waxed this week."

"Good. Shit, girl. If they didn't want you getting attention, this was *not* the right way to go about it."

I don't bother responding, lost in my inner conflict. *Why the hell did he pick this for me?* Or maybe he didn't. Maybe he just pointed at something because he doesn't care what I wear. *Why would he care, London? Ego much? He doesn't care.*

"Are you muttering about Cross?"

I blink and focus on Steph, who's trying not to laugh. "What? No. That's crazy. I was, uh, reciting drink recipes."

She grins. "Sure you were."

"Shut up and help me into this contraption."

After a fair amount of wiggling, tugging, and cussing on both our parts, I'm dressed. Or as dressed as I'm going to be.

"It's actually not uncomfortable," I admit grudgingly.

The thick, tensile fabric of the halter covers my breasts and upper chest, creating flattering lines against my collarbones and shoulders. Even the snug shorts offer more coverage than I anticipated.

Inadvertent flashing of the vag drops off my list of worries, though there's nothing remotely modest about the getup. Once I've wrangled on the knee-high lace-up boots, Steph spins me toward the nearest mirror.

She grins. "You look so badass."

I whistle at my reflection. "You're not wrong. We look like extras in Mad Max."

"Better than Magic Mike, right?" She rubs her palms together. "Ready to rake in the dough, girl?"

"Hell yes."

Chortling together, we put away our personal items and head out, our steps light with excitement.

Not until we're halfway down the hall does it hit me that for a few brief minutes, I forgot why I'm here. Forgot about the grief and rage beneath my human-shell. Forgot why I'm dressed like a sex-doll, bartending for money because my beloved career ended in death and defamation.

I forgot... everything. All because Dominic Cross selected my outfit, and the thought of him seeing me dressed this way hijacked my brain.

My steps falter and slow.

"What's wrong?" asks Steph, frowning back at me. "Feeling okay?"

I swallow the lump in my throat. "Yes, good. Go on out, I'll be right behind you."

"Okay sweetie. Hey, it's okay to be a little nervous. You'll get through it."

I smile weakly. "Thanks."

When she's gone and I'm alone in the hallway, I slump against a wall and cover my face with my hands. My thoughts move erratically beneath the haze of an existential crisis. A fissure streaks through the center of me—who I was on one side, who I'm becoming on the other.

Oh, Paul, what's happening to me?

"Second thoughts, kitten?"

I jerk upright, my hands falling like lead weights. Cross walks toward me from his office, filling the hallway with darkness and danger. The overhead lights seem to dim. The walls pulsate closer. For an irrational second, I think he's the Devil come to collect my soul.

His scent reaches me before he does. Earthy. Mouth-watering. Sucking air into my lungs, I nearly choke on lust. I want... *I want...*

Punishment.

Atonement for my sins.

Redemption.

Why I think this man can give that to me, I'm too insane to care.

"Breathe," he commands from several feet away. "In through your nose. Count to four. Out through your mouth. Two—three—four. That's it. Again. Breathe with me."

His broad chest rises and falls in steady increments. Starved for equilibrium, my body follows his lead. Within seconds, dizziness fades and my mental haze clears.

Cross nods in satisfaction. "Better?"

I shiver as cool air skates across my flushed skin. "Yes, thank you."

My voice is low, hoarse with pain. Or possibly need. Whatever it is makes Cross go very still. Dark eyes narrow on my neck and the pulse pounding there. His eyelashes flutter, then lift to expose a maelstrom of emotion, the most predominant of which is anger.

"Get to work," he grinds out.

I blink, stunned at the shift, and do the only thing I'm capable of in the moment. I flee.

10

I'M SO FUCKED.

Two hours later, that's all I can think as I stare at the man across the bar. He's... breathtaking. Chiseled as all get-out, messy auburn hair, and the brightest blue eyes I've ever seen. Eyes that are currently fixed on me with such intensity I feel skewered.

Steph's elbow in my back keeps me from foaming at the mouth. "Hi," I say too loudly. "What can I get you?"

The gorgeous stranger smiles, those electric eyes crinkling with humor. *Sweet baby Jesus.* "Your name is a start," he says smoothly.

I open my mouth and close it again. Being struck stupid by a pretty man has happened exactly three times in my life, the last two times alarmingly recent. I really hope it doesn't indicate a new trend in my life of spine-less, lusty female.

The stranger chuckles, leaning forward to prop elbows on the counter. The bar is packed with customers, but for some inexplicable reason, he commands a bubble of space.

He reminds me of someone.

Speak of the devil.

A dark, imposing figure approaches the bar, a tanned hand gripping my customer's shoulder. Leftover fear and arousal from our last interaction weakens my knees. I glance at him only long enough for politeness.

"The usual, Mr. Cross?"

"Yes, and scotch on the rocks for my friend. I'm glad you could make it, Liam."

Liam. Good name, but he suddenly doesn't seem as heart-stoppingly handsome as he did a minute ago. Not with Cross beside him. *Dominic,* I think irreverently.

I make both drinks and slide them onto the counter, hearing the tail end of the men's conversation.

"—not an option. Right, London?"

My head snaps toward Cross. "What?"

"I was just telling Liam that you're not available for play."

I glance between the men—one scowling, one grin-ning suggestively. I focus on the blue eyes above the grin.

Strangely, I don't see desire there. Only mischief. Like he's moving pieces on a game board I don't know about.

"What kind of play?" I ask for the sole purpose of annoying my boss.

Cross growls, which seems to be exactly the reaction Liam intended. He laughs uproariously and slaps his friend on the back, then winks at me.

"London, is it?" I nod. "I was merely commenting on your skin. It's absolutely lovely."

More confused than flattered, I mutter, "Um, thanks."

An empty Whiskey Sour slams onto the counter. My gaze leaps up to dark, stormy eyes. "He wants to mark it, kitten. See if it turns as pink as your lips."

A queer feeling unfolds in my gut. I force a laugh. "Well, then." Backing away, I point aimlessly. "I'll just... you know, customers—"

Racing to the other end of the bar, I leave the men to their laughter. *As pink as your lips.* He's noticed my lips. He's thought about my skin.

Has he thought about marking it, too?

Annoyed with myself—my thoughts—my false life— I stack glasses on the back counter with more force than necessary.

"Careful with that one," murmurs Steph from beside me.

I pause, looking up. "Which one?" I deadpan.

She laughs. "Both. Nate told me Cross and Rourke only go for the 24/7 types." At my frown, she clarifies, "you know, subs that *live* the lifestyle. Besides, don't forget rules number one, two, and three."

I nod, flashing her a tight smile, and throw myself back into work. But I'm distracted by thoughts I shouldn't be having—I fuck up three drinks in a row. After I finish apologizing to the last customer, a domme with blue hair and a spiked choker, a stiff finger taps my shoulder.

"Take a break," snaps Charlie.

I don't bother responding, instead nodding briefly and heading for the employee lounge. On my way through the crowds, I happen to glance toward the center of the club. There, in a sunken, circular pit, a woman is suspended in ropes from a contraption on the ceiling. People float around her, touching and teasing. Barely aware of my own body, I slow and stop as a familiar figure steps down into the pit.

Cross—in all-black as usual—looks like a devil amongst lesser demons. Wearing that cold, detached expression of his, he circles the bound woman. Her eyes follow him, wide and blinking. I see her chest undulating as her breath quickens.

My own breath quickens, my feet carrying me

forward. Closer. Unnoticed in the throngs, I edge near enough to see her eyes roll back in her head. The cause? One strong, tanned hand stroking from her hip to her ankle.

My legs quiver.

A low voice beside me whispers, "Houston, we have a problem. Methinks she likes it."

I glance aside at Nate. "What's he going to do?"

He shrugs. "Nothing, probably. But nothing can be a whole-lot of something. Just watch."

I turn back to see Dominic complete a circuit around the woman. The others in the pit have moved back in silent deference, peons before a master.

He touches her three more times. Once on the back of her neck. Once at the base of her spine. Each time, her body goes more and more taut. The final touch I don't see, but nevertheless feel. His hand slips beneath her body, down to the apex of her thighs. Whatever he does makes her jerk and shudder.

The crowd roars.

I look wide-eyed at Nate. "Did he just—"

"Make her come? Yes, London."

"Holy shit."

Nate chuckles. "Aren't you supposed to be on break? I heard you pissed off some customers."

My gaze narrows. "Does anything get by you?"

He grins. "Not much. You might want to look back at the pit, sugarplum."

I do. And immediately wish I hadn't. The devil stands tall and virile, the replete woman hanging before him like an erotic sacrifice.

But his eyes are on my face.

One mocking finger lifts, pointing first at me, then at the woman. The following movement is so swift I barely see it—his hand cracks against her bare ass. She moans; the crowd titters. Even from fifteen feet away, the bloom of blood beneath her olive skin is visible. And I understand the point he's making. If he slapped my ass with even a margin of the same force, my fair skin would turn scarlet.

Shaking for a reason I can't name, I spin around and escape Nate's curious stare, Dominic's devilish eyes, and my own body's inexplicable response. The door to the back hallway slams behind me, dampening the sensual thumping of the club's music.

Steps from the employee room, I stop, panting. Like it's on a string, my head swivels to the Exit sign.

For the first time since being hired, I doubt my ability to do this. *You wear all your emotions on your face.* Bossman was right. I always have. Once, it almost got me killed.

And it killed my husband.

"Calm the fuck down," I whisper aloud. "Remember why you're here."

"And why *are* you here?"

The timbre of his voice pours like a shot of whiskey straight to my stomach, curling warmly and sinking between my legs. I spin around, almost tripping over my own feet, to find Cross right behind me. I hadn't heard the door opening or closing—not over the blood roaring in my ears.

As I see it, my options are to either hump his leg or punch him in the face. Compromising, I hiss, "That was fucked up. Why did you do that?"

One dark brow cocks. "To teach you a lesson, of course."

"You're not my fucking teacher. I'm not your fucking submissive. I'm your *employee*."

He tucks his hands in his pockets and rocks back on his heels. Mirth alights in his eyes. "Do you think cussing makes words more persuasive?"

"Yes, I fucking do."

He smiles. *Smiles.*

Asshole.

"Now, tell me what you were begging yourself to remember. The reason you're here."

"For money," I snarl.

He grunts. "Part of the truth, at least." He takes a

step toward me, eyes fixed on mine. "Ask me why I followed you back here."

"I don't care."

I do, of course, and he knows it. His lingering smile edges toward smug. Two more steps and he's in my face, looming over me with his broad shoulders filling my vision. Blocking me from the world—or the world from me.

I can't seem to get my breathing under control.

"So beautifully defiant, kitten," he murmurs. "I'm here to offer you something."

I stare at the curl of his sinful lips. "What?" I breathe.

"The first is an apology for my anger earlier this evening." He pauses, gaze flickering to the side before returning to my face. "For a moment, I treated you as I would my submissive. Your reaction... it threw me for a loop. But you didn't deserve my harsh words."

"Thank—"

My voice chokes off as he shifts forward until mere centimeters separate us. Heat from his body cascades over me, his scent permeating my nostrils. My mind is instantly highjacked by a fantasy of his glorious, tanned, muscled body against mine. Sweat and friction and a red imprint on my ass.

I screw my eyes shut as my pulse thunders between

my legs. More than anything in recent memory, I want his lips on me. Everywhere.

His breath whispers against my ear. "Ask me for the second offering, kitten, or my hands stay in my pockets."

Annoyance opens my eyes. "You're trying to find a reason to fire me, aren't you?" I demand, though my voice is laughably weak.

He hums agreement. "Ask me."

Poised on the brink of throwing my job away for one measly orgasm, I finally remember why I'm here. Only the reason doesn't seem so important right now. It's all jumbled up with my craving for something else. Something earth-shattering and dangerous and *punishing*.

The thought is just repellent enough for me to regain composure. Turning my head, I lift my chin until our mouths are a hairsbreadth apart. Then I look into his hooded eyes. Despite the shock of what I see—desire to equal mine—I stay the course. He wants to teach me lessons?

Turnabout is fair play.

"There's no point denying it—you do it for me. I've exhausted the batteries on my vibrator once already over you. But if you think I'm going to throw away the first good thing to happen to me in years, you're sadly mistaken. Back the fuck up, *Dominic*, or I'll sue you for sexual harassment."

He blinks, then smiles slowly. It doesn't reflect in his eyes. "Good girl," he whispers, then spins on a heel.

I watch him retreat down the hallway. The door to the club closes behind him, the thump resonating in my chest. As I turn toward the employee lounge, I can't shake the feeling that another door—this one symbolic—closed as well.

A door I wish I had the bravery to keep open.

11

THE NEXT THREE months pass in relative peace. My nightmares, anxiety, and depression begin to fade little by little as I trudge ahead. Willfully surrender to my new existence.

I call this new life—this new *person*—London 2.0, which Paris thought was funny until I told her why. The new version of me is skin-deep. Superficial armor fashioned of denial and survival instinct. On the outside, I'm a confident, put-together bartender who earns great tips and makes her customers and coworkers laugh. No one knows about the darkness lurking beneath my skin, in my soul.

London 2.0 also has a budding social life, comprised mostly of breakfast after work with Nate and Steph. They've taken me under their collective wing, inserting themselves shamelessly in every aspect of my life—which, according to them, is boring as hell.

When they learn I live in a mostly-empty apartment, they bully me into a day of shopping for secondhand furniture and basics like curtains, bathmats, and silverware. After a drunken, pizza-filled evening of decorating, my apartment still doesn't look anything like home, but it does have a new set of memories attached to it. Memories that don't hurt. And my mattress isn't on the floor anymore.

As expected, Crossroads' opening was massively successful. In the weeks following its debut, more staff was hired—cocktail waitresses, performance artists, valets for VIP guests. Nightly entertainment—usually a demonstration of safe bondage or play—takes place in the sunken, central area that Nate dubbed the Epicenter of Sin. And although in the early days I was hit on and even propositioned a few times by customers, it soon became common knowledge that the club's employees aren't in the lifestyle and are therefore off-limits.

The only hiccup in the club's short history happened last Thursday night. I wasn't working, but came in the next day to the aftermath—installation of closed-circuit cameras throughout the club and security personnel to monitor the feeds, as well as a shift to an invitation-only guest list and vetting for all prospective members.

When I finally hear the full details of what happened, it sounds like a horror story. A woman's safeword was ignored in one of the private rooms. As the curtains were drawn over the viewing window, no one knew anything was amiss until it was almost too late. She was whipped so badly an ambulance was called.

"My God," I gasp. "Cross found her?"

Nate, Steph, and I are sharing breakfast at a café on Wilshire, all of us having worked until four a.m. Outside, the sun is just waking, the first touch of dawn coloring the eastern sky.

Nate nods. "I thought he was going to kill the guy. It took four people to pull him off the scumbag."

Steph shakes her head. "So freaking sad. That poor woman. I'm glad about the new security though."

"Me too," remarks Nate. "Just not the way it came about."

Setting down my coffee, I ask haltingly, "What about the woman? Is she okay?"

Sorrow clouds Nate's eyes. "She's okay. Turned down the club's offer to pay for a lawyer."

"Do you know her?" I hazard.

He nods but doesn't say anything else. The look on his face prevents me from pressing further.

"She's not pressing charges?" demands Steph. "That's nuts—why not?"

Nate and I share a glance. I don't know who the woman is, but I can suss out her motives easily enough. I cock a brow at Nate, who waves a hand for me to speak. I turn to Steph.

"I'm not saying she doesn't have a case, or shouldn't seek justice, but let me put it to you this way—I used to be a journalist for a major paper back east. My most valuable asset was my reputation. Anything that might jeopardize that..."

The frown clears from Steph's brow. "Ah, I get it. She might be avoiding the press coverage." She sighs. "I'm not even into kink, but I hate that she has to make that choice. People should be free to explore intimacy however they want, as long as it's safe. And assault is assault."

"Amen," murmurs Nate, picking a napkin to shreds. "Mr. Cross is really torn up about the situation. He truly believes in Safe, Sane, and Consensual and feels like he's failed the community. I guess he always wanted the added safety measures, but Charlie thought it would limit the club's exposure. He blames himself for not pushing harder. She's angry because she thinks he blames her. It's a total mess."

"Aw, your mommy and daddy are fighting?" coos Steph, effectively breaking the dark mood over our table.

Nate throws a packet of sugar at her. She laughs and tosses it back.

"Anyway, enough about work," Nate says on a loud yawn. He grins at me. "You still up for what we talked about?"

My conflicting feelings about what I've learned—specifically Dominic's guilt and the niggling urge to diminish it—vanish at his words. Anxiety shivers down my spine.

"You were serious?" I squeak.

Nate sticks his lower lip out. "Of course!"

"What's this?" asks Steph. "Do tell."

I swallow past a dry throat. "He wants to, uh, photograph me."

Steph's brows lift. "Why does the word *photograph* rhyme with *murder* when you say it?"

Nate chuckles. "Because our London might have been a wee bit drunk when she agreed to pose for my belated grand-opening present for the bosses. I want to do erotic nudes. Black and white. Totally tasteful. Well, except for maybe a nipple here or there."

Steph squeals and shoves my shoulder lightly. "Oh my gosh, that's awesome! Girl, I can't believe I thought you were a prude when we met."

I roll my eyes as Nate laughs loudly. "She's not even as vanilla as she thinks she is, right, London?"

I glare at him, then tell Steph, "Nudity doesn't bother me."

"You should hear about her childhood," Nate provides, "total hippie-parents. Orgies in the backyard, masturbation classes, dildo-making. Didn't you tell me your parents held some big ceremony when you and your sister got your periods?"

Steph gapes at me. I kick Nate under the table. "Remind me not to trust you with any secrets, shithead."

"Oh, come on now." Nate gives me his cheesiest smile. "We're your bffs. No secrets here."

No secrets. My stomach flips. I look down quickly, hoping he doesn't notice the guilt in my expression. Thankfully, Steph speaks up. "So what's the present, exactly?"

"I want to hang the series of photos in the back hall-way." He points a finger at her. "You can't tell anyone, though. It's a surprise, and London doesn't want anyone to know it's her."

"You're not going to let me out of this, are you?" I whine.

"Nope," he replies brightly. A club napkin covered with writing flutters to my empty plate. "We have a contract."

Steph snatches the napkin and reads, "I, London Limerick, do solemnly vow to pose for nude photographs taken by Nathan Amherst, on the condition that my face and vagina aren't in them. I will do this for free." Fighting a smile, she glances up at me. "You both signed it."

"I was drunk," I mumble unconvincingly.

I hadn't actually been that drunk last night, but I *had* just walked down the hallway with private playrooms and seen something I could never unsee. Dominic Cross, shirtless and in black leather pants, standing above a naked woman bound in rope to a high table. She trembled and bucked as he mercilessly held a vibrating wand to her clit.

The image that seared me most, however, wasn't the fierce, focused look on his face or the beautiful stacking of muscles beneath his olive skin. It was the outline of his long, hard cock against the leather of his pants.

I was angry—so angry that he was hard for someone else, that he might *fuck* someone else. Fueled by jealousy and three shots of booze, my only thought when Nate made his proposal was revenge against Dominic for the way he made me feel. Torturing him with images of my naked body every time he walked to and from his office seemed like a perfect plan.

Only in the rising light of day do I realize the stupidity of my impulsive decision. Dominic won't know it's me in the photographs. And even if he does figure it out, he probably won't care one way or the other.

The last weeks have proven that my fascination with him is one-sided. Since opening night, our interactions have been minimal. When they do happen, they're back to the borderline frostiness of our first meetings. And with direct deposit now in effect, I don't even see him to pick up my paycheck.

There's no logical reason I should think of him as anyone other than my boss. But I just can't seem to stop. I fall asleep fantasizing about him and wake up throbbing for him.

The moment we shared in the hallway after his blatant test—that stark flare of desire I saw in his eyes—now seems like wishful thinking.

Maybe I had been drunk last night, after all.

12

JIM AND EMERALD LIMERICK gave my sister and I a gift we can never repay—a happy childhood wrapped in the colorful landscape of their love. The anecdotes I've shared with Nate are some of the wildest—and all true.

My parents aren't weekend-warrior hippies who drop acid at festivals and go to their desk jobs Monday mornings, but the real deal. I'm talking free love and uncompromising personal expression and "accidentally" leaving pot brownies on the kitchen counter when I had friends over as a teenager.

They also had an endless stream of new, amazing, have-to-try spiritual vocations, which despite giving my sister and me an adventurous childhood full of travel and odd characters, also gave us both a need for control and stability as adults. To this day, my mom is baffled by how her children turned out.

I love my parents, but I'd be lying if I said a good part of my early ambition in life wasn't to be different from them. From my teenaged years, I knew exactly what I wanted. Financial security and independence. A home mortgage and retirement plan. A dedicated career that I was passionate about. A family, PTA meetings, and cheering at after-school sports games.

Everything I didn't have as a kid.

Despite my rejection of my parents' life-philosophy, my childhood nevertheless shaped who I am—or *was*. Someone who looked on the bright side and noticed everyday miracles. Saw the beauty in people and nature. Breathed consciously, was present in the moment, and expressed my passions without reservation.

The young woman I once was—ambitious, grounded, perpetually positive—is still inside me, curled up in a dark corner of my heart. She flickers there, in her death throes, as I... exist. Live out my penance. Pretend I'm a normal woman, when all I really am is a shadow of a woman who died with her husband.

My present-day pain has many flavors. Grief, shame, and guilt predominant among them. Their potency shifts day to day, triggered by errant thoughts, random sights and sounds. But losing my only, biggest dream—

the dream of my future and myself—has never dimmed. Every day, it sits sour on my tongue.

A constant reminder of my failure.

AS I WALK INTO A SILENT, empty Crossroads to meet Nate on a Wednesday afternoon, I can taste my usual defeat mixed with trepidation. The emotions are salt and copper and bitter lemons.

What am I doing here?

Why am I doing this?

"Hello, London."

The unexpected voice—not Nate's—makes me jump and gasp. I spin toward the bar, zeroing in on a familiar—if dangerous—face. The man smiles broadly, hands up in a placating gesture.

"I didn't mean to frighten you."

Hand over my heart, I wait a few seconds for my voice to return. "Mr. Rourke, right?"

He nods. "Call me Liam."

"Okay. What, uh—do you know where Nate is? We're supposed to meet." *And the little sneak promised the club would be empty.*

Liam nods toward the door leading to the back hallway. "He'll be out in a few. Tinkering with his camera, I think." At the look on my face, his eyes narrow. "Ah, Nathan forgot to mention he'd roped me into helping? Pun intended, of course."

It's then I notice the coils of rope on the bar beside him. Neat little piles of what looks like braided cotton—a fact I would have been clueless about mere months ago.

Swallowing hard, I meet Liam's amused gaze. "I didn't know you'd be here, no. I guess I thought Nate would be doing the..." I wave a hand toward the rope.

Liam chuckles. "Trust me, you don't want Nathan trussing you up."

Well, I sure as shit don't want you *doing it.*

The thought must reflect on my face, because Liam's smile softens in understanding. "I can see you're uncomfortable. Come, have a seat. I'll pour you a drink and we can chat about what I'll be doing. Very basic bondage, I assure you. I can probably do most of it blindfolded, if you'd like."

The faint, soothing lilt in his voice and his casual manner make it hard to stay on guard. I take a step toward him, then stop. "Just so we're clear, this is a purely professional... situation."

Liam merely nods. "Of course. I would never presume otherwise. Perhaps we should lay down some ground rules?"

Damn, he's charming.

Before I'm fully conscious of it, my feet carry me to the stool beside his. As soon as I'm settled, Liam leans over the bar and snags a bottle and shot glass. He doesn't ask me if I like whiskey, merely pours and hands me a shot. I throw it back without hesitation.

"Well done," he says, and pours me another.

I eye him skeptically. "You're not trying to get me drunk, are you?" I ask, then swallow dutifully.

His eyes twinkle with mirth. "I don't particularly like the company of drunk women, so no, I'm not." He leans an elbow on the counter and fixes me with a bright blue stare. "Tell me, London Limerick, how does a promising investigative journalist end up bartending in a Los Angeles sex club?"

The words burn hotter than the whiskey in my throat. Meeting his gaze, I shake my head. "I don't talk about it, sorry."

He nods, as if expecting the answer. "I understand. For the record, though, I think you deserve a fucking award for going up against Ivan Reznikov, and it's a damned miracle you're alive."

An icy wave breaks across my scalp as my stomach clenches in fear. For a moment, I'm paralyzed by the thought that Liam was sent by Ivan to kill me. That despite our arrangement, he's going to tie up the final loose end from last year. Me.

"You're perfectly safe, London."

Liam's calm, compassionate voice brings me back to the present. Away from the heat of fire, the spray of shattered glass, and the tang of spilled blood. I swallow acid, my fingers shaking as I pour myself another shot.

"How do you know about that?" I ask, focusing on Liam. "About him?"

"Reznikov?" He shrugs. "I know a lot of things about a lot of people. As for what I know about your... circumstances, you could say I specialize in finding things. Information, people, whatever suits my fancy or the fancy of my employers."

A new spike of fear propels a question from my lips. "Did he pay you to find me?" I ask, my legs tingling with the urge to run.

"No, God no. I wouldn't work for that madman if he offered me the bloody moon." Liam sighs, his forehead creasing with remorse. "I'm truly sorry for frightening you, London. Some of the information I gathered made it seem... well..."

Understanding dawns, and with it, a bitter dose of memory. "That I was involved in what happened to my husband," I finish.

Liam winces, but nods.

Familiar footsteps echo behind me. Nate's voice

rings out, vibrating with censure. "Are you getting my model drunk?"

Liam swings on his stool, a shit-eating grin firmly in place, no sign of our conversation in his relaxed posture. "Just getting to know London a bit. She has a weakness for Irish Whiskey." He winks. "And Irish men."

Nate groans and studies my face. "Are you okay?"

I nod, the movement oddly delayed, like I'm not occupying my body but watching it. Nate frowns, not buying it. *You wear every emotion on your face.*

I force a smile. "I'm fine, really. It's now or never."

Nate grins, rubbing his hands together. "Excellent. Let's get this show on the road."

13

WHEN I RETURN to the bar after changing into a thong and robe, Nate and Liam are already setting up. The lattice above the Epicenter is lowered. Liam is busy tying ropes, his hands moving swiftly as he creates some complex rigging system. Nate is testing lighting, using a remote to adjust the overhead spotlight. The rest of the club is still shadowed and empty, but we only have an hour before people start arriving for the early evening shift.

"Ready?" calls Nate when he spots me walking toward him.

"As I'll ever be."

If my parents could see me now...

...they'd be thrilled.

The thought twitches my lips, a welcome reprieve

from lingering echoes of my conversation with Liam. I have questions for him, but they'll have to wait. At least I know he's not going to kill me or deliver me back to Ivan. I can't explain it, but I trust him.

"Okay, London, come on down." Liam's voice is brisk and professional. "As this is your first experience with bondage, I'll walk you through each step. If you feel uncomfortable at any point, please tell me."

Stepping down the short flight of stairs into the sunken area, I begin to pull off my robe. "Is it going to hurt?"

Liam laughs. "Not unless you want it to."

"What the fuck?" bellows a voice behind me.

I gasp, clutching the lapels of my robe over my bare chest. Nate almost drops his camera as he jumps out of the pit and starts babbling at the tall, dark figure just outside the spotlight's glow.

"Hi! What, uh, are you doing here? I thought you weren't coming in until later. This is nothing. Nothing's happening. Just, um—"

"Shut up, Nathan," snarls Cross.

My wide eyes veer to Liam, who doesn't look alarmed in the least. Quite the opposite—he looks downright giddy.

"Dominic!" he says with a jaunty wave. "Good timing. Want to help?"

Silence reigns for three seconds. Then: "London, come here."

Cross's voice is liquid-smooth and utterly controlled. My legs vibrate with the need to obey even as my mind rebels. The pieces of me stretch apart, bound by brittle glue. When those bridges snap, I'm either going to scream, cry, or fall down dead.

Liam murmurs, "Just give in to it. Embrace it."

My feet obey before my mind can catch up. I walk up the stairs, past a shocked Nate, toward the looming darkness of Dominic Cross. I don't look up—can't seem to lift my gaze past his belt buckle. But my mind is quiet. Oddly peaceful.

"Follow me, please."

He doesn't wait for a response before striding across the club. I follow, my bare feet silent, my body relaxed and muscles loose.

Cross doesn't stop at the door leading to his office but continues on to another door at the far rear of the club. I've seen workers come through it with deliveries before but have never been inside. Cooler air skates over my exposed legs as I follow Cross down a short hallway. At the end is a roll-up metal door, currently down and locked. There's only one other feature in the hallway—a black door with gold lettering proclaiming *Private.*

Cross produces a key and unlocks the door, opening it on a narrow stairwell of rich wood and white walls.

"Up you go."

My skin prickles with mingled anxiety and anticipation. Questions ricochet in my head but my tongue stays glued to the roof of my mouth. Clutching the short, silk robe over my chest, I step past him and up. At the top, I pause in surprise.

Cross moves past me, his black dress-shirt whispering against my robe. His scent lingers, tendrils of it curling around my body. I watch him stride across the lavish loft to a galley kitchen.

Without turning, he says, "I'm going to pour myself a drink. Please make yourself comfortable on the couch. To answer your question, yes, I live here. No, I don't publicize the knowledge, and yes, I'm livid right now so you're making the right choice by treading lightly."

He doesn't know what I'm feeling. This sweet surrender, this relief. What I want from him. What I need.

Hell, I don't have a clue what I need. But for the first time in so, so long, I'm one-hundred percent in the present moment. And until Cross tells me otherwise, I'm staying right here, right now.

I make it five steps across the loft before my knees weaken. *Give in,* Liam said. So I do, allowing gravity to carry me to the ground. I sit back on my heels. Bowing my head, I close my eyes and rest my hands in my lap. As I mimic the way I've seen submissives present to their Doms, I'm surprised by how natural it feels. How freeing.

Silence looms against the backdrop of muted street noise, the hum of a refrigerator, and a soft *tick-tick* of a wall clock. Not until my knees begin to hurt on the hardwood, until my calm begins to buckle, until every breath I take becomes overly loud, does Cross move.

Slow, measured footsteps approach me. Circle around me. My skin comes alive at the phantom pressure of his gaze. By the time he stops directly before me, I'm trembling.

"Open your eyes, kitten."

I obey, blinking several times before he comes into focus. Or rather, his *crotch* comes into focus. One broad hand sits on the outside of his zipper, cradling the bulge beneath it. Before I can react, before I can even consider what this means, his nimble fingers reach for the zipper.

"I'm going to fuck your mouth," he says mildly. "When I come, you'll swallow every drop."

"Wha—wait," I gasp, jerking back and falling on my ass. My robe falls open but I'm too stunned to grab it. With humiliation rising like a tidal wave inside me, I stare up at him.

The smile on his face is cruelty personified. Condescending, yes, but more, too... worse. It's pitying.

His head tilts appraisingly, dark eyes gleaming like twinned black holes. "Don't want it after all, do you? That's too bad. I've thought about that pretty mouth choking on my dick." He sighs and turns away. "Get off my floor, London, and cover your tits. We need to talk."

Fueled by adrenaline and rage, I scramble to my feet. Since it's likely I'm about to be fired, I throw caution out the same window my pride plummeted through seconds ago.

"Fuck you, Dominic! Who do you think you are? Is that how you treat your subs? No wonder you can't find a steady one!"

Between one breath and the next, he's in front of me, towering over me with a sucking storm in his eyes. "That little tirade just proved my point. You're not cut out for this life. If you were, I'd be sliding down your throat right now."

The words add salt to my open wound—horrifyingly, tears burn in my eyes. My voice emerges thin and shaking. "You didn't give me any warning. Aren't people supposed to discuss everything beforehand? I've never *done* this before!"

"And you never will," he snarls, then spins away

with fingers clenched in his hair. "Goddamnit, London. Just get out."

"Why?" I yell at his back. "Why are you doing this to me?"

He pivots on a heel, facing me. The look on his face makes me take a swift step back. *Lethal* comes to mind. He blinks, and the momentary monster is gone, replaced by a tired man.

"Do you even know what you're asking for?" he asks, voice raw and threadbare. "I'm not like Liam—like a lot of other Doms—who get off on submission and a little discomfort. I'm a *sadist*, London."

The word hits my ears, then my mind, fitting like a key into a lock. "You like giving pain," I whisper.

He nods curtly, gaze dropping to my mouth before flickering back up. "To be perfectly honest, if I thought you could handle it, I'd have bruised you by now. You're exactly my type."

"Bruise me," I echo dumbly. "Whip me?"

He nods. "Among other things. I prefer flogging."

"Burn me?"

"Possibly. But I'm careful to not leave scars."

I swallow. "Cut me?"

He pauses. "Bloodletting isn't my favorite, but I've done it."

That elusive feeling of earlier is back, threading like

mist through my mind and body. "Can you orgasm without inflicting pain?"

He draws a swift breath, then coughs out a surprised laugh. "Yes, London. Being a sadist doesn't necessarily mean I have sexual dysfunction. Is Twenty Questions over yet?" His voice is dry.

"Almost. I have one more question."

"What's that?"

Here goes nothing.

"Will you hurt me?"

14

"HE KICKED ME OUT."

"What?" barks Nate, lunging toward me from the other side of my living-room sofa. He grabs my arms, eyes comically wide. "What do you mean he kicked you out? What did he *say*?"

I take another gulp of wine. "Literally nothing. He shook his head and pointed at the door. Like I was a dog or a freaking solicitor."

Nate eyes me like I might sprout wings or grow a tail any second. "Why are you smiling? Did he break you?"

I laugh. "No. I'm fine. Embarrassed, obviously, but weirdly relieved."

"Because you unburdened yourself," says Nate softly, his eyes revealing far more wisdom than his age should afford. "There's nothing wrong with wanting to be dominated."

"I know. In theory, at least." I sigh, slumping into the couch and turning my head toward him. "I didn't used to be this way. My husband and I had a great, *vanilla* sex life. Do you think him dying rewired my brain?"

It's the closest I've come to admitting I feel responsible for Paul's death, and Nate picks up on it with a sad smile. "Maybe. But I do know that sometimes submissive are born, and sometimes we're made. In the end, we all want the same thing—freedom from the true bondage, that of our thoughts, our fears, our emotions."

"That's poetic," I muse. "Is it true?"

Nate's smile sheds its shadows. "As true as true can be. If you want someone to teach you the ropes, introduce you to some good Doms—"

"I'll pass," I interject, softening the words with a smirk. "I'd rather keep my job, which shockingly enough I still have."

Nate shakes his head, his frustration evident. "I really don't know why Cross treated you that way. I've only ever heard glowing praise from satisfied women about his methods. What he did—there's no excuse for it, London. If I was braver, I'd tell Charlie what happened."

"Please don't," I say quickly. "If Cross intended to humiliate me and make me think twice about submission, he succeeded. But if he wanted me to feel shame about exploring my desires? He missed the mark by a mile. Hippie parents for the win."

Nate finally relaxes, swinging his feet onto my new coffee table. "Damn straight. I love your parents and I don't even know them. Do you think they'll adopt me?"

I laugh. "Definitely. Nate Limerick has a nice ring to it."

He smiles wistfully. "It does."

We sit in companionable silence for a few minutes, our private thoughts dancing over soft music from nearby speakers. The sting of Cross's rejection has lessoned, due in large part to two glasses of wine and Nate's company. Thankfully, neither of us are working tonight. I don't know if I could have handled seeing Cross again so soon after what happened in his loft.

"Nate?"

"Hmm?"

"If he's really what he says he is—a sadist—then wouldn't he have enjoyed humiliating me?"

"Probably," he replies, then hesitates. "On the other hand, it's not black and white. If he wasn't in a Dom headspace, maybe he was just being an asshole."

I've thought about that pretty mouth choking on my dick.

Oh, he was in a Dom headspace, all right, but I'd bet

the life I have left that he didn't enjoy it. Not for one second. My biggest hint being his lack of arousal, even with his zipper right in front of my face.

"There's a lot you don't know about Cross."

Blinking away my thoughts, I ask, "Anything you'll tell me?" My voice is teasing, but my gut clenches in anticipation. I want to hear something. *Anything* that helps me understand him. That reconciles my sick fascination with the man—a fascination that sadly burns just as bright as it did before this afternoon.

I want to understand *why* he did what he did. The impulse isn't new to me—it's part of what made me a great journalist—and I guess I can be grateful that I'm feeling it. An echo of my old self.

"I want to tell you one thing in particular, but I'm not sure you'll want to hear it. But it's not like it's a secret or anything."

I chuckle a little. "That sounds ominous."

"Yeah, kinda." He fights a private war with his conscience, then grabs my free hand. "You know how I mentioned you look kind of like his ex?" I nod. "Well... that ex was his wife."

"Cross was married?" I ask stupidly.

Nate nods. "I've never seen a man so completely besotted in my life. Obsessed, even. She hung the moon and stars in his eyes."

I eye him carefully. "Why do you sound bitter?"

"Because she used him. Baited him, trapped him, and wrecked him."

I stare at him blankly. "Wow. It's really hard to imagine *anyone* doing that to Cross."

Nate sighs. "Ashley was good, I'll give her that. Played submissive perfectly. It wasn't until they were married for a year that she dropped the act. Refused to let him top her anymore. I don't know all the details, but as you know, I'm good at listening and observing. She waged some serious psychological warfare. Made him think he was a monster. Sick. Threatened to tell people that he was abusive if he didn't seek 'sexual rehabilitation.' He did everything she asked, and she still left him in the end."

"Good God," I whisper. "Why would she do all that? For what possible reason?"

Nate's brows lift. "Haven't you ever Googled him?"

I shake my head.

"Oh, sugarplum, you're seriously the cutest. Cross is ex-Special Forces. Basically GI Joe. Left the military ten years ago and founded Saber Security."

My jaw drops. "The international private defense company?"

He nods. "Yep. Cross started it because he wanted

the freedom to help struggling governments and nations during crises without dealing with miles of red tape."

"What happened?"

"His *wife* happened. His brother David runs the company now, and he turned it into what it is today—a business that capitalizes on war. And shitting on Cross's dream wasn't even the worst thing David did. Guess who he married after the divorce went through and Cross was deemed *unstable* by the Board of Directors?"

My jaw dislocates. "Shut the fuck up. His brother married his ex-wife? Was it a whole setup to push him out of the company?"

He shrugs. "I don't know, but what does your journalistic spidey-sense tell you?"

I sink back into the couch, stunned and deflated. "That Cross's dislike of me suddenly makes more sense. Do I really look like her?"

"Honestly?"

"Yes, honestly!"

He grins. "You're way hotter."

THAT NIGHT as I lie in bed, I think of Dominic and my heart hurts for him. I can't imagine the pain he must have felt having someone he loved—*someone he married* —betray him so profoundly.

Yes, I'm still embarrassed, and angry at the way he treated me, the undeserving lesson he taught me—to be careful what I wish for. But if I've learned anything in the last year and a half, it's the truth is rarely cut and dry. People are rarely black and white, either. Not one- or even two-dimensional, but living, breathing channels of energy and emotion, their experiences strung together, creating a design of identity more complex than the mind can comprehend.

In a weird way, knowing what I now know about Dominic's past makes me feel a kinship with him. We both had our dreams ripped away by others.

As I drift to sleep, I allow myself a few minutes to think of Paul. To appreciate the love he gave me, and the short but happy life we had together. We had our ups and downs like any couple, but at the end of the day, our love for each other was unconditional. He would never have betrayed me as Dominic's wife did him.

PAUL and I married at nineteen, just four months after meeting at NYU. My parents were supportive. His were not. Old Money from Greenwich, Connecticut, they couldn't fathom their son marrying a girl from podunk, upstate New York. Nor did they approve of Paul's decision to drop out of college and enter the Police Academy. Maybe that's why I wholeheartedly approved, having been subtly conditioned toward rebellion against social norms by my eccentric parents. Who the fuck knows.

I was so young. Stupid. Full of aspirations about doing good in the world. Paul was terminally optimistic about his career path. Arresting criminals. Making the world a safer place. As disapproving as his parents were, they nevertheless pulled strings. Big strings. Their son wasn't going to be a run-of-the-mill beat cop if they could help it.

Right before Paul planned to officially withdraw from NYU, he begrudgingly accepted an offer from his father to play golf. It was no accident that they were joined by Rudolph Schultz, head of the New York branch of Homeland Security. Those eighteen holes would change Paul's life—our lives—forever.

Despite their role in altering his career trajectory, Paul's parents still blame me for his death. Most of the time, I believe I deserve their loathing. But what they don't know is how frightened I was when Paul came home that day full of bright-eyed passion about going after terrorists, drug cartels, and sex traffickers as an undercover ICE agent working with Homeland Security.

In their quest for Paul's longterm stature, his parents never grasped one of the fundamental facets of his personality. Specifically the focus—or limitation, in their eyes—of his ambition. Paul didn't want to sit behind a big desk and issue orders, or stand behind a microphone and spew rhetoric to the masses. He wanted action. To be in the middle of events. To exact *real* change.

I couldn't stop him. My fear didn't sway him. But over the years, while he completed his degree and started his training, my trepidation faded. I'd found my own trajectory in studying Journalism. I had my own plans. And for a while, we were happy. Paul's parents made sure he got the job he wanted, working in New York, and I landed my own dream job at the New York Independent, a small newspaper that specialized in investigative journalism.

We were both bound to our separate passions and each other, wearing matching cement boots we couldn't feel. The only difference is Paul's life ended and I'm still breathing.

But I'm still underwater, in the murky dark.

15

NOW

"You have two choices."

The rough, accented voice jars me from the empty space between sleep and waking. My head lifts defiantly, my gaze narrowing on the face of the man crouched before me. He's at the top of the food chain of guards. I think of him as Cinder because it looks like someone once hit him in the face with a cinderblock.

"No thanks," I rasp.

He grins, eyes flat and pitiless. "I'm going to tell

you your options, then let you think about it for twenty-four hours." A blunt fingertip taps my nose. I recoil, which only makes him laugh. "First option is hot shower, massage, food, a bed. Nice dress, pretty heels, makeup, the works. You play nice and get rewarded. Find a high-roller to buy you, make us a pretty penny. You live glamorous life keeping him happy."

"Never," I seethe.

"Tut-tut. Wait for me to finish. You might think differently when you hear the alternative."

Beside me, the teenager shifts subtly away, responding to the rising menace in our captor's voice. She shushes the toddler when she moans. To my relief, he doesn't look at them.

"What's Option B?"

His false smile vanishes. "I make you choose one of your companions here. My men and I—we rape her, then kill her in front of everyone."

Blackness swarms on the edges of my vision. I suck in air past a hammering heart. Around me, women shudder and cower together. Someone sobs.

"No," I gasp.

He rises in a smooth pulse of muscle. "Like I said, you have a choice. Twenty-four hours, little shlyukha."

Little whore.

A minute later, a door slams and a heavy lock slides closed. The space erupts in chatter, a mixture of languages from English to Spanish to Chinese to Russian. Eyes watch me. Hopeful eyes. Fearful eyes.

"What are you going to do?"

They're the first words the teenager has spoken, to me or anyone else. Her eyes—unblinking, empty—fix on my face.

"Don't worry," I whisper.

She blinks and looks away.

16

THEN

I'M NOT five steps into Crossroads the next evening when I'm summoned to Charlie's office. The messenger is Steph, and from her expression I surmise I'm not about to be offered a raise. After an encouraging squeeze of my arm, she wishes me luck and disappears.

As I walk toward the back hallway—and potentially my last paycheck—I can't summon remorse. Sure, my impulsivity yesterday might have just gotten me canned, might force me to move if I can't find another job by the end of the week, but I still don't regret what happened.

That feeling, for brief minutes, of relief. Or as Nate called it, freedom from inner-bondage.

I remind myself that working at a sex-club was never my career of choice, but rather a bandaid on bills until I could figure out how the fuck to live again. I'm not there yet—don't know if it's even possible—but Crossroads can't be the last house on the block for me. Whatever happens right now, I'm not giving up. No way in hell I'm going back to New York.

In the hallway, I glance past Charlie's door to the next, wondering if Cross is in his office right now. If he knows what's happening or feels guilty. Then I concede that it's probably better this way—if he apologized, it would make everything harder. My emotions where he's concerned are tangled up enough already.

I knock and Charlie calls, "Come in!"

Her office couldn't be more different from her partner's, the decor matching the theme of the club itself—all white, gold, and silver. Silk tapestries, a delicate gold chandelier, and a gleaming glass and metal desk opposite plush floor cushions. It's a bright, serene, harem-esque cave perfectly suited for making visitors feel welcome. A gilded trap to trick the unsuspecting into letting their guards down. But Charlie isn't nearly as scary as she thinks she is.

I've been in a *real* predator's trap.

My mind flashes back to a room many times the size of this one, with thousand-dollar rugs and custom furniture. With open windows letting in the mingled scent of roses and jasmine along with brilliant natural light. Priceless artworks. An entire wall lined with books. A place of culture and refinement. A place I first loved, then loathed.

Forcing the foul memory from my mind, I close the door and face Charlie. "You wanted to see me?" I do my best to sound normal, not like I just had a flashback that made my skin crawl and armpits damp. I do my breathing exercise, imagining my lungs are gills.

I'm okay.

Charlie, sitting behind her desk, looks up from some paperwork. She has her poker-face on, but her eyes are tight at the corners. She's either too focused to notice my disquiet, or I'm getting better at hiding it.

"Have a seat, London."

I glance at the floor pillows. "I'm okay standing, thanks. What's up?"

Her lips pinch. "I heard a rumor. A very distressing rumor that you've broken one of the cardinal rules of Crossroads. Do you remember rules one through three?"

I wilt inside. *There goes my job.* "No fraternizing with the clients."

She cocks her head. "You're not going to deny it?"

I shrug. "What would be the point? I'm assuming Cross told you his version of what happened."

Her brows skyrocket. "What does Dominic have to do with this?"

My brain slips sideways. "What? What are you talking about?"

Charlie sits forward, disturbing papers. A pen clatters to the floor. "I'm talking about *Liam Rourke*. Now tell me what the hell happened with Dominic." Her voice is clipped and icy, the tip of an iceberg hiding miles of ruin-your-vacation feelings.

I just stepped into a shit-pile of my own making.

"Uhh—"

Charlie's gaze flies over my shoulder a moment before a dark voice says, "Nothing happened. She's likely referring to when I interrupted them and hauled her out of there for a reprimand. Which you know, since you watched the video feeds."

Oh my God. The new security cameras. Nate and I are officially idiots.

"Forgot about those, did you?" Cross murmurs for my ears. His voice is closer than before, though I might be imagining the heat of his body on my spine.

Charlie's eyes narrow, glittering as they veer between me and the man I haven't turned to look at. I can barely keep my breathing under control as it is. The last thing I need is to see his eyes, his stupidly perfect face.

"And how did you reprimand her?" Charlie asks him tightly.

"I told her to suck my dick. She quickly decided she didn't want to play at being submissive, after all. Lesson learned."

Charlie sputters in unfeigned surprise. I gasp, hot mortification flooding my veins. Mortification and *anger*. My weakness forgotten, I spin and glare up at Cross's expressionless face.

"You have no right to make it sound that way! I wasn't doing anything wrong."

Darkness flickers in his eyes. "Weren't you? You're not a submissive, London. You *thought* you might like it, but when push came to shove, you were just pretending."

I gape. "Do you have selective amnesia?"

Will you hurt me?

The words ricochet like a bullet between us, taking pieces of us and leaving wounds behind. Exposing the ugly truth—our fear of what we want, tied inexorably to our primitive needs.

Cross's eyes drop to my throat. Mine veer to his jaw, clenched tight, a muscle ticking as he grinds his teeth.

"You could have been kind," I hiss.

"Yes, I could have been," he grinds out. "But that's not what you want, is it?"

The blow lands squarely, taking my breath. "You don't have a fucking clue what I want." My voice wavers. "You're too wrapped up in your self-hatred to see it."

His eyes widen, then narrow with a look that makes me want to run. Fast and far and immediately. But my feet are glued to the ground. Even when he steps so close the toes of our shoes connect, I don't move.

With my job gone, I've got nothing left to lose. I don't even know why I'm arguing—what I'm fighting for—but it feels more important, bigger and more real than anything in recent memory. *More than anything since—*

"Say it again." His voice drops like a machete through my thoughts.

"Say what, exactly? That hating yourself is no excuse for treating me poorly?"

"Whoa!" shouts Charlie. "Mind clueing me in on what the *fuck* you two are talking about?"

"No," snaps Cross.

Without breaking eye contact with Cross, I tell Charlie, "I asked the oh-so-respected Dominic Cross to hurt me. Safely, sanely, and consensually. Because the more I think about it, the more I want it. *Need it.* And he refused because he's had his head up his ass so long he can't see I'm not his fucking wife."

17

"I'D SAY THAT WENT WELL."

I lift my arm long enough to give Charlie a disbelieving look, then relax again into the pile of pillows. I shouldn't have hated on them earlier; they're ridiculously comfortable. A surface depresses near my hip as Charlie's weight settles.

"Why didn't you tell me?" she asks softly.

I snort. "Because you're scary and I didn't want to lose my job. And frankly, I didn't really know *what* I was feeling."

Charlie sighs. "I'd never, ever stand in the way of someone wanting to explore kink. But London, listen to me." She waits for me to lower my arm and meet her gaze. "Dominic is in a tough place. He hasn't had a steady sub since Ashley, and that was years ago."

"I was a real asshole about his wife, wasn't I?"

She smirks. "He needed to hear it. But since you know some of what happened, maybe you can understand why it's hard for him to trust it when a woman offers him what he most needs. Something he denies himself."

The words bring me upright. "But—I saw him in one of the rooms. With a sub. And don't you…"

"Something you don't understand—yet, at least—is it's not always about sexual gratification. In Dominance and submission, a huge part is the emotional experience, a catharsis found for both parties through the transfer of control. What I'm saying is, Dominic hasn't let himself be physically satisfied by a scene in a long time. Honestly, I'm not even sure he's being fulfilled emotionally anymore. He's still an amazing partner, one of the best Doms I've ever been with, but something's missing. That bitch took his mojo."

"What does that even mean?"

Her brows lift, a teasing glint entering her eyes. "He doesn't have intercourse with his partners. Not even me —unfortunately."

For the third time in an hour, my jaw hits the floor. "Are you saying he's…" I can barely get the next word out, "celibate?"

She laughs. "If your definition of sex is penis-enters-vagina-and-ejaculates, then yes, I suppose Dominic is celibate." I flush, feeling foolish, and she touches my hand gently. "Don't be embarrassed. I can see why Nate likes you, why Dominic does—even though he probably doesn't want to. You're curious, straight-forward. Unafraid of asking questions."

"Even if the questions make me look stupid?" I guess dryly.

"No," she says, squeezing my hand. "It's a gift, London. Being teachable is a greater gift than you know, especially to someone like Dominic."

The full magnitude of the situation starts to sink in. I rub my face with my hands and mutter, "What did I agree to again?"

Charlie pats my back. There's laughter in her voice when she answers, "Think of it as an adventure. At the end of the adventure, you'll know without doubt if the lifestyle is for you. There's no better teacher out there, London. You're in the safest hands."

Dominic Cross's hands.

WHEN I ENTER the employee lounge ten minutes later, Steph jerks up from her seat on the floor in front of my locker. She darts across the room and grabs my shoulders.

"What happened? I heard yelling. Did you get fired? Tell me you're not fired."

I wheeze out a laugh. "No, I'm not fired."

I still don't understand it myself. One minute, I was yelling in Dominic's face, and in the next, we were standing before Charlie's desk like schoolchildren before a headmistress. She talked. We listened, nodding and shaking our heads as she asked questions and swiftly drafted a contract between us.

A contract between a Dominant and a submissive.

I don't even remember most of my hard-limits. Blood-letting, I think. Hopefully fisting. Charlie gave me twenty-four hours to modify my choices. A copy sits folded into a thick square in my back pocket, and I plan on making Nate go over it with me. Once I can think straight again.

"Then what was the yelling about?" asks Steph, wide eyes unblinking.

I glance at the several other employees in the room, dressing and loitering before the club opens in a half-hour. "Can I tell you later?"

She groans. "Yes, even though I'm dying of curiosity. Breakfast in the morning?"

I nod. "Definitely."

"Ten minutes, people!" chirps one of the cocktail waitresses. I think her name is Susanne. Nate calls her Teacher's Pet behind her back.

Steph gives her a cheesy thumbs-up, then turns to me. "You'd better get a move on. Wear the lipstick I gave you and no one will notice your sad lack of makeup."

I roll my eyes. "Whatever you say, boss."

She winks and heads back to her locker.

By the time I'm dressed—including startlingly red lipstick—the employee lounge is empty. A glance at my watch tells me I have forty-five seconds to get behind the bar. Slamming my locker closed, I hustle out of the room and run smack into someone striding past the door.

From the electric awareness that alights beneath my skin, I know who it is even before I look up.

Dominic cocks a brow and checks his watch. "You're late."

I have thirty more seconds!

I bite my tongue on the words, aware of my impulse toward defensiveness in a way I've never been before. Lowering my gaze, I say, "I'm sorry, sir."

His exhalation—*relief? annoyance?*—grazes my bare shoulder. "I was actually hoping to find you before your shift. To tell you I understand if you change your mind about the contract. You were put on the spot earlier, and Charlie can be... persuasive."

"I haven't," I say quickly, "and I won't. Sir."

In the following pause, the urge to see his expression is an almost physical pain.

"Very well." The bland words contrast sharply with the tension in his voice. "The schedule says you're not working tomorrow evening. Is that still correct?"

"Yes, sir."

My voice is thready with excitement, but I can't help it. I want this. *Him.* So much it scares me. Which I also like, the pulse of fear elevating and sharpening my conviction. The disturbing realization comes too late—I'm already off the cliff and soaring toward either doom or salvation.

"I'll expect you at my loft, then. Six p.m." He pauses. "Here's your first lesson, kitten. On-time is late, early is on-time, and late is unacceptable."

"Y-es, sir."

A warm finger beneath my chin draws my face upward. The gentle touch floods my limbs with languorous warmth. My knees locked against weakness, I hold my breath as his eyes find mine. They're so dark—the pupils barely visible—but they're not empty or cold.

They're burning.

"You'll bring the signed contract with you, complete with any changes. We'll review it together tomorrow evening after dinner."

"Okay," I breathe. The spark in his eyes makes me blurt, "Sir."

He smiles slowly. I watch the progression like a blind woman who's never seen the sunrise. It peaks in his eyes with all the warmth and brilliance of a star.

"Do you have any questions?"

I shake my head.

He pinches my chin lightly, then releases me. "Good. I expect you to be productive tonight and treat our customers with utmost respect. And under no circumstances will you flirt with anyone. Man or woman. Consider this a trial run. An assessment of your commitment. You're *mine*. Mine to care for, mine to command, and mine to hurt. Understood?"

"Yes, sir."

The words pass my lips for the first time without even the shadow of intellectual resistance. With complete surrender. And it's then that sweet bubble of relief closes around me. Cocooning me. *I'm not alone. I'm his to care for.*

Cross makes a sound, low and strained. "Get to work."

I nod and dash down the hallway, the tone of his voice adding another layer of comfort. Because this time, there's no censure, no irritation in the words. There's a promise.

Mine.

18

BREAKFAST WITH NATE and Steph goes much as I expected—with a generous amount of gasping, cussing, squeals of approval, and heckling. Nate follows me home after and guides me through the contract line by line, offering insights from his years of experience with different Doms and Dommes.

Not counting the obscenely-long checklist of limits, the bulk of the contract is concise—less than two pages of text with our names in Charlie's writing peppered throughout. The more times I read it, the more beautiful the verbiage becomes, the more it resonates in my mind. The essence of it is a simple vow. One of trust and mutual respect between two people. Between Dominic Cross and me.

"I can't believe this is happening."

Nate, curled up under a blanket on my bed, gives me a sleepy smile as he watches me pace. "You need to get some rest, London. Come cuddle me."

I give him a surprised glance. "I shouldn't. Right?"

"Pfft. Cross won't care. He doesn't want you flirting with other *Doms*." He pauses and sighs. "No, you're right. You should ask him how he feels about it, though. I like cuddling with you. And God knows nothing else would ever happen."

I roll my eyes. About a month ago, after a rowdy night and way too many drinks, Nate and I shared an awkward kiss. We laughed after—mostly in relief—at the utter lack of spark. A happy side-effect of the failed experiment is now Nate occasionally stays over after work, and I don't have nightmares when he's here. Something about a warm, safe body next to me at night keeps my demons at bay.

I wonder if I'll ever sleep next to Cross, and whether or not I'll dream.

I come to a stop at the foot of the bed and shake Nate's foot until he opens his eyes. "What?" he groans. "Just put pillows between us if you're worried. It's too bright in the living room for me to sleep on the couch."

"There's one thing still bothering me."

"Is this about the piss-play? I'm telling you—"

"No, no. I can't stop thinking about what Steph said

once, about Cross wanting only the 24/7 types. What if he wants that? I can't do that, all the house-slave type stuff, being told when to eat, to shower. I need space, my own time, freedom to—"

"Whoa there!" Nate fumbles from beneath the blanket and comes to the edge of the bed, taking me by the shoulders in a firm grip. His gaze is clear of sleep and direct. "Listen. The biggest pillar we uphold is *consensual.* It says right in the contract that either of you can terminate the relationship at any time."

"Right," I confirm, nodding quickly. "You're right. Okay."

"London," says Nate gravely, "Cross is super smart and perceptive, but you also can't expect him to read your mind. You need to be honest with him about how you're feeling. As you get to know each other, he'll be able to anticipate your needs better and whether or not they align with his. Maybe one of you will come to realize the relationship isn't working. It happens all the time."

My breathing is shallow and choppy; I pull at the collar of my t-shirt, feeling confined. "You keep saying *relationship,* and it's freaking me out." I laugh shrilly. "Shit, shit. Oh God, I can't do this."

Nate pulls me onto the bed, wrapping an arm securely around my shoulders. "Slow down, sugarplum.

That's it, deep breaths. Now tell me what you're so afraid of. Are you second-guessing submitting to pain? Pleasure? Or is it the emotional exposure?"

Calm and numb now, I answer, "A bit of the second one, but mostly the last."

Staring at the bare wall opposite the bed, I see another room, another wall, this one a rich navy-blue color. I remember the day Paul and I painted it, about three months after we moved in. How we measured and bickered and laughed over which photographs to hang and where. And after, the sight that greeted us every morning for years—a collage of love and happiness. Our wedding day. Felix on the grass with his tongue hanging out. Our families, our friends... our life.

That blue wall is gone now. Maybe it's a different color, or maybe hanging on it are someone else's framed memories. The tokens from my past life—as far as I know—are still sitting in boxes in my parents' garage. All those messy, beautiful years ended with a car bomb. One click. One second. Everything gone.

I drag myself from the memory and look at Nate, at his concerned face and red-rimmed eyes. We both need sleep badly, the lack no doubt contributing to my anxiety. But either way, I can't ignore the fear gripping my body and mind. Unlike the threat of consensual, physical pain, this fear doesn't excite me.

Deep down, in the darkest corner of my heart, the shadow of the woman I used to be lifts her head. Listening. Waiting. She senses my fear; it ignites something in her. Dread, or possibly hope.

Can I keep her hidden from Cross? What if I can't?

Nate strokes my hair, tucking strands behind my ear. "I get it. You're afraid he'll see you. The real you. The you that you keep on lockdown all the time, even from me."

The words are without judgement, but I jerk just the same. "Nate, I—"

"Don't," he says gently. "Trust me, London, I understand. I've been exactly where you are. But I won't lie to you—whatever happened to you, whatever you went through, it's going to come out in a scene whether you want it to or not." He pauses. "Do you believe things happen for a reason?"

"No," I say harshly.

His lips quirk. "I do. I think there's a reason you and Cross are in the same place at the same time. Why you've had a thing for him since day one."

I don't even deny it. "And what's the reason?"

He shrugs, leaning forward to kiss my cheek. "Time will tell. Be the brave, badass bitch I know you are. Maybe it's time to set the old you free."

19

OUR LAST FIGHT was one of those stupid arguments between couples who've been together a long time. I can't even remember the subject. He didn't put the toilet seat down. I forgot to pick up the dry-cleaning. Felix got into the pantry again because one of us forgot to close the door before bed. *I closed it—no, you didn't.*

It doesn't matter. It doesn't even matter that the last words Paul and I spoke to each other were in anger. Even when we were pissed, we shared the unbreakable safety-net of our love. Our arguments, few and far between, invariably ended in laughter, gentle affection, and finally, confessions about what was *really* bothering us. Something from work, or a troubling phone call, or some random insecurity triggered by comparing ourselves to others.

That's what would have happened, had that final day gone differently. I'd planned on stopping at his favorite Vietnamese restaurant on the way home and picking up dinner. We'd have eaten together, then taken Felix for a walk. Gotten ice-cream, maybe some hot tea. I'd have pretended not to notice when he smoked a cigarette, but would've made a face when he tried to kiss me. We'd have talked it out. Brushed our teeth side by side. Lit candles and made love. Fallen asleep in each other's arms.

That's the story I tell myself, at least. A lie, one atop many, but I don't care. It's a worthy fantasy. A happy dream of what might have been.

No one who hasn't been through losing their closest loved one understands the aftermath. The fundamental shift in how you view the world. In the early days, when I only rested thanks to sleeping pills and my mother's arms around me, I used to try to put a name or shape to the pain. But it has no name, and there are no edges to define it. It's merely *absence*. In my warped, grief-stricken mind, I theorized that if the soul was infinite, and someone punched a hole in it, then the hole itself was infinite by association.

When that piece of my soul—formless, nameless— was torn out, its ichor stained what was left of me. Even the idea of a sharing tender intimacy with a man makes my hackles rise. A relationship? Shared dreams and long talks and private laugher? Panic-inducing.

Cross was right—I don't want him to be kind.

I'm not so far gone that I can't admit I'm not a pillar of psychological health. If Cross knew the real reason I want him, he'd never have agreed to our arrangement. Yes, I want his touch. His mouth, teeth, hands. Other parts of him, too, if I'm honest with myself. But sexual gratification and emotional catharsis aren't my end goals.

I want punishment.

AT EXACTLY 5:50 p.m. that evening, I ring the bell beside the black door. A small crackle from an intercom precedes a curt, "It's unlocked. Come up. Present at the top of the stairs."

Am I doing this?

I'm doing this.

I open the door with a steady hand and slowly ascend. Each step brings me closer to *him*. Closer to what he can give me. Excitement trills in my blood; my heart flutters and accelerates.

If it wasn't for Nate's coaching and help this evening—not to mention his soundtrack of obnoxiously catchy dance music—I might be more nervous. But there was something calming about the lengthy routine. Showering, shaving, slathering on almond body-oil. Drying, then straightening my hair. Putting on the lingerie that Nate surprised me with, brand new with the tags still on. The flirty red dress, the sky-high heels.

Steph arrived halfway through to apply my final layer of armor—makeup that transformed me into a sexy version of myself. The process and result reminded me of tagging along with Paris to college parties and clubs, and special night's out with girlfriends.

This night is special, too.

When I reach the top of the stairs, I stop and clasp my hands before me. Head lowered, I wait. Soft music filters through the loft, along with street noise from an open window. The air is cool, scented with savory aromas from the kitchen.

Finally, soft footsteps pad across hardwood until his legs fill my line of sight. "Hello, London."

It's *that* tone. I haven't heard it since my interview months ago, and then it wasn't even directed at me. Smooth and rich, indefinably powerful. A voice that doesn't demand obedience but *manifests* it.

My skin tightens. My knees weaken.

"Sir," I squeak.

"Take off your shoes."

I toe them off. One of them falls over. I stare at it, frozen with uncertainty. *Do I pick it up?*

Cross reads my mind. "Leave them. I'm going to walk you through how I'd like you to present yourself for our assignations. On your knees."

I release a pent breath and drop to my knees.

"Sit on your heels. Hands in your lap. Yes, like that. Shoulders back. Perfect. This is how you'll present unless I specify otherwise. Now, lift up and tuck your toes. Spread your knees. Further... there. Hands laced behind your neck. When I ask you to *display*, this is how I want you."

Obeying him is surprisingly easy. Intellectually relieving, even. Here and now, I don't have to be in charge of my life. I could never live like this day in and day out, but for brief periods? So far, it's fucking magical.

My breath comes raggedly, audible to my ears. The position isn't comfortable, its intent obvious. My back is slightly arched, my breasts straining against the bodice of my dress. And if I was naked, I'd be completely exposed. The thought brings warmth to my chest and face—and a throbbing awareness between my legs. Closing my eyes, I imagine it. Having his eyes on me, watching, wanting...

Giving voice to my fantasy, he says, "You present or display for me naked, London. Do you have a problem with that?"

I shake my head.

"Good."

The edge of satisfaction roughens his voice, and pleasure swells inside me. I remember Charlie's advice, to think of this as an adventure, at the end of which I'd know if the lifestyle is for me. But she was wrong. I already know.

"Look at me, London."

I lift my head, feeling drugged and loose-limbed. Standing above me, his hands tucked into his pockets, his black dress-shirt unbuttoned at the neck, he looks anything but aroused. Severe. Coolly judging. Not angry, but tense with purpose. It's exactly what I wanted —exactly what I need. I don't know what's coming, but I hope it hurts.

A small softening of his intensity. An infinistirmal curl of his lips. Then: "Do you like chicken piccata?"

Thrown, it takes me a few seconds to reply, "Yes, sir."

Cross nods. "Up you go, then. Take a seat at the table. White wine or water?"

He walks away, leaving me wide-eyed and slack-jawed. Halfway to the kitchen, he glances back. His lips quirk higher.

"We're having dinner, London. Then we're talking

about the contract." His head tilts. "I didn't take you for the house-slave type."

"I'm not, sir," I say quickly.

He watches me a moment more with that level stare that does spirally, tight things to my core. "Do I need to tell you again to sit at the table?"

I scramble to my feet.

"Since you didn't answer my question, you're having water."

20

DINNER IS UNCOMFORTABLE. An awkward first date with stilted conversation. Not helping is my general edginess as I try to act like I'm supposed to while also keeping up with boring small talk. And saying *sir* a lot, which is starting to grate on my nerves.

Cross sits opposite me, but he might as well be in another room. He eats as he does everything else, with purpose and poise. In a conversational lull, I try to picture him as a young soldier, bright-eyed and smooth-faced. It's hard. On the other hand—thanks to Hollywood and his physique—I can easily imagine him as a super-soldier. Face camouflaged with black paint, a wicked knife in his hand. Big gun strapped to his back with ammo wrapped around his torso. Running toward an enemy yelling, "Yippee ki-yay motherfucker!"

I cover my smile with my napkin.

"You're not eating."

His voice wipes the smile off my face. "I'm sorry, sir."

Cross throws his napkin on the table. "For fuck's sake, London, look at me."

Startled, I meet his gaze, taking immediate note of the ticking in his jaw. My stomach sinks. "Sir? Have I done something wrong?"

He swipes a hand down his face, mulling thoughts, then sighs heavily. "Your behavior during dinner has been perfect, but I'm not interested in a slave. In fact, I wish you'd stop acting like someone you aren't."

I blink. "I thought... um, how do you want me to act, sir?"

Cross leans forward, features tight and fierce. "Cut the shit and tell me what you want."

My palms are sweating, nerves clamoring. *No, no, I'm ruining this.* Looking around the loft wildly, my gaze hits and snags on a St. Andrews Cross. It's beautiful, handcrafted wood. Oak or maybe Ash. Black restraints wait for wrists and ankles. The piece dominants a white wall; subtle lighting makes the wood glow.

"You want that, do you?" he asks, tone lightly mocking.

I gaze at it another moment, then meet his stare.

"Yes, sir." My voice—unlike the rest of me—is calm and confident.

At my answer, something changes in him. Nothing quantifiable. More like a door opening in another room, or a shift of light just before dawn—too faint to see but nevertheless detectable to the senses. The air changes between us. Crackling with promise that wipes away the last forty minutes of superficial chitchat about the weather, current events... All of it disappears.

My breath hitches. His gaze narrows.

"I want pain," I tell him. Unspoken is the conclusion, *You want to deliver it.*

"Give me the contract."

I jump to obey. In reaching for my purse, I knock a fork off the table. My face hidden beneath the surface, I freeze, half in embarrassment, have in excitement. *Will he punish me now?*

"Nervous little kitten," he murmurs. "We're not playing yet."

The words are flame to dry kindling. I'm instantly aching. Singular in my want. *Him.* And when the thought arises that I've never felt this intensity of need before, I slam it down. *It's just been a long time. It's the newness. The illicitness.*

"Quit stalling," he snaps.

All doubts and insecurities dissolve in the onslaught

of nuclear desire. I grab the fork and the contract, handing the latter to him and setting the former near my plate with a trembling hand. Cross scans the contract, spending long minutes on my checklist of limits. Though he wears a detached expression, I sense his readiness. He is predator in repose, ever aware of his prey, merely waiting for the perfect moment to act.

Finally, just when I think I might die without some release of the pressure inside me, he looks up and smiles. Slow and satisfied. It's not a nice smile—not kind—but it's everything I want.

Everything.

"Stand up, kitten."

I stand, my bare toes curling against the wood.

"Listen very carefully," he says, standing and walking around the table to my side. Pinching my chin lightly, he lifts my face and catalogues my features with precision; memorizing me, unmaking and remaking me. "From this moment on, you do exactly as I say when I say it. If you don't want to do something, you use your safe word. What is it?"

Staring at his firm, perfectly shaped mouth, my own lips part. "Felix, sir," I whisper.

He nods, expression hard and sharp. "Very good. I'm in a giving mood tonight. I'm going to whip you, and then I'll make you come. If you come before I give you permission, I'll forgive you this once. But from now until this is over, your orgasms belong to me. Understood?"

All I can manage is a nod.

"Voice," he snaps.

"Y-yes, sir."

Touch me more. I'm burning. Please, please.

Cross steps back. My chin tingles with an echo of his warm fingers. When his lips curl again, there's the undeniable edge of cruelty. He knows exactly how aroused I am—and he likes denying me pleasure. It's a torture I didn't consider, didn't crave. But I understand now that it's pain. Different, but just as exquisite.

"Stand facing the cross. Dress and bra come off. Leave the panties."

My feet barely acknowledge the ground as I walk across the room. I'm not sure how I make it to the cross without falling on my face, but I do. As I draw down the side-zipper and let the dress pool at my feet, I have no shame at my near-nakedness. Still none when I unclasp my bra and it falls atop the dress. My loose hair slides across my bare back, heavy and soft.

Staring at the subtle whorls in the wood before me, I feel... weightless. Insulated. Sensual. Like an ancient goddess readying for a mighty ritual. Like nothing and no one can touch me.

Cool air on my spine is the only warning I have

before my head is jerked back. Pain shimmers white at the edges of my vision. The thick cable of my hair secured in one hand, Cross steps close. Hard thighs meet the curve of my ass, my thong a laughable barrier for the thick ridge of his cock. Lowering his face to the exposed side of my neck, he breathes against my skin. There's no contact other than breath, but my body reacts almost violently. I barely hold back a moan.

"Did you really think it was linear?" he whispers. "A to B, pain then pleasure? Oh, little kitten, you have so much to learn."

His lips find my neck, grazing, then pressing firmly. Kisses trail from my ear to my collarbone, each sensation compounding until I'm lost in soft, hazy pleasure. For a moment, I wonder if this might be enough, that perhaps I don't need—

Vicious teeth.

"Oh, God," I rasp, jerking against unforgiving wood.

A second later, my ass is on fire. When my brain catches up, I realize he spanked me hard. *Really* hard. Pain in my neck and ass curls together with the arousal in my blood.

"What's my name?" he asks mildly.

"Sir, sir, sir," I chant, sagging against the cross.

Gentle stroke of his palm over my stinging backside.

"Mmm, look at that bloom. Better than I imagined. Are you ready, kitten?"

"Yes, sir." My voice is a thready moan.

He mutters something under his breath, then: "Flat to the cross. Arms up, legs out."

My cheek pressed to the wood near one arm, I glance back, seeing first his face—expression shockingly soft and human—then his hand at the apex of his thighs, curled around his daunting erection.

Before I can stop myself, I ask, "Second thoughts, sir?"

A dark brow arches. "Not remotely, though I'll consider a gag if you sass me again."

The way he says it, like he *wants* me to talk back, hits my system like a drug. With sudden insight, I understand why this is referred to as *play*. My safe word holds the boundaries, but like an unsupervised playground of youth, anything goes. The last thing I expected was to have fun, but here I am, hiding my smile with my bicep as smooth strides carry my salvation to me.

He makes quick work of my wrists, then crouches to attach my ankles to the wood. The rope is smooth but not soft, and a few experimental movements confirm that I'm well and truly bound. Before I can even consider panicking, warm fingers skate up my bare legs. They tease my knees, swirl across my trembling thighs, and finally stroke outside the edges of the flimsy fabric between my legs.

"Second thoughts, kitten?" he mocks, punctuating the words by dragging his thumb over my swollen flesh, bound in its own way by black lace.

"Fuck no," I whisper. "Sir."

Whack.

The sound arrives first. Then the pain, radiating angrily from my inner thigh. I gasp, my eyes screwing shut on instantaneous tears. A second later, one long finger sinks inside me and curls. The edges of agony blur and reshape. I catch a sob with my lips, but he hears it anyway.

My relief given voice.

A soft kiss presses to my shoulder. "Welcome home, London."

21

NOW

There are no clocks in this place. No light but artificial, dim and flickering far above us. I don't know how long has passed since Cinder was here. Since the ultimatum. Minutes. Hours. An entire day?

I don't know why certain people last longer under abuse or deprivation. Don't know which layers of the mind must be hardest, thickest, to prevent fracturing. What makes a survivor? What determines how many layers must crack before the vulnerable core of a person is exposed? I only know that what's on the inside of a person can't be determined by what's on the outside.

Some of the women have broken already. No commonalities have existed between them—old and young, hard-eyed or not. When they break, their wails are piercing. Unearthly. They throw themselves at the walls or the heavy doors, hands bloody, faces bloody, nails scraping skin, cracking against metal.

The guards let them exhaust themselves. Let the women sag, fall like puppets with cut strings. Then they haul them out.

Where do they go?

Nowhere.

22

THEN

"LONDON?"

"Hmm?"

Nate's frowning face fills my vision. "Damn, sugarplum. I've called your name probably ten times. Have you been in bed all day?"

Yawning, I stretch my arms over my head, then halt with a wince. "Ow."

Nate chuckles knowingly and plops onto the bed near my hip. Sunlight haloes his fair head. "I can't believe you slept all day with the curtains open. But actually, I can. You look used good. Did he drive you home at least?"

I nod and sit up, groaning at the stiffness in my muscles. "What time is it?"

"Close to three."

My brain awakes in fits and starts. Images carousel in my mind. Sound and sensation.

Crack. You look so beautiful covered in my marks. Red haze. Two more, kitten. Can you handle it? Too much —yes, sir. More, sir. You were so good, such a good girl. Soft kisses tracing lines of pain over my shoulders, back, down my legs. Hands on my ass as he kneels behind me. His tongue... You taste like heaven, kitten. Now for your reward...

Nate's fingers snap before my nose. "Earth to London?" His voice is teasing but his eyes are not. "You're freaking me out. Come on, out of bed. Show me."

"I'm okay," I say, but accept his help as I carefully maneuver to standing. I couldn't bear wearing anything to bed, so Nate's reaction is immediate.

"Jesus-fucking-Christ, you took a beating." I close my eyes and sway. "Minimal bruising, which is great, but it's too early to tell how long recovery will be."

"I've always healed fast," I mumble.

His sigh makes my welts burn. "I need to ask you—did you agree to this?"

"Yes," I say on a strangled laugh. "And I'd do it again."

"Uh oh," he mutters. "Stay put, I'm going to get my kit from the living room."

I glance back. "Kit?"

His brows lift. "Survival and recovery kit. You know, for when your Dom beats the shit out of you. At least tell me he gave you decent aftercare."

Weightless in his strong arms. Soft, satiny sheets against my stomach and breasts. Cool, thick salve quenching the fires of pain. Wrists and ankles covered in warm, wet washcloths.

"Do you know how difficult it was for me not to fuck you, London? Not to shove my thick cock in your tight little cunt?"

"Please, sir..."

"Soon, kitten. You have to earn it."

Nate's gaze is sharp and amused. "Rocked your world, did he? Damn, I really wish he liked dick."

My lips twist with wry humor. "He's everything they say he is. Even the word cunt sounds good when he says it. How is that even possible?"

Nate explodes in laughter. "Mysteries of kink." Still chuckling, he leaves the room and returns with a small black case. "Facedown on the bed. Let's get you lubed and drugged."

I groan. He cackles.

———

THERE'S NOT enough ibuprofen in the world to tackle the full scope of my misery. An afternoon of resting while Nate pampered me, fed me, and eventually helped me shower was challenging enough. I figured working tonight would be hard, but worth it for the chance to see Cross.

So wrong.

"Whoa, you okay?" Another bartender grabs my shoulder as I sway toward a stack of glasses. I can't prevent a tiny moan as he inadvertently touches the edge of a welt.

I step away from him, nodding spastically. "Good, fine."

He follows me—*what's his name again*—and lays a hand on my forehead. It feels wrong, too slim, too cold. "You don't look so good. Hey, Jack, I'm going to help London to the back. She needs to sit down."

"Okay!"

"London?" Steph's face swims into view. "What's going on? You sick?"

It's too loud. Too bright. I can't find my voice to protest when a heavy male arm comes around my shoulders. My whimper is pitiful, lost beneath music and revelry. I'm guided to the end of the bar, out through the small portal, and toward the back hallway.

A shout somewhere in the club: "Master Cross!" I recognize Nate's voice, urgent and panicked.

"What the—" mutters my well-meaning captor.

"Release her right fucking now."

I sag with relief at the dark, edged voice. When I'm released like a leper, my knees buckle, but strong, familiar arms catch me and hoist me up. Miraculously, his embrace avoids all points of pain. *He knows exactly where he marked me.* The thought is unaccountably soothing. *I'm safe.*

Steady, long strides carry me away. I tuck my face into his warm chest, breathing him in, relishing in the momentary absence of pain. Like his very presence is morphine. A door opens, music fades. Another door, then stairs. Scent of the loft—leather and spice.

"Damnit, London," he mutters, "I told you to call me if you couldn't work tonight. I knew I should have cancelled your shift. What the fuck was I thinking?"

"I missed you."

The words slip out, divorced from rational thinking. I'm so loopy, I don't take them back. Cross pauses for a moment, then continues across the loft and into the dark bedroom. Setting me carefully on my feet, he bends to pull back the coverlet.

"Undress. On your stomach."

It's more painful getting the dress off than it was getting it on. The only item from my work wardrobe that promised to cover my marks, the dress is high-collared and long-sleeved, made of snug, tensile material. As much as I want to, I don't ask Cross for help. He probably wouldn't give it, anyway. I recognize the tone of reprimand. I'm being punished for foolishness.

By the time I'm naked except for underwear, I'm shaking and sweating. My back is aflame, pulsing in time with my heart. Whimpering, I crawl onto the bed and collapse.

Cross sits beside me and opens the drawer in the nightstand, removing a tub of salve and uncapping it. The mild scent of Arnica floats to my nose, stimulating memories of last night.

"How do you feel?"

"Sleepy, sir. Relaxed. Thank you."

"It was my pleasure, kitten. Stay in bed tomorrow. Do you have ice-packs at home?"

"No, sir."

"I'll give you a few to take with you, and I'll have Nate check on you in the afternoon. You'll call me if the pain is more than you can stand."

"Yes, sir."

He sighs, rising from the bed. I miss the heat of him instantly. "I'm going to pull the car around, then I'll come get you." Bare footsteps pad across the room. When they stop abruptly, I open my eyes to see him paused in the doorway.

"London?" he asks softly.

"Yes?"

"Thank you."

Now, the man who blew open my universe last night sits frozen on the bed, salve in one hand and his other clenched in the thick hair of his crown.

"Jesus, I'm sorry." He sounds choked.

"What? No." I reach for him, laying my palm on the small of his back. He flinches but doesn't move. "Sir? *Dominic.* I'm fine, really. Just stupid. I should have called out today."

He glances back, brow furrowed. "Last night I

treated you as I would a seasoned submissive. The blows you took..." He shakes his head helplessly, gaze tracing the welts. "You were so unbelievably perfect—your pain threshold is incredible. I hit the zone fast and forgot how green you are. It's inexcusable."

The vulnerability in his voice triggers alarm bells in my head. The earth is shifting, quaking and opening beneath us. Something huge waits in the steaming fissure. Something I don't think either of us are ready for. I'm sure as hell not.

"No." My voice is sharp enough to wipe the softness from his expression. "I fractured my arm at summer camp when I was a kid. I thought it was a little bump and a bruise. It barely hurt. The whole thing swelled up like a balloon before anyone thought something might be wrong."

He's skeptical. "Is that true?"

"One-hundred percent. I've always had a high pain tolerance. My older sister is the opposite—cries when she stubs her toe. Total sissy."

A smile flirts with his lips. "You are definitely no sissy."

I grin. "I know, right? I'm badass."

He laughs, the sound rich and warm and utterly intoxicating. It does horrible things to my body, causing my heart to squeeze, my stomach to dance. And I realize my error. In trying to veer the conversation away from the cliff of intimacy, I inadvertently drove us right off the edge.

"You can't have it both ways, you know," muses Cross, his smile gone, his keen gaze on my face. "Trust me, I've tried."

My breath stills. "Can't have what?"

"The benefits of a Dom/sub relationship without emotion of any kind. At the very least, we have to be friends for this to work." His eyes crinkle at the edges. "I can't handle another boring dinner."

A short laugh escapes me. "It was bad."

"So bad."

"Friends?"

He nods. "Friends who play." Shifting on the bed, he scoops out a wad of the salve and warms it between his hands.

Tension drains from my body, and with it the majority of my pain. I'm still going to let him massage me, though. He has a magical touch.

At the first gentle touch, I sigh and close my eyes. "I can do friends, Dominic, but that's it."

Whack.

"Ow!" I shriek. My efforts to bolt upright are

thwarted by a forearm on my now-screaming ass. Grumbling, I relax again. "No calling you by your first name?"

"Good catch." He's smiling. "Like my cock, you have to earn it."

I roll my eyes, but I'm smiling into the pillow.

"Yes, sir."

23

I'M DREAMING. I know I am, but I can't escape. I'm in the airy, elegant room with its library and fresh floral fragrance. Midday, bright sunlight. The air is cool, the breeze warm. A man sits in one of the high-backed armchairs before an open window with a view of the garden and groomed acres beyond.

"I know why you're here, London."

My feet carry me toward him... this man who destroyed my life. Destroyed my dreams, my hope, my love. When I reach him, he smiles up at me, blue eyes crinkling warmly. Grey-haired, handsome and distinguished. The look, as always, is grandfatherly. Full of acceptance and affection.

Lies, all of it. All of him.

"Why?" I ask him.

He shrugs. "'*If you gaze for long into an abyss, the abyss gazes also into you.' Better to be the monster than be eaten by one, no?*"

I grip the back of his chair, the urge to strangle him visceral. "*Don't quote Nietzsche to me, you pompous, arrogant fuck. Tell me WHY!*" The word is a scream of primordial rage. It echoes in the dream, shattering the windows. Glass rains down like harmless confetti, disappearing before impact.

He sighs, smoothing a hand down his silk tie, his gaze on the lush garden. "*Do you remember what I told you the night we met, London? No? I do. I told you to be careful, because there would come a time when you would have to choose between instinct and self-preservation.*"

"*You always were a cryptic sonofabitch,*" I snarl. "*Is this the time? Am I choosing now?*"

"*You were the daughter I never had,*" he says wistfully, "*and Paul was like a son. I'm truly sorry it's come to this.*"

Pressure on the back of my head. The cloying smell of gun oil. I don't look back. Don't need to see who it is—I can smell his distinctive cologne.

The man I loved like a grandfather stands and straightens his suit-jacket. He's not smiling anymore.

"What will it be, my dear? Will you join us at the top of the world, or will you hold to meaningless ideals?"

I spit in his face. *"Fuck you. Just kill me."*

The sad, blue gaze lifts over my head. He nods, and the world explodes white, then black.

"HEY, hey, it's okay, you're safe."

I open my eyes to Cross's face above mine. My mind is fuzzy, my mouth dry. I'm still in his bed, still naked, but cradled in his arms against the headboard. His bare chest is a furnace against my cool, damp skin. The lights in the bedroom are off, but there's an ambient glow from the living room. Enough to register his concerned expression.

"What..." I trail off, my brain stalling in confusion.

A warm hand strokes my sweat-soaked hair. "I gave you a little something to help you sleep, remember? You were out for a few hours, then had a nasty nightmare. It took me a while to wake you up."

It all comes back—the dream-memory, the betrayal, the blackness and bleakness... I feel it again like it happened yesterday, not eighteen months ago. Mortified and near-tears, I try to jerk away, but Cross's arms only tighten.

"PTSD is nothing to be ashamed of," he murmurs, gentling his grip as I surrender to his embrace. "Neither is asking to die. Trust me, I've been there."

I screw my eyes shut at the realization I must have been talking in my sleep. *Just kill me.* "It's not what you think." The words are empty, blatantly false.

"Mmm." The noncommittal hum vibrates his body, sending soothing waves through mine. I begin to relax in earnest, a detached calm stealing over me.

"He didn't," I say vacantly, "kill me, that is."

"Who?" Curious, but without expectation.

"The man who murdered my husband."

Cross goes still. Almost inhumanly so. In the silence, I imagine him weighing the pain in my voice against his own pain, trying to find common ground where there is none. His wife used him, betrayed him. My husband died to protect me—to protect innocents.

Sparing us both, I say, "I don't know why he didn't follow through. Sentimentality, I guess. But he ended up killing me in other, just as permanent ways."

Torching my reputation. My career. My *life*.

"This is what you were talking about," he muses softly, "when I accused you of being a criminal."

My laugh is soundless, mirthless. "Yes."

"Someone orchestrated a smear campaign against you," he deduces. "I'm guessing you discovered or learned something you shouldn't have. And your husband... he was law enforcement?"

"Good guess. ICE agent working for Homeland Security. I thought you Googled me," I add wryly. "That didn't come up in your search?"

"I didn't read past the first few headlines. I'm not in the business of judging people by their pasts."

I snort. "Didn't seem that way."

"Yeah, it probably didn't. You were right to tell me off that day." He pauses. "If it matters, I never actually thought it was true."

I look up, startled. "Why not?"

"I've only known you a few short months, but there's no way you seduced a fat-ass Russian mobster and asked him to kill your husband. No-fucking-way." The words are calm, matter-of-fact, and their certainty nearly bring tears to my eyes.

"Thank you," I whisper.

His brows lift, eyes soft and unguarded. "For what?"

"Believing me."

He smiles slightly. "In my former line of work, the ability to read a person's character sometimes meant the difference between life and death." There's a layer of darkness beneath the words, an unspoken current of history. His instincts failed him when it came to choosing a wife.

I want to ask—want to know—and the impulse shocks me enough to remember how dangerous Dominic Cross is. Especially this version of him, the man whose presence makes me feel... *safe*.

I need to get out of here.

"I... I think I'm okay to drive home." I shift in his arms, angling for escape, but his laughter stills me.

"Not happening. It's four in the fucking morning, and even though you don't feel it now, you're going to be in pain in about an hour."

I still, narrowing my gaze on his face. "That wasn't Tylenol?"

"It was. The kind with codeine."

My eyes widen. "You drugged me?"

"Oh, kitten. That's cute. It was just enough to take the edge off." He chuckles, big body shaking beneath mine and bringing immediate attention to the thin sheet separating us. His lack of pajamas. His swiftly thickening cock, which sits nestled against my core.

Gasping, I squirm again toward the edge of the bed.

Only to be reeled back in.

"Relax," he says chidingly. "It's just an erection. You're going to have to see it eventually." My face flames, my gaze averting from his teasing grin. Now that I'm aware of his nakedness, I can't seem to think about anything else—or stop myself from teetering toward intimacy I don't want.

"I can't right now," I whisper, "not after talking about... that."

His hips subtly flex, teasing my softness with hardness. "I think you can."

Low, controlled voice. *The* voice. My limbs go liquid with surrender. With relief. For an instant, I quail at the transition that seems so divorced from my control. I'm like Pavlov's dog, rolling over on command. But as he effortlessly shifts my legs so they fall open on either side of his hips, then drags me directly atop his long, thick ridge, I realize that giving in is a gift.

There's no memory here—just feeling.

His hands cradle my neck, fingers massaging, drawing a soft sigh from my lips. "There you are. Do you feel me?"

"Yes, sir."

Another, stronger movement of his hips. Sensation unfurling, heat cascading. My head falls back into the support of his hands as my body obeys a biological command to move. To seek and find the perfect friction, the perfect rhythm.

"Don't stop until you come, kitten. And don't forget to ask for permission." His dark head lowers to my chest, sucking and biting, devouring one breast, then the other.

"Oh, God, sir, don't stop."

He hums in pleasure, one hand falling to my hip, anchoring me, moving me faster and harder against him. His groan lights every nerve ending in my body. "I can feel you dripping on my cock. So wet. So hot. Fucking you is going to be so good."

"Please, please," I chant.

He bites my nipple so hard I see stars. I cry out, seconds from falling apart. "Don't you fucking come."

"*Please.*"

"Not yet," he snarls. "I want to feel it." My thong is wrenched away, three thick fingers shoving inside me without warning, curling and mercilessly massaging my g-spot.

I scream through my teeth. "*Please, sir!*"

"Kiss me, kitten."

Our open mouths collide and fuse in savage darkness. It's not a kiss. It's a battle for power on the only level playing field between us. As he claims me, I claim him, my fingers clenched tight in his hair. As he devours my cries, I devour his groans and hissing breaths. All the while his fingers pump inside me, his shaft tight against my clit. His taste, scent, grace, power... it's ambrosia. Perfect agony.

Teeth clamping on my lower lip, he growls, "Now."

I'm gone.

And I don't care if I come back.

24

ON THE NIGHTS I work at the club, it's business as usual. Dominic broods and prowls, monitoring the playrooms and the Epicenter. I work my ass off, fast becoming one of the most popular—and lucrative—bartenders. I even earn a special drink called The London: an Earl Grey Martini with lavender-infused simple syrup and a twist of lemon peel. Charlie's idea, coinciding with her new playmate, who's one of the city's top mixologists.

The community at Crossroads is familiar now, full of faces and personalities instead of nameless customers. Everyone knows I'm Dominic's submissive, but I'm not treated or spoken to any differently. At least not to my face. Nevertheless, I'm mindful of avoiding rumors of special treatment, and offset the risk by working as hard —if not harder—than my colleagues.

Nate, Steph, and I still meet for breakfast after shifts. We do occasional movie nights, dinner dates, or shopping excursions for more accessories for my apartment. I talk to Paris several times a week, and call my parents every Sunday. I pay my bills and funnel money monthly into my savings account. Once in a while, I let Steph drag me to get manis and pedis. In my private time, I binge-watch *The Walking Dead* and *House of Cards*, or read whatever latest Science Fiction novel my dad has recommended.

And yet, despite what could be labeled as normalcy in my life, the axis of my world has drastically shifted. The rotation was slow and subtle over the course of weeks. I barely noticed it happening, and only occasionally do I glimpse the full scope of my transformation. When I do, it's mind-blowing.

I'm no longer an automaton going through the motions. *Work. Eat. Sleep.* Now, I am *more.* Changed. Myself and not. London 3.0, perhaps, if I didn't recognize that thinking about myself in the third person was fundamentally bizarre.

If my axis had a wheel, Dominic Cross's hands are on it. Since our first night together, my unconscious—my subconscious—all of me—has been consumed by him. I exist in a new state of sexual awareness and craving. Even the sight of his broad shoulders moving through the club accelerates my heart. And his touch?

I'm an addict—he is my drug.

We meet in his loft approximately twice a week. On the nights I have to work the next day, he takes it easy on me. Relatively. The other nights, though... we are gods who pray only at each other's altars. Sacrifice and surrender, brutality and succor. And each time we're together, I see him forgive himself a little more. Accept himself a little more. Honor himself a little more each time he honors my needs. My pain. He takes it, or maybe I give it.

Whatever it is, whatever is happening between us, it's unlike anything I've experienced with another person. Despite my past, which is firmly in the *do not talk about* category, with Dominic I'm honest in a way I've never been before. I'm free to speak the truth of my body.

I don't know what will become of me—or rather, who I will become. And I would be lying to myself if I said I'm not still haunted by demons, don't have trouble sleeping on the nights I'm not with him, or never think about Paul and the past. But when I'm with Dominic, there are no ghosts.

There is only him.

AT WORK, we pretend we don't seek each other out, watch each other, or trade a thousand punishments and pleasures in one look. We've never been to a playroom on my off hours. We don't hide in a closet to make out. Far from it—he hasn't kissed me since that night I woke up from a nightmare in his bed.

But there are other ways he shows me he thinks of me when we're not together. A brush of his fingers on mine as we pass in the hallway. A book of erotic poetry left where only I would find it. And notes in my locker almost every day. I look forward to them, feel fluttery and hot with anticipation every time I get to work.

No underwear tonight

How does your ass feel today?

You didn't call me when you got home last night

How bad do you want my cock, kitten?

The answer is *bad*. The pleasure I've felt at his hands far surpasses any I've experienced—or even dreamed of—but as the days and weeks bleed by, there's a rising emptiness inside me only his body can remedy.

Before Dominic, I never would have thought it possible to get sick of a man eating me out, fingering me, or using any number of toys to get me off. But I am. At this point, I'm not sure who he's punishing, himself or me.

But the alternative is to walk away, and I can't. Don't want to. Might not ever.

In addition to the notes, Dominic also likes leaving little presents in my locker, usually with brief instructions. Ben Wa balls. A butt plug. A tiny vibrator with a wireless remote—which I learned about the hard way while chatting with a customer.

If you come, you're in trouble

Put it in. Use spit for lube

Don't spill any drinks

If I was a whole woman, I'd be halfway in love with him. As it is, my pain and pleasure take the place of my heart. My body is his playground, his canvas, his instrument. His inhuman restraint is my greatest agony.

I want him to break—or maybe I want him to break me. He seems to know, and before every scene he reminds me of my safe word.

I haven't used it. Don't want to.

Might not ever.

25

ON A THURSDAY EVENING IN AUGUST, I take matters into my own hands. Dominic has been out of town the last three days visiting his parents in Napa Valley. In lieu of pining in his absence or stalking his social media for updates on his whereabouts, I've spent the time brainstorming with Nathan on how best to seduce my Dom. I even picked Charlie's brain. As awkward as that conversation was for both of us, I learned some essential facts about Dominic. Facts I'm going to use mercilessly against him tonight.

I spent the afternoon getting everything ready in the loft. I'm wearing his favorite color—blood red—from panties to dress. I've made his favorite meal, chicken cacciatore, and his favorite Miles Davis album is queued on the record player. All that's left is to wait and try not to chew off my lipstick.

Thanks to Google, I know his flight landed forty minutes ago. He should be here any minute. Every sound outside makes my heart leap and fools my ears into thinking it's his key in the door.

Another twenty-five minutes pass. The oven goes off. I pull out the chicken and promptly start worrying it will be cold by the time he gets here. To distract myself, I re-toss the salad, fuss with my hair in the bathroom mirror, and wipe off then reapply my lipstick. Dominic has taught me plenty about patience, but it's still not my strong suit.

When I finally crack and grab my phone to call him, it rings in my hands. Sighing in relief at the sight of his name on the screen, I answer.

"Sir?"

"Room six. Now." The line goes dead.

Lowering the phone from my ear, I consider that all my preparations are for naught. I glance at the counter where our dinner is rapidly cooling, then at the candles flickering merrily on the table.

I laugh and bend over to blow out the flames.

Screw the chicken.

IF I DIDN'T KNOW the club like the back of my hand by now, I might be nervous walking down the shadowed hallway housing the playrooms. But though I've never *used* a room, I've seen firsthand what each has to offer.

Knowing he wants room six fills me with a delicious mixture of anticipation and dread. Among regulars at the club, it has the nickname Devil's Den. Like something out of a gothic horror novel, the playroom has dark walls, minimal lighting, and an antique-flare with accents of crimson and navy. One wall is covered entirely in tools of the trade—gags, cuffs, harnesses, hoods, spreader bars, clamps, paddles, floggers, hooks, ropes, chains...

It's a torture chamber.

When I reach the room, I'm breathing heavily, fear spiking as I see the curtain drawn over the viewing window. I wonder what he has planned for me. If I can stand it—if I want it.

Despite my nerves, the answer comes swiftly. *Yes.* Yes, I want it. Anything and everything he has to give me.

I don't care if my needs classify me as a masochist. If some might think me weak, or damaged, or lacking self-esteem. They don't know shit. And I don't care, either, that to the general population Dominic's desire to deliver pain is considered a mental illness. To me—*for me*—he is an iron glove swathed in velvet. Redemption at the end of a whip.

Before my fingers touch the doorknob, the wood swings open. Air leaves my lungs in a rush.

All the furniture save one piece has been removed. Candlelight glows around the thick, padded bench set perpendicular on the opposite wall. Shackles hang from it, waiting for my limbs. A thick collar also rests on the black surface, its attached chain linked to the wall. Soft, lush music drifts from speakers, the rhythm fluttering against my skin. But what makes my pulse pound in need is the man waiting for me.

"Good evening, London," says the demigod in leather pants and nothing else. A smile teases the corner of his lips. "Are you ready to play?"

There's only one answer.

"Yes, sir."

He nods. "Clothes off. Hands and knees on the bench."

I rush to obey, stripping out of my dress and lingerie with Dominic's searing gaze caressing my every move. His appreciation glows in my chest, spins my anticipation to new heights.

The supple leather of the bench is cool under my palms and knees.

"So beautiful," he murmurs, warm palm sliding

down my spine, making me sigh in relief. "You have no idea the things I want to do to you."

"You can do whatever you want, sir."

"Mmm. Is that so? Head up."

As I obey, he lifts my hair from my nape and reaches for the collar. The interior is soft, the buckles clinking softly as he fastens them. In short order, my ankles and wrists are shackled. I squirm, testing the limits of the chains.

"One more," he says, reaching overhead to a thick belt that hangs from the ceiling. He fastens it around my waist, pulling the chain until my spine is straight. The support is a false promise—it only means I can't lower onto my forearms without hurting myself.

When a tremble shakes me head to toe, he sighs in pleasure. "You love not knowing what's coming, don't you?"

"Yes, sir," I whisper, my head dropping forward.

"Head up," he snaps, "unless you want me to tighten the chain on your collar."

I jerk my chin up, my eyes fluttering closed. "No, sir."

"I thought not. Point your toes. Like that. Are you comfortable?"

"No, sir."

He chuckles darkly. "Good. Maybe this will help."

I know by the tone of his voice that whatever *this* is, it's only going to heighten my anxiety. Sure enough, a strip of dark fabric covers my eyes. There's a tug as he ties it, a small pinch in my scalp as my hair pulls. I whimper.

He strokes my shoulder, my flank, then gently squeezes my breasts. Pleasure spreads in waves from the contact, then turns on itself as clamps bite down on my nipples. Because of my inverted position, the pressure is more painful than usual, but I welcome it. Embrace it as the high-pitched hum of a vibrator fills the air, as he attaches it to a mount and positions it between my legs.

I'm not ready for it, the vibration on my clit an unwanted shock. I squirm helplessly to escape even though there's nowhere to go.

It sets the tone of the evening.

Whatever's on his mind tonight gives him an edge I haven't seen, brings a rawness to his actions, makes everything brighter and more potent.

Whistling whip.
Searing fire.
Pulsing heat.
Warm glow.
Crack—crack—crack.
Stinging feet.

Shoulders.

Ass.

Harsh commands.

Filthy purrs of approval.

I break, and break, and break.

Merciless pleasure. Pitiless pain. I'm ready—exultant—when the sweeping wave of surrender takes me. I belong to pain and him, and they belong to me.

My pain is *my* choice.

I'm his therapy and redemption as much as he is mine. The taste of our communion is bitterness laced with cream. Sugary arsenic. For what I want, he doesn't give, in the end spilling his seed on my back instead of inside me.

Never inside me.

Sadist.

But also my savior, for when he's unraveled me to the most fundamental level of my humanity, the greatest gift arrives. Whispery nothingness. Floating peace. If not exactly forgiveness, it nevertheless feels like acceptance.

Each time he breaks me, I rebuild a little more.

After, he holds me as I come down, his face tucked into my neck. My fingers play in the soft hair at his nape.

"Are you okay?" I whisper.

He nuzzles me, holds me tighter. I don't protest—it's

worth the discomfort. "I am now," he answers at length, lips against my pulse.

"Do you want to talk about it?"

His smile curls against my skin. "I just did."

I huff out my amusement. Beneath it, though, is a tingle of intuition coupled with fear. The good kind of fear, like falling with a parachute.

"You just missed me, didn't you?"

He nips me lightly. "You're pushing it." No bite in the words, only soft affection. Content with my sleuthing efforts, I snuggle deeper into his embrace.

26

"SO..."

"So, what?"

"Come on," whines Paris. "We don't keep secrets, remember? Spill."

"I have no idea what you're talking about."

She laughs at my horrible attempt at lying. "Bullshit. Something happened. Something's changed. You sound..." her voice softens, "more like yourself. Like the baby sister I've missed so much."

The words are double-edged. Sweet and painful. My chopping of lettuce pauses, then resumes with more force. "Maybe it's just time, you know? I'm finally getting used to... it."

"So you don't have a boyfriend?" She doesn't bother masking her disappointment. "I thought maybe—"

"Nope," I interject. "No boyfriend."

Just a Dom.

A Dom who still won't fuck me. He'll whip me, flog me, tie me up, hang me from the ceiling of his bedroom, play my body and senses and make me orgasm like it's his freaking job, but he has yet to make good on his promise. *You're going to have to see it eventually.* He won't even let me touch it or taste it, no matter how much I've begged. It's frustrating. Painful.

I love it.

Smiling to myself, I separate the lettuce onto three plates and top the salads with pine nuts, crumbled gorgonzola, and thin slices of bell pepper. Across the country, Paris is calmly asking my niece why she decided to cut the hair off her Barbies. My smile widens as Suzie states her case and runs, squealing, from the room.

"Lord, did you hear that?"

I chuckle. "Seems logical. No hair, no lice."

She groans. "A kid she goes to school with had lice last month, and the school did a big assembly on it. Put ideas in her head."

"At least she didn't cut her own hair, right?"

"Oh, shit, I didn't even think of that." She pulls the phone away from her face. "Josh! Will you hide all the scissors, please?" There's an indistinct male response in the background. "Gah! I gotta run. He's is in one of those moods where he pretends he doesn't know where anything is. I swear, there are days I want to strangle—" Sharp gasp. "London, God, I'm so sorry, I wasn't thinking."

I laugh past the sharp pain in my chest. "Hey, stop that. I don't want you to walk on eggshells with me. It's been almost two years."

She hesitates. "Are you sure?"

"Positive," I say, though I'm anything but.

"Okay. Love you. Talk soon?"

"Yep."

I end the call just as there's a knock on my front door. Without waiting for permission, Nate and Steph enter in a frenetic cloud of fragrance, glitter, and night-club attire. Within minutes, the conversation with my sister is forgotten as we dive into salads and fresh bread rolls and chat about what bar we're hitting before dancing the night away.

Shocking everyone—myself included—I was the one to suggest going clubbing. Nate initially wanted a low-key celebration for his twenty-fifth birthday, but I couldn't allow that. Twenty-five is the last great measuring stick of youth—you're finally allowed to rent a car in most foreign countries. For my own milestone,

Paul surprised me with a trip to... yes, London. And of course, I did the honors of renting us a car.

I can't take Nate somewhere exotic, but I can make sure he has a memorable birthday.

"Oh here, before I forget." Grabbing the small, wrapped package from my purse, I hand it to him.

"I told you not to get me anything!"

"Just open it.

After another look of censure, Nate tears the paper off and opens the little cardboard box. He reads the note inside, then gapes at me. "Are you serious?"

"What is it?" demands Steph.

I wink at her. "I got him a spot in that photography workshop he's been talking about."

Nate grabs me in a spine-cracking hug. "Oh my God, London! That workshop has been booked for months! How on earth did you manage this?"

I giggle. "Trade secret."

"Whatever, I don't even care if you sold your soul for it. I'm so freaking stoked. You've made my day, month, year, et cetera."

I kiss his cheek. "You're welcome."

"At least my card was really funny," grumbles Steph.

Laughing together, we head into the night.

BY 3 A.M., I'm ready to call it quits. Even though working nights has recalibrated my biological clock, there's a huge difference between bartending for six hours and dancing in heels for the same amount of time. If someone threw a pillow into this dark booth with me, I could pass the fuck out.

Seeing Cross last night also took a lot out of me. It was a new experience—he spent close to an hour crafting a complex masterpiece of rope and my naked body. By the time he attached me to the ceiling and slowly elevated me, I was half-asleep in my rope hammock and painfully aroused.

Then he kissed me on the cheek and left.

I'm still processing the mind-fuck he put me through, and the emotional hangover from learning that he was only gone for fifteen minutes. Those fifteen minutes felt like fifty. The combination of pressure and weightlessness mixed a cocktail of anxiety, claustrophobia, extreme sadness and equally potent euphoria. And finally, peace.

When he returned, lowering me and cutting me free, I ugly-cried in his arms for another ten minutes. After... well, that's a big slice of the mindfuck. Cross carried me to the bathroom and lowered us both into a cool, lavender-scented bubble bath. He fed me chocolate and strawberries and washed me head to toe, even conditioning my hair. And though he was naked and hard against the crevice of my ass, I didn't even try to look. Sex was the absolute furthest thing from my mind.

And that's not even the weirdest part. We didn't speak one word to each other the entire night, and we *still* haven't kissed since our first and only, but the intensity of the suspension and his tenderness after opened a portal inside me. One I thought forever closed—the conviction that I could easily spend eternity in someone's arms. *His* arms.

Dominic Cross is fast becoming an axis in my world. As much as I can't allow that to happen, I'm powerless over it. Powerless over what he makes me feel. How much I'm coming to depend on him as the one who will catch me when I fall.

27

"I'M DYING," pants Nate, sliding into the booth opposite me. He grabs a stiff drink coaster and fans his flushed face. His pale hair curls damply against his temples.

I smile. "You look radiant."

He grins. "There are so many hotties here tonight. It's too bad you're not single—don't give me that look, you know what I mean. We both know why you skedaddled when that sexy-as-fuck guy started rubbing on you."

I open my mouth, then close it. It's no use arguing that Cross isn't my boyfriend. Whether I like it or not, our arrangement is monogamous. *Isn't it?*

"Hey, Nate? Cross made it clear I wasn't allowed to see or be with anyone else, but do you think he's, um... shit, we didn't actually discuss exclusivity on his end."

He laughs. "Word on the street is that he's off the market, but that might be because we all saw him go caveman when that other guy touched you. Just ask him."

I down the remains of my Jack and Coke. "Yeah, right."

Nate's gaze roams the club. "What does it take to get drink service in this—" His voice chokes off, then resumes with a laugh. "Speaking of your booty's boss, he's up in VIP. You should text... oh, *shit*."

My head jerks up so fast a muscle in my back protests. Following Nate's line of sight, I look up to the second-story balcony opposite us. A large booth of men and women is front and center, with a bird's eye view of the club below. The scene almost looks staged—a perfect tableau of The Rich and Beautiful. The table's surface is covered in drinks, both empty and full, and the visible faces are laughing or engaged in animated conversations.

No one is flushed and sweaty from dancing. No one's hair is a lank rat's nest, and no one's makeup has worn off over the hours. And that's just the women—the men are suave, polished, each possessing that singular air that comes from money and big cocks.

Cross sits in the middle with his arms stretched across the back of the booth. The women to either side of him are close. Too close. They're talking to each other while Cross chats with someone a few seats down. As I watch, one of the women reaches out—ostensibly to grab a drink—and rubs herself all over his chest. He doesn't move, just glances down with a smile and a wink.

A *wink*.

"London, calm down. You don't know what he's doing. Cross isn't the type to go behind your back." When I don't say anything, his voice gets louder and higher. "Well, this is a fucked-up bit of synchronicity, huh? Since we were just talking about it. Kinda funny, right? What a perfect opportunity for you to—"

"Shut up, Nate," I say without heat. Dragging my gaze away from VIP, I bare my teeth. "It's all good. He's not my boyfriend. We're not emotionally involved or anything."

"That's a scary smile you have going on there," Steph says as she slides in beside me. She wipes her glistening face with a cocktail napkin, belatedly noticing Nate's furiously shaking head. "What? What's going on?"

"Nothing!" I chirp. "I'm going to dance. Who wants to come?"

Nate jerks forward in panic. "No! Are you nuts? He might see you!"

"Who?" asks Steph, utterly confused.

"Mr. Cross," growls Nate, and Steph gasps.

I laugh carelessly. "Come on! Our arrangement begins and ends when we're actively together. He isn't my Dom when I'm working or when I'm at home. He doesn't control my life. And clearly I don't have any sway over what he does with his free time, either!"

I sound like a maniac, angry while grinning like a loon. My gaze swings between my friends, both wide-eyed and visibly freaked out. I'm an actor in a B-movie with no handle on my motivation. I'm jealous, I'm giddy, I'm... *relieved?* There's no time to process the clash of emotions inside me—my animal brain is screaming for me to do *something*.

Nate says, "Please, London—"

Steph interrupts, "This is some juicy drama. I'm in!" Before Nate can protest, she grabs my hand and hauls me from the booth.

Steph charges across the club, onto the crowded dance floor, and straight to the middle of the madness. Her fierce energy and copious tattoos ensure us safe passage. Some people even jump out of her way. I'm laughing hysterically by the time she's asserted control over a space big enough for us both to let loose.

This close to the DJ and sound system, the bass vibrates in my bones. Rihanna is singing over a mixed track, her velvet voice and the heady beat making movement mandatory. Swept up by the distraction, I embrace my body's demand.

Before two tracks have passed, my skin and hair are damp again and I'm having the time of my life. When male arms come around my waist, I don't immediately jerk away. From the wicked grin on Steph's face, he's good-looking. All I know is he smells good. And more importantly, he doesn't smell like Dominic Cross.

My mystery partner and I move together, though I'm careful to keep space between my ass and his crotch. No point in letting him think this is going anywhere, like to his apartment. But in all other respects, I flirt with my body, inhibited and without care.

"You are too sexy," a deep voice whispers in my ear.

I make a face at Steph, who laughs. "Thanks!" I say and decide its time to end this pointless game. But when I start to pull away, he drags me flush against him.

A thick, strong hand closes around my throat, fingers digging deep. Sparkling tendrils of fear move through me. We're not dancing anymore, but in the chaos and crazy lights, no one notices anything amiss. His grip tightens, cutting off my air. My head swims. My knees lock. I'm frozen, unable to do more than gasp Steph's name. By chance or luck, she looks over in that moment. She's instantly charging toward us.

"Hey, asshole!" she shouts. "Let her go!"

Warm breath bathes my ear. "I have a message for you, Mrs. Kirkland. You haven't been forgotten. The Old Man says hello."

His fingers vanish, as does his body. Steph grabs me, arm tight around my waist as she spins around. "Where did he go? Shit, let's get out of here."

I nod, my hand curled protectively around my throbbing neck. Steph guides me off the dance floor. Away from the screaming crowd and press of bodies, I gulp in cooler air.

"I'm so sorry, London. I didn't see what was going on. Are you okay? Did he hurt you?"

From behind me comes a chilling, familiar voice. "Did he, kitten? Because I seem to remember that being my job."

Steph whispers, "Oh, fuck."

THE ALLEY IS DARK, the air chilled with pre-sunrise dew. It doesn't smell great, but the overall aesthetic is a fitting backdrop for the worst conversation of my life.

"Say that again."

"I—don't—remember," I snarl through my teeth.

"Why, London? Why are you lying to me? I *saw* him say something to you. I *saw* the horror on your face."

Shivering, I wrap my arms around myself. "Nice of you to intervene on my behalf." My voice is as acidic as my roiling stomach. "Oh wait—no, that's right—you were too busy flirting with two bimbos in VIP. Why do you care, anyway? It doesn't matter. It's over."

"Sir?" asks Nate timidly. "It's super late and security keeps giving us looks. Maybe we should—"

"Not until she tells me the truth."

I snort. "You could always beat it out of me." The flash of hurt on his face is so quick I convince myself I imagined it.

Expression hard, Cross reaches for me. "I'm taking you home."

I shuffle back, jabbing a finger in his direction. "No. I'm going home with Nate."

He glances to the side. "Nathan, leave."

"Uhh—"

"Don't order him around!"

"Now, Nathan!"

Nate looks from Cross to me, and I know I've lost. "I'm sorry, London," he whispers, then races down the alley.

I grab my hair at the scalp and scream through my teeth. It doesn't help, so I unleash on Cross, shoving him as hard as I can. My efforts result in low, dangerous laughter. In a second flat, I'm trapped in his arms, my back to his front. Of course the position is purposeful, a reminder of another man's recent embrace.

"This is your fault," I seethe. "I wouldn't have been out there at all if I hadn't seen you winking at some slut upstairs when she shoved her tits in your face."

More laughter, this time surprised. "Oh, really? That bothered you?"

"No! I don't care who you fuck. You're obviously

getting it somewhere since you're not getting it from me. Is it her? That brunette?"

His chest vibrates against my spine. "Jealousy brings out the kitten's claws."

Anger and helplessness spiking again, I thrash in his arms. "Let me go."

"You're only hurting yourself," he says with insufferable calm. "Calm down and let me show you how to break free."

The words finally register. I go limp, physically and emotionally spent.

"Good girl," he murmurs. "Now, step your feet forward to allow space between us. Lean back."

"I'm going to fall," I protest.

"An attacker isn't going to let go that easily. In fact, they'll most likely try to drag you backward." He demonstrates, my heels digging into asphalt a few feet before he stops. "Once there's space, make a fist and punch backward. Aim for the junk. If you miss the first time, don't give up. Keep pounding away."

Hands in fists, I hesitate. "I don't want to, um, hurt you."

He laughs in delight. "You won't, kitten."

"Are you saying I *can't*?" I stiffen with affront. "What's the point, then?"

"No," he says with barely restrained mirth. "I'm

saying that ninety-nine percent of the male population can't defend themselves like I can."

Basically GI-Joe.

"Right. Okay." I swing my fist back, landing a pitiful impact on his thigh.

"Do you even know where a man's dick is?"

I swing harder. Alternating hands. He dodges every blow, but murmurs encouragement. "Yep, got him. Again. Nice. Good job. Make sure you keep your feet forward or he's going to pull you back and you'll lose the advantage."

Panting, I sag. "I'm still stuck."

"Only because I need to guide you through what happens next." His arms fall, robbing me of his heat. I scowl at him and wiggle my fingers for him to hurry up. Smirking, he points at my legs. "Those are your best weapon, especially with heels. Sometimes, a punch where it counts will be enough for you to get away and run. But it's best to kick immediately after he releases you, while he's still standing and not hunched over mourning his shriveled balls."

I gape at him. His eyes are alight with passion, his voice instructive and encouraging. He looks... happy.

His brows lift. "What?"

I shake my head quickly. "Nothing. You were saying?"

He waves me forward and taps his chest, then his stomach. "Aim here or here depending on height. Kick high and hard, then run. Let's see it."

"Let me guess, I can't actually hurt you?"

He chuckles. "Come on, kitten. Don't be shy."

This time, I don't give him any warning. I aim a kick at his stomach, using the skills from years playing soccer as a kid. He doesn't flinch as he catches my spiked heel millimeters from his abdomen. We stare at each other for a pregnant beat, then with a soft stroke of fingers on my ankle, he release my leg.

"Nice form," he says, lips twitching.

"Told you I'm a badass."

A smile breaks free. "Do you feel better?"

I nod, blowing out a breath. "I do."

"Good. I want you to sign up for weekly self-defense classes. When you've done that for a month, you need to start running. A mile to start, then increase until you can run five miles without stopping. Understood?"

"You're joking."

"Do I look like I'm joking?" He steps close and cups my face with warm hands. "It's important to me that you know how to protect yourself if I'm not there. Can you do this for me?"

I swallow hard. "Okay."

"Thank you." His forehead drops to mine. "I couldn't get there in time. I'm sorry."

Off-kilter, I mutter, "Not your fault."

Kissing my forehead, he draws back to look me in the eyes. "It was. I'm not seeing or fucking anyone else. I shouldn't have allowed that woman to touch me. It was disrespectful to you, and I'm sorry. Which is the *only* reason I'm not going to punish you for dancing with that dickhead. But if you do something like that again, I guarantee you won't be able to sit comfortably for a week."

Heat funnels through me as I imagine what that might entail. My mouth parts on a shallow breath. "I'm sorry."

He smiles softly, thumb grazing my cheek. "Don't be. You answered a question that's been bothering me for a while."

"Huh? What question?"

"Whether you give a shit about me beyond what I do to you in my loft." Without waiting for a response—not that I have one—he wraps an arm around my shoulders and guides me out of the alley. "Let's get you home. And by home, I mean shackled to a bench."

"I thought you weren't punishing me!"

He grins down at me. "Who said anything about punishment?"

Oh.

29

BY THE TIME Cross is done with me, I'm boneless and teetering on the edge of sleep. He lays me gently on his bed, tucking blankets around me. They smell deliciously of him.

"Sleep, sweetheart."

I do. Mercifully, I don't dream. No nightmares, nothing. When I wake, it's to soft, masculine voices in the living area of the loft. Rolling over, I grab my phone off the nightstand to check the time. 10:47 a.m. Thanks to the heavy blackout curtains, I missed the sun rising and most of the morning.

Though I only slept a little over five hours, I'm alert and refreshed. Even when in the past I've caved and popped a sleeping pill, it's rare for me to experience rest free from any dreams. *Is this how normal people feel in the morning?* I don't remember anymore.

Stretching lazily, I focus on the voices. Cross and... Liam Rourke. Their tones are low, but bits and pieces hit my ears.

"...security feeds caught him leaving right after..."

"...staying in the city?"

"...LAX this morning. Missed him."

There's a long pause, then Cross mutters, "What the hell is she hiding?"

Sitting up fast, I clutch the blanket to my chest. Last night comes back in a vicious surge. *You haven't been forgotten. The old man says hello.* Delayed fear makes an appearance, shooting chills down my body.

Stupid. So stupid to think he'd let me go, let me live free of his influence. His evil. Of course he knows where I am, where I live, work. He probably has my phone tapped, my bank accounts watched.

What does he want from me? Better yet, what do I have left to give him?

He's already taken everything.

"You're up. Did we wake you?"

Cross leans on the doorjamb, arms crossed over his bare chest. Low-slung pajama pants hug his lean hips and show off his inhumanly-cut physique. Normally, the visual treat has a notable effect on my lady parts. Not this time. He told me once I wear every emotion on my face, but when I look at him now, I'm blank. Empty. He sees nothing because I *am* nothing.

"It's all right." I swing my legs off the bed. "Mind if I shower before heading home?"

His eyes narrow. "That's fine. How are you feeling?"

I smile. "Good. Great, actually. Thanks for, um..."

He smirks. "Three orgasms?"

"Yep! Slept like a log."

"Good. I forgot to ask—how did Nathan like his gift?"

"He loved it. Thanks again for the hook-up." Dragging the blanket with me, I edge toward the bathroom. "Is Liam still here?"

Cross watches me with predatory focus as I shuffle across the room. "He just left."

I nod. "Okay, well..." I'm almost there.

"London."

"Yes?"

"While I can respect your need for privacy, our conversation last night isn't over. When I said you were mine, I meant it. I *will* find out what you're hiding from me."

My shell cracks. Staring into his dark eyes, my conviction wavers. Maybe I can trust him. Maybe he can help me. Then I remember—the last person who tried to help me is dead. The possibility of Cross suffering the same fate has my walls closing high and tight.

"It's none of your business, Dominic. I appreciate your concern, but I don't need your help. Or Liam's."

He doesn't react to my use of his name other than to take a step into the bedroom. "Then you won't care that we discovered the identity of the man who accosted you last night and have a good idea who he's working for."

I shrug. "None of that means anything to me."

"You're getting better at lying, I'll give you that." His voice is mild, in sharp contrast to the ferocity in his eyes. "I certainly won't beat the truth out of you, but I bet I could fuck it out."

"Ha! Funny man. I didn't realize your cock was truth serum. Is that something you learned in the army?"

His smile dims. "I was a Navy SEAL, actually. Do you want to see my dog tags? Hear about my last mission? Know how many people died on my watch? See the scar where I almost lost my leg and my life? I'll warn you, though, you'll have to get up close and personal with my dick if you want to check it out."

Appropriately chastised, I say, "No. I believe you."

Another step toward me; no trace left of lightness or humor in his bearing. "You don't want to know anything about me. You might start to care, and that's not an option, is it? You've been burned, I get it. So have I."

He's close now, all that bronzed skin scattering my thoughts, battering my walls.

"But what I don't understand," he continues, "is how you give me your body like a sacrificial offering for my darkest desires, how you fall apart so perfectly for me, and still somehow keep most of yourself locked away."

"I—"

"Don't bother," he says on a sigh. "Last night, when you acted jealous, I thought..." He shakes his head, gaze lowering to the floor. "I knew this was a mistake. I should have listened to my gut. You'd think I'd have learned that when it comes to women I want, they're always liars."

This is it. The moment I either walk away or tell him everything. I didn't think it would come so soon, had selfishly hoped we could stay as we were—Dom and part-time submissive, sadist and glutton for pain. The thought of losing him now, so suddenly, takes my breath away. I want to run, I want to fall... I don't know what I want anymore.

"Dominic," I whisper. "You don't understand. I'm not... not right. Most days I don't even feel alive—that I'm still breathing isn't a relief. It's a curse. I don't want to hurt you. I didn't know you even..."

"Cared about you?" His head lifts, a sour smile on his lips. "Christ, London, the only reason I haven't fucked you is I'm afraid I won't be able to get enough.

Tell me you don't feel anything when I dominate you. That it's just scratching an itch, and you're just a pain-slut looking for a good time."

Even though the moniker isn't said with any judgment, I suck in a breath, my stomach clenching. "You're right. That's what I am."

He moves too fast for my eyes to track. One second, we're several feet apart. In the next, my back hits the wall by the bathroom and his fingers encircle my throat. He isn't squeezing, but his grip is firm enough that I know he's in control. Despite the parallels to last night's assault, in every way that matters this is different. My head knows it. And my body's reaction?

Damning.

"You want me to believe that any Dom could touch you like this and you'd react the same? You're pupils just blew. I can *smell* you, London. I know just how wet you are right now. Know exactly how you'd taste on my tongue. If I ordered to you display right now, you'd do it. Not because you want pain, but because I'm the one giving it."

He's right, and I would. God help me, I would drop to my knees right now if he told me to.

"Please," I whisper, "I can't."

"Can't what?"

Have feelings for you.

Trust you.

Need you.

I give him the only safe fact: "I can't tell you the truth, and I can't tell you why. I'm sorry."

His fingers gentle, feathering my skin as he retreats back a step. For a pregnant moment, his gaze takes in my features. Then he nods and leaves the room.

WHEN I'M SHOWERED and wearing the spare set of clothes I keep at the loft, I walk out of the bedroom. The space is empty—he's gone, and I have the sinking feeling he's not coming back. My gaze stalls on the dining table. Breath shallow in my chest, I walk toward what he left for me.

Our contract—torn cleanly down the middle. A note rests over the breach, and I lift it with numb fingers.

London,

I'm terminating our contract effective immediately. Whatever we both thought going into this—that we could keep it casual, friendly—was wrong. I don't want to be your friend, and I don't want to be the only one invested. Seems I have learned something from the past, after all.

If you want to renegotiate our contract, I think you know what it will require. The ball is in your court. But I do want you to know that whatever trouble you're in—you have my number. Use it if you need it.

Sign up for those self-defense classes. It's not an order, but rather a very strong suggestion from someone who knows how violent the world is.

Don't worry—you're not fired.

Take care,

Dominic

Blinking away the sheen of tears, I whisper, "Good for you, sir."

30

NOW

"I want something in return."

My statement is met with a raspy chuckle. "You're not in a position to bargain, Blondie. Either you come, or one of these women gets special treatment."

Behind Cinder, two other guards joke quietly in Russian, their attention on a pair of young women who look like sisters. Their glazed eyes stare back unblinking.

"Maybe your friend here." Cinder's big boot kicks at the curled-up legs of the teenager, who shifts protectively around the toddler. Though I told her several times to move somewhere else, to get as far away from me as she could, for some inexplicable reason she didn't listen.

Then again, this is a house of insanity. And the gamble I'm about to make proves it.

"No," I say, hauling myself to my feet. Blood rushes from my head, my vision momentarily darkening. I brace a hand on the wall behind me and lift my chin. "I have conditions. I want cots in here, one for each woman. Pillows and blankets, too. A fresh, hot meal once a day, and fresh milk for the child. Clean water to use for bathing, a tub and a privacy screen. And you get a doctor in here. I'm sure there's one on the payroll. Some of the women have been sick for a week. They need medicine—"

For such a brutish man, Cinder moves like the wind. My head slams into the wall as his fingers seize my throat. "Who the *fuck* do you think you are?"

"You tell your boss my terms," I grind out, stretching to gasp air, blinking dark dots from my eyes. "I'll play his little game *when* and *if* I get what I asked for."

Rage purples his face. He squeezes harder, severing my claim to oxygen. I'm too weak to fight back. My vision slowly dims, and I wonder if my last sight on this earth will be the angry vein throbbing in his neck.

With a beastly roar, he tosses me to the ground. On my hands and knees, I cough and retch until I'm choking on bitter, unhinged laughter. Sagging back against the wall, I palm my sore neck. When I look up, I laugh harder at the comprehension in Cinder's eyes.

"That's right," I mock hoarsely. "You *should* be scared. You can't hurt the stable's prize stallion, can you? It might upset their owner. And we both know what happens when he's upset." I mimic a slice across my neck.

He snarls something in Russian and spits, a fat glob of phlegm landing near my feet. "You'll get yours, American whore."

I grin. "And so will you."

When they're gone, I look around at silent, staring faces. Beside me, the teenager whispers, "Who *are* you?"

I shake my head. "No one."

31

THEN

The warmup, as always, is slow and delivered with care. Tickles and taps from the flogger's leather tails on my thighs, stomach, breasts. A tease, a foreshadowing of what's to come. The blindfold is thick and tight, no light leaking through, enhancing my other senses and keeping my nerves on edge. I tremble on the cross, fingers and toes twitching. Ready for worship. Enthralled by his devotion.

THE MEMORY IS A FAVORITE—IF it was a timeline-bead, it would be worn, smooth from over-handling. But I don't care. It's mine. I can do whatever the hell I want with it, even if it means rolling it around and playing with it until there's nothing left. Which is doubtful. I'm not sure a blow to the head and amnesia could extract Dominic Cross from my marrow.

"Do you want to talk about it?"

Charlie's office has recently become my refuge. Much to her annoyance. But at least here I don't have to pretend, smile and laugh with colleagues and clients like nothing's changed. Like I can't see him every time he moves through the crowd. Like I don't miss him.

Not the cross, cuffs, or clamps. Not the wax, rope, whip, or flogger. Just him. His laugh, rare and contagious. His loathing of socks, obsession with Cary Grant movies, and habit of touching me. Always, anywhere, whenever we shared the same space. A hand in my hair. A foot against mine under the table. His fingers grazing mine as we passed in the back hallway of the club.

A handful of nights together and it feels like a thousand. One kiss amidst a lifetime of surrendering to pain and pleasure at his hands. It's insanity, the hold he has over me. I've never even seen his dick, for shit's sake.

"I don't even know what he *was*, you know?" I

mutter at the ceiling. "We weren't lovers. He wasn't my boyfriend."

Charlie looks up from paperwork. "He was your Dom, London. Sometimes that means a whole lot more than those other labels." She sighs, pulling cat-eye glasses from her nose. "If you don't give me details, I can't help you. All this vague, love-sick shit is getting old. Either tell me why he called it quits, or get out of my office. Shouldn't you be getting ready for work, anyway?"

She's still scary—but not nearly as scary as she was before this whole thing started. Or before two weeks ago, when I cried like a baby in her arms during a break the night after he ended things.

But I can't tell her the truth, any more than I can tell Dominic the truth. There's no way through this. No happy ending. *He* made sure of that two years ago. The visit from the thug on Nate's birthday only confirmed what I already knew: I will never be free of the past.

Charlie merely frowns when I make excuses—*look at the time*—and head across the hallway to get dressed for work. For the first time in nearly two months, I pull out my opening-night outfit. I haven't worn it since my first time with Dominic. Since he put his first marks on me. But my body no longer shows any signs of a sadist's barbed care. I'm exactly the same as I've always been.

On the outside, at least.

ANOTHER THREE WEEKS PASS. I return to my pre-Cross routine. Work, eat, sleep, and withstand the nightmares. The only change has been on my days off, when I religiously attend self-defense classes at a gym in my neighborhood. As I get stronger, faster, and more agile, I experience moments of pride. And gratitude. Because of Dominic, I now know exactly what to do if someone assaults me again—and they will. The echo of that stranger's hands on my throat lingers. *He* isn't done with me yet. It wasn't a message but a warning.

I buy mace. Hide a knife in my nightstand. Consider, then discard, the idea of purchasing a gun. I keep going, *living*, in the twilight.

Every night I come into work, I dread hearing that Dominic will be publicly participating. Doing an instructional scene in the Epicenter for the delight of the crowd, or worse, taking a sub into one of the playrooms. There are times, too, that what we shared feels like a dream. That nothing ever changed between us—we are barely civil, rarely in the same place at the same time.

On a Saturday night, five weeks after ultimatums and torn contracts, I arrive at work to find Nate waiting for me in the employee lounge. The look on his face—part sympathy, part frustration—tells me everything I need to know.

My heart contracts painfully.

"Charlie wants to see you," he says softly.

I drop my purse in my locker, avoid the curious stares of others, and follow him from the room. Nate knocks twice before opening Charlie's office door. She looks up from her desk, nodding at him before focusing her dark gaze on me. Nate slips out, closing the door silently behind him.

After a few moments of appraisal, she sighs. "Christ, you look like shit."

I smile tiredly. "Having a hard time sleeping lately."

"And when you were serving Cross, did you sleep?"

The question throws me. "What?"

Domme-vibe in full force, she snaps, "Answer the question."

"Y-yes."

Charlie nods grimly. "Listen up. You're not working tonight—not behind the bar, at least. I'm renegotiating your employment contract on your behalf."

I frown. "I'm lost."

She stands, rounding the desk with a sharp smile. "I know. In three hours, at midnight, Cross is scheduled to demonstrate proper technique for caning."

I shudder. Of all his toys, the cane is my least favorite—it delivers a vicious, all-consuming pain that cannot be quelled by pleasure. And yet... the idea of him giving that pain to someone else makes me wild with jealousy.

"Don't like that idea, do you?"

I shake my head. "No."

"Good." Her smile spreads. "How would you like to be the sub he canes tonight?"

My brain screeches to a halt, then shifts into overdrive. "What? No! I can't do that to him, surprise him like that—he'll be so pissed. Are you nuts?"

Charlie gives me a flat look. "Dominic is a professional. He might yell at you after the fact—and me, no doubt—but he'd never allow anger to affect the scene. Do you want to do it or not?"

As the idea sinks in, my heart picks up pace. "Yes, absolutely, yes. Why are you doing this for me, Charlie?"

She returns to her desk, sliding gracefully into the chair. "My reasons are my own, but I'll say this: as much as I begrudgingly like you, London, I'm not doing this for you. Take the bag by the door on your way out. Nate will help you get ready in one of the playrooms. Don't disappoint me. Or Dominic. Understood?"

Swallowing inane laughter, I bow my head. "Yes, madam."

32

"TEN MINUTES."

I nod from my perch on a padded table in Playroom Six. The curtain over the viewing window is drawn, only Nate as witness my lip-chewing, foot-tapping state. We've worked our way through a handful of risqué knock-knock jokes and compared favorite movies and books. He's doing his best to distract me, and I'm doing my best not to bolt.

"Oh—I forgot to ask. You're not on your period or about to get it, are you?"

My head swings toward him. "What the hell? Why?"

He shrugs. "Pain receptors are more active during that time, apparently."

"I'm good," I mutter, screwing my eyes shut. "I can't

believe I'm doing this."

"The caning or the blatant manipulation?

I shake my head. "The audience."

Nate laughs shortly. "I can. Didn't your parents force you to vacation at a nudist colony one summer? This is nothing."

I groan, but laugh in spite of myself. "That was the worst. Who takes teenaged daughters to a nudist retreat? Scarred us for life."

"Speaking of—have you told your parents yet?"

"About letting someone tie me to a pole and beat me with a belt? No. No, I have not. They'd probably throw a party."

He laughs and glances at his watch. "Five minutes. Up you go."

With a jolt of adrenaline, I slip off the bench to my feet. The floor-length silk dressing-gown whispers against my legs, rippling like crimson water. Nate approaches me with the only other item that had been in Charlie's bag. A full-face hood. Not latex or leather— thank everything that's holy—but black lace with intricate designs over the eyes and mouth.

Nate carefully rolls it down from my crown, over my face and under my chin. The light in the room dims, filtered by the thickness over my eyes. My lungs protest to the restricted airflow over my mouth. I breathe slowly through my nose until claustrophobia fades.

"Okay?" he asks, adjusting my low braid over one shoulder. I nod and he steps back, a wistful expression on his face. "It's... breathtaking. I wonder where she found it."

"It was probably a gift for you," I quip, tilting my head side to side to get used to the light pressure and constriction.

Nate snorts. "Definitely not. Oh—hear that?"

I do. The playrooms are close to sound-proof, but not completely, and the noise of the crowd in the main club filters through. Having witnessed it so often from behind the bar, I can easily envision what's happening. The music softening, the lights dimming. Masked employees bringing the velvet-swathed cross into the Epicenter. The soft spotlight slowly intensifying as the crowd surges to the railings, ready for action.

Nate offers me his arm. "My lady."

His stoic expression gives me pause, and stills the nervous quip on my tongue. I take his arm. "Thank you."

We make it to the door before he hesitates. "Are you sure you don't want Advil? Or something stronger?"

My breath shudders out, warming the lace before my mouth. "No." I leave it at that.

Pain slut.

Maybe I am. But as we leave the playroom and walk down the hallway toward the cheers and shouts ahead of us, I'm not ashamed of who I am. Of what I want. And with new certainty, I know that Dominic was right. My pain belongs to him, because he's the only one I trust to take it from me.

When the edge of the crowd notices us, a low murmur ripples outward and a path opens up. As we walk forward, from the corner of my eye I catch nods of respect from submissives and Doms alike. And I take a moment to appreciate Charlie's genius. If I was already naked, gagged or blindfolded, my reception might be different. Debasement. Demeaning shouts or harsh touches. But covered completely by the mask and robe, I'm a dignified sacrifice on the way to the altar. No one touches me. No one dares.

It's a heady feeling. Undeniably erotic.

We reach the short steps that lead down into the Epicenter. The space is empty, the cross unveiled and waiting. Nate stops. With a final squeeze of my arm, he whispers, "Good luck," and disappears.

My hand on the railing, my heart pounding a staccato rhythm, I stare at the cross. The crowd is remarkably silent, the faces around me disappearing into darkness after the first few rows.

Two tall, masked men step into the pit and take up

position on either side of the cross. My cue. I step down on weak knees and walk the short distance to my altar, then reach for the ties on my robe. My shaking fingers struggle, then find the release. Fabric slithers down my body and flutters to the floor.

My mind goes still, my ears filling with an electric hum. The men take my extended arms and guide me face-first to the wood. Their touch is brisk and impersonal as my wrists and ankles are secured in cuffs. When their task is done, they, too, melt away. I shift, getting used to the position, and glimpse expressive faces above me—encouragement, apprehension, excitement, arousal... But none of it matters. None of them matter.

My cheek against the main support beam, I close my eyes and wait. I don't know how much time passes before I hear his name—first in whispers, then shouts.

"Cross."

"Master Dominic."

My eyes shut, I still feel him when he steps into the Epicenter. A hush moves over the crowd—*a response to his reaction on seeing me?* My question is answered a second later as a warm, bare hand floats up my spine and grips the back of my neck.

"Bad, bad kitten," he whispers against my ear.

"I'm sorry, sir."

His grip firms, fingers massaging the tense muscles in my neck. "I won't go easy on you."

I squirm in readiness, in fear, in anticipation. "I don't want you to, sir."

His chuckle is dark and sultry. "So be it." He moves away, cool air rushing over my body and making me shiver. "Tonight, I'll be demonstrating cold caning."

There's a uptick of surprise from the crowd. Gooseflesh ripples down my body as the words sink in. *Cold caning.* Caning without a warm up.

Oh, fuck me.

"The most important thing to remember when caning is the necessity of a pause-period after a strike."

An ominous whistling of air is my only warning before the slender, rattan cane lands on my ass. I jerk against the cross, yelping from the immediate, brutal sting. Just when the pain begins to fade, when my heart begins to slow, the second wave of sensation hits—an intense burn radiating from the offended spot. I groan, twisting fruitlessly in effort to escape it.

"...seconds to a minute, so your sub can experience each strike fully. Cold caning should never be done lightly—as it's extremely painful—and never on an inexperienced sub. But this little kitten knows what a cane feels like, don't you?"

"Yes, sir," I gasp.

"Are you thankful?"

"Yes. Thank you, sir."

"Do you want another?"

Overriding every instinct, I say, "Yes, please, sir."

Over the roar of the crowd, I still hear the whistle of air.

Again.

And again.

Waves of pain hit, one after the other, until endorphins finally flood my system. My mind hovers, quiet and peaceful, even as my body sobs, thrashes, and screams. There's no pleasure, no space for it at all in his beautiful cruelty. But that in itself is a type of pleasure. At least for me.

"Three more," he promises, strain in his voice.

"Yes," I whimper. "Again, sir."

Again.

And again.

33

CHARLIE AND DOMINIC are yelling at each other, a pointless volley of accusations and insults flying over my head. I'm still naked—which is surprisingly easy when you're in excruciating pain—and lying facedown on the couch in the loft. Nate's beside me, stroking my hair and distracting me from the fire that's taken residence on the back half of my body.

"I've never been so disrespected!"

"Well, you've never been this stupid before!"

"I almost lost it, Charlie! I could have really hurt her, and it would have been your fault."

"Bullshit. Not in a million years would you have hurt her."

I almost laugh, but it's not funny. I'm in pain, yes, but Charlie's right—I'm not hurt. The blows were perfect. No broken skin, which is a miracle in and of itself. Just a world of discomfort on my ass, thighs, and shoulders.

Charlie continues, "Stop second-guessing your instincts. Stop trying to be someone you're not!"

"Watch yourself, Rhodes."

"*You* watch yourself, you arrogant shit. If Liam won't give it to you straight, then it's up to me. That woman lying there dropped out of the fucking sky and straight into your lap. She's everything you want and need, but you threw her away!"

"Because she lied to me!" he roars. I flinch at the raw feeling in his voice, glad for the cool washcloth over my eyes so I don't have to see firsthand how angry he is. Nate's hand stills, then resumes.

Charlie's voice lowers, becomes almost gentle. "It's not the same, Dominic. Can't you see that? London isn't using you, manipulating you—"

"Oh, really? What do you think tonight—"

"Just shut up and listen! We both know she would never have blindsided you like that if I hadn't orchestrated it. Yes, London has some shit in her past that she doesn't talk about. But so do you. So does Nathan. It took him two *years* to tell us what happened to him. And last time I checked, I still don't know what made you leave the Navy!"

Do you want me to tell you about my last mission? How many people died on my watch? See the scar where I almost lost my leg and my life?

I twitch, feeling like the worst kind of voyeur. Give me pain any day of the week, but witnessing someone else's? No way. Especially when the pain is wrapped up with almost-intimacy. *Would he have told me? Given me a truth he hasn't even shared with Charlie?* I don't want to know the answer—it scares the hell out of me, how much I want it to be *yes*.

The wall around my heart shivers. Inside me, the shadow-me looks up, waiting. Hoping for a ray of sunlight in the dark. Tears burn in my eyes. I'm so tired. So fucking tired of being alone. Of not trusting anyone. Of the nightmares, the duplicity. The daily pretenses I maintain.

"...do this again, Charlie. I really can't. Ashley—"

"Is a dirty twat who almost landed you in a looney bin!"

"Enough!"

Charlie growls—literally *growls*. Her heels pound away from the couch toward the kitchen. Leather creaks as Nate leans down, his breath tickling my ear.

"Hey, you're shaking. Are you laughing or crying right now?"

A muffled sob escapes with the lie, "I'm okay."

"No, you're not," says Dominic, voice reedy with exhaustion.

"She's dropping hard," murmurs Nate.

"Give her what she needs," snaps Charlie from across the room.

I barely hear the words, the dissolution of my reality all-consuming. Dominic's voice hums beneath my misery, then two sets of hands lift me gently to my feet. Like a flower seeking sunlight, I melt into the warmth and scent of my Dom. One arm braces me mid-back, the other arm sweeping me up from beneath the knees.

I whimper with relief, then in pain as he walks toward the bedroom. "Hush. I'm here."

"Dominic." His name is thick and slurred. "I'll tell you. Everything. Please, don't go."

His arms briefly tighten. "I won't."

As I slip deeper into the void-like space in my mind, I hope against hope that he means it.

I WAS AMBITIOUS. Too ambitious, according to some. Borderline reckless in my pursuit of a story. But with each new exposé, my reputation grew, and reputations required maintenance. More—they demanded *better*. Bigger. My editors had come to expect it. My readers wanted it. There were even whispers in some circles of a Pulitzer on my horizon, and I believed with near-fanaticism *this* would be the one to catapult me into the realm of journalistic greats.

The interviews with the young women weren't enough on their own. Despite the atrocities they recounted for me, despite the revulsion I felt listening to them, my logical mind knew I needed more. More than the word of three drug-addicted Russian teens who talked about famous, rich men paying for them, about escaping from labor-camp conditions only to be forced into prostitution just to eat.

I needed a connection. A name. And now I had it, via a photograph of a highly recognizable man leading a barely-legal young woman into the back of a limousine. The same young women who, one week ago, showed up in the morgue with an execution-style gunshot wound in her forehead. The man was Jeffrey Donalds. Supreme Court Justice. Willing participant and benefactor of an international, illegal sex trafficking ring operated by the Russian mob in New York.

Bingo.

I immediately sent the photograph to a tech who could tell me if it had been doctored in any way, then printed it and sent an additional copy to my personal email. Electrified at the possibility of renown, I ignored the voice in the back of my head warning me about risks. Stepping on the toes of law enforcement. Jeopardizing undercover work, Federal investigations... But I shut that voice up with rationalizations.

I was exposing one man—a criminal who didn't deserve to sit on a bench of public office. Sure, the mob would be indicated, but really, who'd be shocked? Not them, certainly. Though I would be pointing a finger in their direction, I had no hard evidence of their involvement. And they knew it.

My recent interview with Ivan Reznikov, the suspected head of the Russian mob, had been both terrifying and exhilarating. He'd been amused by me, laughing often as we shared drinks and ceviche. A robust bear of a man in his fifties, I could tell he was attracted to me.

Despite my wedding band, he made no fewer than ten passes at me over the course of our time together. So I used it. Flirted and smiled. And Reznikov enjoyed the game, though he was too slick to take any of my bait. A master of evasion, he offered only the barest hints of culpability, and nothing that could be used against him in a trial.

Jeffrey Donalds's life would go down in flames, and my praises would be sung far and wide.

34

IN THE WARM SUNLIGHT, the truth is starker. Everything is brighter, harsher. The glimmer on the water, the coarse sand beneath my bare feet. The shrieking of children nearby and the crash of waves. Even though my ass is still tender, I'm glad to be sitting. The story is pummeling me as it comes up and out. I'm weak. Lightheaded.

The man beside me stares at the water. I can't see his eyes, hidden beneath a tattered baseball hat and sunglasses. But he's listening. I notice small signals—twitching of fingers, compressing of lips.

After a fitful few hours of sleep, I woke this morning to coffee and an offer to help me dress. I barely had time to process the fact he'd kept my remaining "aftercare" clothing before Dominic grabbed his car keys. Wearing drawstring pants, a t-shirt sans bra, an oversized cardigan, and flip-flops, I followed him numbly downstairs and into the crisp morning. I figured this was it—he was taking me home, he didn't want to hear the truth, didn't want to deal with my crazy. I couldn't blame him.

But instead, he drove us to the beach in Venice. A cloudy morning, the white sands were vacant except for several clusters of homeless and black dots of surfers in the water. Over the last hour, as I've haltingly started my tale, the clouds have burned off. The sun now beats warmly down. Vagrants have been replaced by families toting umbrellas and coolers, and pairs of young women in skimpy bikinis.

Covering my eyes from the glare off the water, I watch a toddler dodging small waves on the shoreline. Nearby, his mother takes pictures.

With a deep breath, I continue my story. "I was unbelievably stupid to think Reznikov wouldn't care. That he'd even enjoy the bad press. Get a laugh of out it. I was living in a fantasy-land. Those women..." I falter, clearing my throat, "Those women trusted me. They gave me their truths, and I got them killed."

Dominic stirs, head turning toward me. "How?"

"Reznikov found them," I whisper brokenly. "It was the night before the story broke. Someone must have leaked the article, I don't know... Three hookers winding up dead is rarely newsworthy, except I was still getting alerts. Same MO as the first victim. I went to the morgue to see for myself. It was them. They were executed for speaking to me about the trafficking ring."

Instead of offering empty platitudes, Dominic nods. "Sounds likely. What did you do?"

Another layer inside me crumbles, revealing deeper, darker shame. "I went home and told Paul everything. He didn't even know about the article. I'd kept it secret because..." My vision blurs with tears.

Memories of that night are jagged, malformed with emotion. Fear, anger, betrayal. I'd never seen Paul so infuriated, so violent. He'd thrown a chair across the room. So much yelling and name-calling. Panic and darkness. I'd begged for him to help me make it right. He'd threatened to have me arrested.

"Because...?" prompts Dominic.

I swallow hard. "My first lead on the story came from a phone call between him and his superior. He didn't know I was listening. I heard a few Russian names and started there."

He's silent for long moments, then: "You used intel from a private conversation between Homeland Security agents to launch your own investigation?"

"Yes," I whisper.

He whistles softly. "I would have been pissed, too.

So Homeland Security was going after the trafficking ring, and you, what, thought you could singlehandedly bring them down first?"

"No. I don't know. I tried to resist the pull of the story. I swear I did. First it was a few calls, then a few more. A name here, a name there. I didn't know that anything would come of it, but I couldn't seem to stop myself. I knew it was wrong, that I should tell Paul, but I... I couldn't. I was a stupid, naïve, selfish woman whose pursuit of fame killed four people."

And my beloved dog.

Dominic's silence lasts so long I'm certain his next words will be a goodbye. I tell myself I'm ready for it. That I'll be okay, even though there's nothing further from the truth.

"I made a call that killed six men." His voice is soft, hoarse. "We had orders to retrieve an informant who'd been compromised. The intel was good—we knew where he was being held in the compound, how many insurgents were there. It should have been cut and dry. But I heard kids. Crying."

Dominic grips the bill of his baseball hat, bending it, his knuckles white. "I sent three men to find our guy, and the rest of us started sweeping the place for those kids. We didn't have much time. The drone was in the fucking air, and that compound was going down whether or not we were still in it."

My heart pounds, chills racing down my arms. "Did you find them?"

"No. It was a trap—a recording attached to a remote bomb. In the seconds before it went off, we learned the informant was already dead. Two of my men were caught in the blast. Through the coms we could hear the other team take fire. It was a massacre. Total chaos."

His breathing is heavy, shoulders tense. Without thinking, I clutch his fist, half-buried in the sand. He jerks, then slowly relaxes.

"If we'd stayed together, we could have made it."

His voice has the familiar, bitter flavor of guilt. I don't say anything. Not because there aren't a thousand words, but because he wouldn't appreciate them. Just like he knew I wouldn't.

"You made it," I say softly. "And that's what hurts the most, doesn't it?"

He glances at me, offering a short nod. "I was carrying a wounded teammate, fighting assholes in every corridor and trying to get out of that sandstone maze. I got stabbed in the groin. It was just a kid. No older than eleven or twelve. He came after me again and I knocked him out, then fell on my ass. Only then did I realize the man I was carrying was dead. I tied off my leg as best I could and crawled the rest of the way out. Dragged myself up a hill and tried to get the drop called off, told command there were men inside. But it was too late. I watched the bombs drop from the sky. Heard the last communication line with my men die. Heard their final shouts."

A sudden gust brings a hint of sea-spray to us. I draw the fresh air into my lungs, feel the expansion, the beat of my heart. Proof of life. Never has it felt more real or heavy.

"I'm sorry that happened to you," I tell him.

He pulls off his sunglasses, revealing tired eyes. "When I was told the higher-ups wanted to give me an award for valor, I left the Navy. I couldn't do it anymore. Couldn't stop thinking about that kid stabbing me, how he truly believed I was the enemy. After taking some time off, I decided to start Titan. Where other private defense companies were commodifying war, I wanted to see if I could use my skillset for peacekeeping efforts."

"A private NATO," I muse.

"Yeah, without the politics." He snorts grimly. "I'm sure you've heard how that turned out, my big dream. I guess we were both naïve."

I laugh, the sound startling us both. "You're a hero. I'm basically a criminal. I appreciate the effort, but there's no comparison."

"I'm no hero," he says gravely, "and you're not that person anymore, London."

My laughter is hollow. "Then who the hell am I?"

"Among other things, a survivor."

I avoid his gaze. "I haven't told you everything."

"I know." He stands, dusting sand from his pants and offering me a hand. "You're taking the night off work, by the way."

My head shakes. "I can't afford—"

His eyes narrow. "Are you saying no?"

That voice. It fills me up, bubbles through me like fine champagne. I didn't realize how much I missed it, longed for it, until this moment.

"No, sir," I whisper.

Strong fingers thread through mine. He lifts my palm to his mouth, pressing a kiss to the sensitive skin. "Good girl."

Before I can stop myself, I ask, "Why aren't you running away?"

His brows lift, a smile teasing his mouth. "When I'm afraid of something, I don't run away from it. I run toward it. And kitten, the only thing on this planet that scares me is you."

35

THE TRUTH CHANGED things between Dominic and me. Pulled threads, scattered beads, reworked patterns on our timelines. Created overlap.

When I look at him now, I see more than the promise of punishment. More than a man I respect and desire, who plays my body like an instrument made for his hands. He's multi-dimensional. Imperfect. Emotional. *Human.* Warm and sensitive, mature and thoughtful. I'm not sure how much longer I can protect my heart. Or if I want to.

Vulnerability didn't used to scare me. My parents encouraged it when I was young, helped us map our emotions and communicate them in positive, loving ways. As an adult, I enjoyed the freedom and intimacy of it in my marriage. Or thought I did—before I fucked everything up. After, I was resigned to never experiencing that freedom again.

Now, by some trick of fate, here it is—a man who heard the absolute worst about me and isn't running. Or if he's running, it's to me instead of away. Those words... they rocked me, illuminating deeper crevices of pain.

Paul ran.

He didn't want to hear my apologies. Couldn't. That night, after telling me I wasn't the woman he thought I was, that he didn't know me at all, he took his car keys and slammed the front door on his way out. I didn't hear from him for three days. At that time, they were the worst three days of my life.

I had no idea what was in store for me.

My guilt hasn't been diminished by my confession. It's still there, round and hard and dark on my timeline. A black diamond nothing can scratch. I failed Paul. Failed *us*. And after he died, my shame was so great I couldn't tell my parents what really happened. Not even Paris knows everything. The bargain I made. The sacrifice.

I told myself it was to protect them, but in reality I was protecting myself. Shielding myself from the truth.

There's no running from the past, but until today, it never occurred to me to run toward it. Dominic Cross is either the wisest or most foolhardy man alive.

Wherever you go, there you are.

"AGAIN."

"I can't, Dominic. I—"

"Again!"

Cursing under my breath, I lift my arms, the muscles quivering like jello. The boxing gloves weigh a hundred pounds each. Sweat stings my eyes. My shoulders burn, my abs burn. *Everything* burns.

"Any day, kitten."

"For the love of—"

"One more set and I'll fuck you tonight."

I flush bright red as musical laughter floats to us from outside the boxing ring. "Oy, Dominic!" calls Liam. "Give her something she actually wants!"

I aim a feeble swing at the pads attached to Dominic's hands. He bats me away like I'm a bothersome fly. I stumble, righting myself with a groan. In contrast to my pathetic state, Dominic bounces lightly on the balls of his feet.

"You're a savage," I pant.

"You're weak," he taunts, effortlessly dancing toward me and back. Muscles ripple on his bare chest; knowing him, it's an intentional distraction. "I thought you were taking self-defense classes. You do know yoga doesn't count, right?"

I swing wildly. Miss him by an embarrassing distance and almost fall again. Dominic grins, eyes twinkling. Wiping sweat from my eyes with my forearm, I scowl.

"Let's see *you* take ten cold hits from a cane, Mr. Tough Guy."

His smile turns devilish. "I'd put that on the table, but there's no way you'd follow through."

He's right, the bastard. Not in a million years could I do to him what he does to me. Even the thought of caning him makes my stomach turn.

I look over at Liam, whose garage-turned-home-gym provides the backdrop to my misery. "What are you getting out of this?"

He laughs. "Free entertainment."

Surrendering to gravity, I crumple to the mat. The bruises on my ass protest, but right now they're the least of my pains. "I'm done. I can't feel my arms."

Dominic drops to a crouch before me, athletic shorts stretching over a certain part of his anatomy. "Eyes up, kitten," he says with mirth.

Though rare for me, I disobey. "You're not, uh, wearing underwear."

Liam explodes in laughter. "You've just noticed?

How the hell did you miss his giant cock flapping around in those shorts?"

"Feel free to get lost," growls Dominic.

"Bah! You're no fun. I've got a date, anyway. See you at Crossroads later?"

Dominic pauses while removing the pads from his hands and glances down at me. "Not sure yet."

Liam aims a cheeky wink my way. "All right, then. Lock up when you leave." Whistling, he saunters across the garage and into the house.

"How do you really feel?" asks Dominic, brushing a sweaty lock of hair off my forehead. The graze of his hot fingertips spark a warm, drifting sensation in my belly.

"Pretty good." Surprisingly, I mean it. "Hungry. Like *really* hungry."

Grabbing my gloves, he hauls me to my feet, ignoring my muttered curse as muscles scream. He starts unwrapping my hands. "Food, then sleep for my brave kitten."

"Sleep?"

Dark, sparkling eyes flicker up to my face. "Depends."

My breath comes short. "On what?"

"On whether you can run a mile." He glances at his watch, then nods toward the treadmill.

I gape. "Right now?"

Slow, devilish smile. "How bad do you want me?"

A rough, disbelieving laugh barks out of me. But it only takes another few seconds for me to toss my loose gloves on the ground and hobble to the treadmill.

Jamming my finger into the start button, I grumble, "That cock better taste like candy and vibrate."

To the sound of Dominic's booming laugh, I run.

STRONG HANDS WORK over my skin, melting knots in my legs and back. I'm far past any embarrassment at my periodic, unrestrained groans of pleasure.

"Ohh, right there."

Dominic goes after a knot in my shoulder blade. The pain is exquisite. I breathe through the bright pulsing, sighing as the tension unravels. His hands retreat. Sheets rustle.

"Turn over, kitten."

I flop onto my back, yawning as I blink open my eyes. Dominic's soft smile greets me. "That was wonderful, thank you."

"You're welcome."

His gaze drops, tracing my throat and down, lingering on my breasts. I've been naked before him so many times—been denied the full pleasure of his body— it doesn't occur to me that tonight's any different. The afternoon was just a tease. His speciality, maybe even more so than pain. He'll tuck me in and leave like always.

Only... he's not leaving.

Awareness frissons down my spine, wrapping around my torso and stiffening my nipples. A broad, tanned hand cups one breast, kneading and plucking the tip. I squirm, arousal turning on like a flipped switch. My legs squeeze beneath the thin sheet covering my lower half.

Time slows, pauses for my memory to capture the moment. Candlelight in the shadowed bedroom, the scent of coconut oil and lavender. The soft waves of his dark hair. Thick lashes shadowing midnight eyes, the curve of firm lips. Broad shoulders rising, then falling as he sighs. The soothing warmth of his hand on me, familiar and not. He's never caressed me without some part of me being immobilized.

I'm afraid to say the wrong thing, make the wrong move. Afraid he'll leave, and this small, precious space between us will vanish like smoke. Afraid, too, of that space. Of how badly I want to dive into it, regardless of whether or not I remember how to swim.

His hand slides across my ribs to my other breast, owning it with the same commanding touch. "London," he murmurs, voice low and raw. Tormented eyes find mine. "Tell me you want this."

The fog of arousal clears momentarily, and I finally understand. He isn't asking if I want to have sex—he's asking if I want to *make love*. My heart burns, an inferno of need and twisted hope. Brilliant light shines in it's darkest corners, searing through shadows and webs of fear. I'm powerless over the truth. And I don't care anymore.

I cover his hand with mine. "Everything I have left to give is yours to take. I'm yours, Dominic."

36

I'M KNEELING on the bed, waiting for him. Toes tucked, knees spread, sitting on my heels with my head bowed and my hands laced together behind my neck. It's not the first time I've been in this position, but it feels that way. The give of the mattress under my knees makes the position difficult to maintain. The burn in my overused muscles has gone from unpleasant to excruciating. Then again, at this point I'd be willing to walk over hot coals for sex with Dominic Cross.

"You're shaking, kitten," he purrs from somewhere in the room. I think he's in the armchair beside the window, but I don't dare look up.

"Yes, sir. I want you, sir."

"What exactly do you want? Tell me the truth."

I suck in a breath, my mind filling with carnal

images. Him behind me, my ankles tied to the bedposts as he drives into me. Face-to-face, slow and needy and vanilla. Tied up and dangling from the ceiling at the exact height necessary for…

"Say it."

"I want to touch you, sir," I blurt. "I want to suck your cock. I want your arms around me as I ride you and you bite my breasts. I want you to kiss me and fuck me and make me come." I gasp into silence, a hot blush blooming under my skin. As much as I've thought the words, I've never in my life spoken so brazenly.

After a pregnant pause, I hear the music of his belt buckle. "Your wish is my command. Come here, London."

My mouth waters as I scramble off the bed. I was right—he's in the big leather armchair—and when I get a good look at him I almost trip. Shirtless, his hair mussed, candlelight making poetry of his face and torso. Slouched with his elbow propped on the armrest, one fist supports his cocked head while the other lazily strokes the most beautiful dick I've ever seen.

"Any day." His voice is wry and satisfied.

"Yes, sir," I breathe, falling to my knees between his spread legs.

"Hands behind your back. Good girl. Come get it."

The first taste of him on my tongue is perfection—

salt and musk and power and servitude. When he breaches my lips, I'm the one who groans in pleasure. And when he hits the back of my throat and I gag and swallow, his voice comes strangled and dark, "Fuck, that's good."

I find a rhythm that makes his hips twitch, alternating my attention between the thick, flared head and testing the limits of my deep-throating skills. His fingers thread through my hair, gripping hard, sending crackles of pain through my body and drenching my inner thighs. When he takes control, I relinquish it gladly.

Never has submission been more empowering than now, with his breathy grunts above me, the muscles of his thighs quivering. His filthy whispers of how beautiful I look doing what he's wanted for so long—choking on his cock. I've never been so turned on in my life, and when he draws my head away, I whimper in protest.

Gentle hands cup my face, thumb dipping into my mouth, fingers wiping saliva from my chin. Panting, I stare up at him. Whatever he sees in my eyes brings an unrivaled intensity to his expression. I can only imagine I look exactly how I feel—devoted, trusting.

In love.

The revelation shimmers through me, finding no resistance. And suddenly my loving him is a foregone conclusion—a fact divorced from fear, regret, and grief.

It doesn't feel new or even surprising. Of course fate brought me here. I belong with him. To him.

"I feel it too," he whispers, then sweeps me up into his lap. I throw my arms around his neck, my head turning, our mouths meeting in seamless, soul-melting grace.

He tastes like home.

For endless, blissful minutes, he devours the offering of my mouth and gives my hands free reign. I read him like Braille, caressing the dips and swells of muscle. His throat. Behind his ears. Hollow of his bellybutton. Ridges of his abdomen. The smattering of dark hair on his chest and arms. I lose myself in his artistry until he dips fingers between my legs. I gasp into his mouth, reverting to carnal need.

With a low groan, he propels us to standing. I hang from his shoulders, my palms memorizing the pull of muscles in his back as he walks us to the bed. Kicking off his pants, he sits once more with me in his lap, scooting back until he leans against the headboard. Gravity rewards me with friction and hardness where I need it most. I grind against him, mindlessly seeking my deepest urge.

Dominic hisses, teeth sinking into the meat between my shoulder and neck. "Take what you want."

He doesn't need to tell me twice. My hands dive between us, my eyes following as I fit him to my entrance. He draws my hair back and up, clenching it in a fist, and we watch together as I sink slowly down. To my shock and pleasure, he breaks first, his head falling back against the headboard.

"So fucking tight," he growls.

And it is—a tight fit. Exactly as I knew it would be and so fucking much more. I clench around him, already close to climax from what feels like the longest foreplay known to man. When I'm fully seated, I go still, gasping at the sensation that's so much deeper than physical penetration. My nails dig helplessly into his shoulders. Against my better judgement, I look up, straight into his eyes.

His thumb traces my lower lip. "Hi," he whispers.

A tear spills down my cheek. "Please," I breathe, not knowing what I'm asking for.

But he knows.

My throat is captured by a strong hand. His other traps my wrists at the small of my back, pulling until I'm curved back, strung tight as a bowstring. I shudder in relief at the strain in my shoulders, the pressure on my airway.

"Get to work, kitten."

With a ragged moan, I swirl my hips, seeking and finding a rhythm that makes my eyes roll skyward. Dominic murmurs approval, his mouth falling to my breasts. He's gentle at first, licking and sucking, worshipping my nipples. Then, as I move faster and harder against him, his teeth sink deeply into soft flesh. Marking me without apology, knowing exactly how much I can take. The pressure on my neck increases, my oxygen slowly diminishing.

"Oh, fuck, fuck," I chant.

"Do you want to come?" he growls.

"Yes, please, sir, please."

"Say it first."

Teeth graze one ultra-sensitive nipple, then the other. Our bodies slide into that space of pure synchronicity, moving together like ripples over water. My orgasm barrels toward me, unstoppable, and for the first time, I doubt my ability to obey him.

An anguished wail rises inside me. "Please!" I scream.

With a yank of my wrists and push of his body, I careen onto my back. My legs find purchase on his hips, the only remaining control I have. Even my voice doesn't belong to me anymore, emerging in hoarse groans. Dominic hovers above me, his chest sliding against mine, his thrusts now impossibly deeper and harder.

"Look at me, London," he snarls. "Tell me, and you can come." The second I open my eyes and see his—dark as sin and hot as fire—I lose the fight.

"I love you," I sob.

And with the admission comes my release. Cataclysmic. Too hot and bright. My bones melt to liquid pleasure.

"Thank you," he whispers.

With a final, jerking thrust, he spills inside me. Each quiver of his body hits me like a drug, blissful and sedating. I float, half-asleep yet more conscious than I've been in years, as he releases my wrists and gently draws my hands out from behind my back.

Dropping his elbows to either side of my shoulders, he presses his forehead to mine. Sweat from his brow drips onto my cheek and mixes with my tears.

"Told you I'd fuck the truth out of you."

I laugh, then sob.

His lips find mine and he whispers against them. "I love you, too."

37

NOW

Cinder is here.

"Time to deliver your end of the bargain."

When I don't immediately move, I'm yanked roughly from the ground. Broken, silent dolls watch. Maybe they're glad to be rid of me, despite the recently delivered commodities.

As I'm hauled forward, I glance back. Meet the teenager's jaded eyes. Find some satisfaction in the sight of her cuddled with the toddler beneath a thick blanket on a simple, military-style cot. She mouths, "Thank you."

I nod. Numb to the pain of Cinder's grip. Numb to the ache in my bones. My itching skin. My brokenness. I know where I'm going. Who's waiting for me. I'd rather die than give him what he wants.

So I'm numb.

Empty.

Gone.

38

THEN

DOMINIC'S BEDROOM is my favorite place in the loft, and not just because of what happens inside its boundaries. Or the bed he had specially made for seemingly endless variations of bondage, only a fraction of which I've experienced. Or the reinforced hooks in the ceiling. Or the silver chains dangling on the rightmost wall beside a display of his favored whips and floggers, clamps and ropes.

Every once in a while when I walk into the room, I imagine what an average, sane, well-adjusted woman might think seeing his private domain. The shock, the budding disgust. I imagine their outrage, their righteous pseudo-feminism, and it makes me laugh. Because they don't know what I do—never have I felt more powerful than I do when submitting to him. Power isn't about control, like we've been taught all our lives. I know now that true power is freedom of choice. Freedom to trust. Freedom to own your wants, give life to desire, and embrace yourself exactly as you are.

But none of those are the main reason I love his bedroom. Oddly, I love it because it reminds me of my old room in my parent's house, long since converted into a mediation/yoga room. But it holds a special place in my memory, as it was the first and last bedroom I decorated during my formative years. There'd never been a reason before since we moved so often, always renting in case a new opportunity for spiritual evolution presented itself to my parents.

But the summer before Paris' senior year of high school and my junior one, they decided it was time to put down roots. Their decision may or may not have had something to do with the ultimatum Paris and I delivered: we stay in Naples, a town about an hour south of Rochester, New York, until both of us leave for college, or we ask our boyfriends to get us pregnant. On the other hand, our parents had found a close group of likeminded friends in the year we'd been there, and maybe they were tired of moving just like we were. Either way, the reason was far less important than the result—the stability we craved.

Victorious and settled for the first time, Paris and I were ecstatic to shop for paint colors, curtains, and new bedspreads. And while Paris went full-on gender-stereotype with her space, opting for a thousand shades of pink, I chose a more neutral color palette. Serene grey walls, navy curtains, and fun, bold accent pillows on my white taffeta bedspread. I spent long hours on that bed reading, journalling, or talking on the phone with friends. It was an anchor during my late teens and early twenties. A safe place. A home.

When I wake up in Dominic's bedroom, I have the same expansive feeling. A sense of belonging and peace. And when I wake up the morning after having sex with him for the first time, I feel it tenfold. There's no judgement here, where parted navy curtains bathe the pale walls with warm, golden light. In this bed where cream-colored sheets are soft against my naked skin, and heat radiates onto my back from a warm, big body.

Stretching and yawning, I roll over to face the man who, over the last months, painstakingly extracted the poison from my deepest wounds, restarting my dormant heart.

He's awake. Sleep-eyed and smiling. "Come here."

I scoot under his lifted arm, burrowing into his chest. His heart thumps, steady and slow, beneath my ear. "I could stay here forever," I say into his skin.

"Mmm. Me too. But if we stay here, I won't be able to bring you breakfast in bed."

I pull away and point to the door. "You're free to go."

With a small chuckle, Dominic sits up. Instead of standing, however, he pivots and tackles me flat to the bed. I put up a decent fight, but I'm laughing and don't actually want to escape. My hands are stretched over my head, my legs pinned beneath his. The weight and heat of his body on mine, the morning sun on his grinning face, the ease and lightness of the moment...

"Am I dreaming?" I whisper.

His smile softens, eyes molten chocolate and brimming with the same feeling that's overwhelming me. "I meant what I said, London, even if you said it under duress. I love you. I love your guardedness, your pride, your intelligence and ridiculous sense of humor. I love your insane childhood stories, and the fact that your feet are always freezing."

My face hurts from smiling. "Oh, really? Maybe you just run hot."

He nuzzles my nose with his. "Do you know what else I love?"

"My ass?"

"Yes. I love spanking it, squeezing it, marking it, putting toys in it, and hopefully sometime soon putting my—"

"Wow!"

He laughs and kisses me soundly. "But that's not what I was going to say. What I love most is how hard you fought not to love me back. But I knew you did. I just didn't know which part of you—London, or the mask you wear—would win the fight. Do you want to know when I figured it out?"

My head spins. "When?"

He releases my hands to cup my face. "When you wouldn't tell me what that asshole at the club said to you, because you thought you were protecting me."

Every ounce of the peace inside me coalesces and dims, robbed of life. I stiffen. "Dominic, you don't—"

He puts a finger on my lips, not backing down. The light in his eyes is fierce—more fierce than I've ever seen it. A barely-leashed predator lurks close to the surface. If I didn't know he would never hurt me, I might feel more afraid. As it is, I'm only afraid of his next words.

"I understand far more than you think. For example, I know creep from the club works for the Russian mob, but wasn't sent by Ivan Reznikov."

"Stop," I gasp.

Dominic ignores my plea. "Turns out he was on loan to someone far more powerful. And far more dangerous. The name Rudolph Schultz mean anything to you? Former Director of Homeland Security, currently a senator in the state of New York?"

My heart whacks my ribs with bruising force. Adrenaline floods my body. I push up and wiggle, but he's too heavy. "Dominic, please. Let me up."

He lets me move to sitting but doesn't release me, cradling me against his chest. Slowly over the course of minutes, his embrace and steady heartbeat counteract my panic attack.

"That's it. Breathe with me." He strokes my spine with a steady hand, anchoring me to the present. The world outside is dark, foreign and terrifying, but a small part of me understands I'm still okay. Still alive. Right here, right now, I'm safe.

"Tell me, London. Please. No matter what it is, I'll protect you. I won't let anything happen to you."

Too late.

My voice emerges brittle and robotic: "He'll kill my family. My parents. My sister. Niece."

His embrace tightens, hands stilling. "Schultz?"

There's surprise in his voice, but not much of it. After all, he's someone who knows how violent the world is. And because of his brother and ex-wife, I imagine he also knows just how corrupting power can be. The thing with Schultz, though—that I found out far too late—is that he wasn't corrupted. He was *always* corrupt. But so, so good at pretending he wasn't. So good at it, in fact, that I think he might actually believe himself irreproachable.

He's a fucking psychopath.

"Tell me," begs Dominic.

I take a breath that sears my lungs with fear. And with freedom. "It started with a golf game."

39

THE FIRST TIME Paul and I were invited to dinner at the Schultz residence, we felt like kids playing dress up and pretending to be our parents. Not *my* parents, obviously, but Paul's—dignified, refined, exuding class from their tailored threads to their wrinkle-free foreheads. Only we were twenty-three, recent graduates of NYU, and scared out of our heads about embarrassing ourselves.

Three years before, when Paul and his father played golf with Rudolph Shultz, he'd been head of the New York office of Homeland Security. Mere months later, he was promoted, then promoted again. All the while, he kept tabs on Paul. Reached out with friendly phone calls and encouragement.

Paul's parents were thrilled Schultz had taken their

son under his wing. Especially when Schultz left New York for Washington DC in pursuit of a political career. With his history—active military service, Harvard Law degree—and his shining public persona, no one doubted he'd make it to the upper echelons of power.

And yet, despite his status as a shooting star and increasing demanding calendar, Schultz never forgot Paul. Though their phone calls had slowly transitioned to sporadic emails, Schultz truly cared about Paul and by proxy, me. However nervous we were that night, Schultz put us both at ease within minutes of our arrival. He had a unique approachability, an intelligence and charisma so powerful it was blinding.

I remember that night like it was yesterday.

SEVEN YEARS AGO

"LONDON, Paul tells me you're a fan of literature." Warm blue eyes smile into mine.

"I am, Mr. Schultz," I reply, my fingers sweating on the stem of a wine glass that probably cost more than last month's rent. I hope he doesn't notice the tremor in my voice. My parents definitely didn't prepare me for this.

Rolling a joint, yes. Mingling with the wealthy and powerful? Big fat *no*.

The handsome older man grins. "Please, call me Rudy. I already think of you as a daughter, after all. Come on, I want to show you something." Without waiting for a reply, he calls across the room, "Paul, I'm stealing your wife!"

My husband, engrossed in conversation with the flawlessly beautiful Mrs. Schultz, laughs and nods. "Just bring her back."

"Eventually."

With a hand on my lower back, Rudy steers me from the sitting room at the front of the house and down the long, marble-floored hallway. We take a turn and come to a stop before double doors. His spicy, expensive cologne teases my nose as he reaches past me to open them.

"After you, my dear."

I take several steps inside before awe freezes my muscles. Behind me, Rudy chuckles. "I was hoping this would be your reaction."

In the golden dusk, the massive room is ablaze with beauty. I'm sure there's a name for it, something fancy like *gallery* or *great room*, but to my eyes it's simply a wonderland. A wall of high, iron-bracketed windows face the back of the property and beyond them is a riot of greenery—groomed gardens, fountains, fruit trees. But it's what's inside that holds me captive. Opposite the glass, the room extends into a beautiful library. Floor-to-ceiling bookshelves bracket an elegant collection of chairs and couches.

My feet carry me toward the books. The air grows cooler and heavier against my skin, as though welcoming me. Or warning me—this is a place I could get lost in and never find my way out.

Rudy walks past me, the arm of his suit whispering against my shoulder. "This section, I think, will be of particular interest to you." He glances over his shoulder. The sunset catches in his eyes; for an instant, they flare red. "Some of the greatest thinkers and essayists are here. Everyone from Hitchens to Emerson."

I manage a little laugh. "This is amazing. I would have loved this during school."

A tawny eyebrow quirks. "Now that you've graduated, you don't have any more interest in learning?"

That, I would come to find out, was a signature Rudy statement. An insult delivered so graciously, that cut so swiftly, the pain registered on a delay. In just a few short words, he introduced a new emotion to my human experience. *Shame.*

"No, of course I still want to learn," I stammer. "I only meant—"

"I'm only kidding, of course," he interjects smoothly, a wide, disarming smile on his face. He seems so authentic my embarrassment slides away. Removing a small volume from a shelf, he walks back to me. "Can I offer a bit of advice, my dear?"

Off-kilter, I nod. "Of course."

"Are you aware of Nietzsche's concept of *will to power*? The instinct we all possess to dominate—be better than—our fellows?" He waits for my bemused nod. "I see this instinct in you, London. The passion for perfection. My advice is this—when the time comes for you to choose between instinct and self-preservation, choose the latter."

I can't contain my frown. "I don't understand."

From what I can recall, Nietzsche proposed that man's highest challenge was to refine his so-called *will to power* in order to be free from all outside influences, thereby creating his own set of values. Was he telling me to ignore my instincts or to embrace them?

Rudy chuckles; I don't know if he's laughing at me or not. "Don't fret, my dear. When the time comes, you'll understand."

A knock on the open library door turns our heads. A liveried servant bows stiffly from the waist. "Dinner is served, Mr. Schultz."

"Thank you, Jerry."

Rudy extends the small book to me. It's an older publication of *Beyond Good and Evil* by Nietzsche, the spine well-worn and pages yellowed. I don't know why he's giving it to me, only that there's a reason. Just like I know I don't want to read it but will, simply because he expects me to.

"Thank you," I say faintly.

He nods, no longer smiling. "I'll expect you to have read it and be ready to discuss its contents before Sunday dinner next week."

My head comes up. "What?"

He watches me. The sunset flares once more in his eyes.

I stammer, "Yes, of course."

40

"AND THAT WAS THE BEGINNING," I say, and pause, shaken by my trip to the past.

"Do you know why you were targeted?" asks Dominic at length. The question is mild, but the look in his eyes is complex—curious, wary, and not a little confused.

I shake my head and hug my knees tighter to my chest. "No, and I doubt I ever will. There were even times I concocted wild fantasies that he was my real father. That I'd been stolen or given up for adoption and he'd tracked me down."

To his credit, Dominic doesn't laugh. "He manipulated you."

I nod. "I was so young, so eager for his attention—this wealthy, powerful man who showered me with books, taught me about everything from politics to wine to which utensil to use at what time during a five-course meal. He even introduced me to the editor of the New York Independent. When the job offer came, he told me to take it. I didn't question him, just did whatever he said."

Dominic's arm tightens around my shoulders. I soften against him, resting my head on his chest. After a few moments, he asks, "Did he ever..." He clears his throat.

"No," I whisper. "It wasn't like that. I never got the sense that he wanted me... that way."

"Even after his wife died?"

"Never."

A freak car accident had taken Mrs. Schultz's life less than a year after that first dinner. Rudy's grief had seemed so real that even now, after everything, it's hard for me to imagine him responsible. But I personally witnessed multiple altercations on my visits to the house. Mrs. Shultz overindulged in wine and pills—Rudy was sick of cleaning up her public messes. He never yelled at her, never lifted a hand, but when all that charisma turned dark and jagged, it was chilling to behold.

I sigh into Dominic's chest. "He loved Paul, too. Or pretended to. Rudy would fly from DC to New York every weekend. He and Paul played golf almost every Saturday."

"What did they talk about?"

There's urgency beneath his words, and I wish I could give him an answer. Instead, I shake my head. "Paul never told me, just like I never shared what Rudy and I talked about Sunday afternoons before dinner."

My mind struggles futilely in the sticky web of regret. Each strand a happy memory turned sour, intimacies cast in a new, sickly light. Only now do I recognize those omissions as the first wedge between Paul and me, driven there by a man we loved like a father.

"There was one night," I begin haltingly, "I started to question things. It was just before everything fell apart—the exposé, the fallout. Paul was out of town on a case. Rudy had been elected to a New York Senate seat by this time, and Sunday dinners had become fewer and farther between. But... everything was good. I was happy, or thought I was. My career was taking off. Paul and I were talking about having kids—"

I stop to catch my breath, my heart suddenly racing. Dominic's fingers begin playing in my hair. He kisses my temple softly, then again. Slowly, his touch filters through, grounding me. I inhale and try again.

"When I told Rudy about possibly starting a family, he had the strangest reaction."

"He was angry," guesses Dominic.

"Yes," I say, turning to him with surprise. "How did you know?"

His lips thin, then release. "Because you were asserting independence. You were deviating from his design for you."

Goosebumps march down my body. I nod slowly. "Yes, I can see that now. But back then, I was hurt and confused. Fuck, I'm still confused. What was point of it all? Of cultivating my ambition? Was it to tear Paul and I apart? Is Rudy really just a sick motherfucker who played with us because it was fun to control our lives?"

"There's another option," murmurs Dominic. "He gave you a choice the last time you saw him, right?"

Will you join us at the top of the world, or will you hold to meaningless ideals?

I pinch the bridge of my nose. My fingers are icy, half-numb. "How could he have thought for one second I would join him? As what? His side-kick? The publicity manager for his criminal empire?"

"As his daughter, London. His *heir*."

You were the daughter I never had.

Cold radiates down my spine. I shudder, and Dominic holds me closer. "Why kill Paul?" I whisper. "Was it because he was given the same choice and like me, chose wrong?"

"Maybe, maybe not. The man sounds like a real psychopath. Who knows what's going on in his head." He pauses. "Will you tell me more about that last meeting?"

I close my eyes. Memory paints vividly across my eyelids. Unlike my recurring dream—which always takes place at midday—the last time I saw Rudy it had been night. My hair and clothes smelling like smoke. My arms and shoulders aching from being held back by firemen. My face raw, eyelashes and eyebrows singed from being too close to the explosion that took my husband and dog.

"Reznikov was there," I tell Dominic. "I didn't know he was, not at first. I was... blinded by rage. I wasn't thinking about anything but killing Rudy. I used my key to get inside the house and found him in the library."

"How did you know, London?"

Shame, oily, slick, coats my next words. "Paul and I were barely civil the last few weeks of his life. Our marriage was falling apart—I couldn't do anything to stop it. He wasn't even sleeping at home. I was desperate and paranoid and had him tailed to see if he was with another woman."

Deep breath, lungs expanding like gills. I'm still alive.

"He wasn't," I continue hoarsely. "He was staying with Rudy, which made sense. I was relieved, even, just knowing he was somewhere familiar. On the afternoon he died, I... I got word that Paul was at the house. Our house. I raced home from work, thinking it was my chance to talk to him, figure things out—" My voice fails.

"It's okay," whispers Dominic. "Take your time."

I lick my lips, tasting tears. "When I got there, Paul was loading his car with suitcases. He refused to look at me or acknowledge I was even there. But that wasn't what made me lose my shit—he had Felix, our lab, already in the backseat. *My* dog, who he hadn't even wanted at first. I freaked out, screamed at him and tried to get Felix out, but he locked the doors. Felix was barking, panicked. Paul... he lost it right along with us. He grabbed me and pulled me back. I tripped. Fell on the ground beside the car."

Turning in Dominic's arms, I search his eyes, wondering if it's the last time I'll see love in them.

41

"I SAW THE BOMB," I whisper. "The black box, the wires that didn't belong. I knew it was there, but I still let Paul get in that car with my dog and turn the key. I could have stopped him. I could have saved their lives."

Dominic's brows draw together, his eyes softening with sympathy. "Oh, London, no you couldn't have. How long were you on the ground before you jumped up? Seconds, I'm guessing. And how many bombs have you seen? Are you trained in explosives? Did you know it was armed? Did you know without a shadow of a doubt what you saw was a *bomb?*"

I shake my head helplessly. "I've asked myself those questions a thousand times, and all I can come up with is that some part of me wanted—"

"No," he interjects, his arms tightening around me.

"You aren't that person. But you *are* the type to beat yourself up over something you couldn't have changed. Mix memories with trauma, regret, and grief, and you can easily put yourself in the center of blame. Believe me, I know. I did it to myself, too, before someone put things into perspective for me."

My conviction falters. "But—"

"But nothing. It wasn't your fault and you had nothing to do with Paul's death."

I almost smile at his tone—firm, commanding, final. I can easily envision him speaking to his team the same way. Imagine how much they must have trusted him... and how horrible it must have been for Dominic to lose them.

And that's when it happens. My dark knot of shame quivers and begins to unravel, tiny threads loosening, disintegrating. The abyss inside me shrinks as light grows around it. As I realize I'm not alone in my pain. Or my healing.

"Thank you." My voice is soft and thick.

He doesn't ask for what—he knows—and his only response is a small smile. "How did you figure out it was Schultz?"

My mind cycles back, populating with snapshots, colors and sounds. A lawnmower somewhere in the neighborhood. A plane overhead. The smell of cut grass and gas fumes. Our garage door open, Paul's car in the driveway.

"It was something Paul said—*yelled* actually. That it was Rudy's idea for him to come get Felix, because my coping mechanism was work and I wasn't home enough to care for him. It sounded exactly like something Rudy would say—shit, he'd said it to my face before—except for the fact I'd found out recently he was allergic to dogs. Rudy wasn't *that* generous. But it only registered after the fact, after it was too late—"

"Breathe."

I fill my lungs. Exhale. Fill them again.

"The blast threw me backward, across the front yard. The last thing I saw before I blacked out was an SUV across the street. I recognized the driver. Saw his smile." I shiver on the last word, remembering so clearly that evil smirk. "It was Reznikov."

Dominic grunts. "Figured as much. The police report said the bomb was similar to ones he's been suspected of using for years. Using the same design made perfect fodder for a rumor about him murdering your husband at your behest."

"Yes, it did." It still hurts, how easily my friends and colleagues believed the lies and turned against me. Like grief, I don't think that kind of betrayal ever completely loses its sting.

"And then?"

"When I woke up with paramedics over me, it was like all the fog in my head had cleared. I knew, *knew* Rudy was behind everything. I wasn't concussed—just some scrapes and bruises—so I refused the ambulance and drove to his house. I confronted him. He quoted Nietzsche, the smarmy fuck, then Ivan put a gun to the back of my head. Rudy asked me to join him, I said no. That's all I remember. Besides waking up in a hospital with a lump on my head and my sister sobbing in the chair beside my bed."

Almost there. Finish it.

"Two months later, I received an untraceable email detailing what I had to do to keep my family safe. Leave New York, don't deny the allegations against me, and drop any and all efforts of investigation into the Senator, his connections to the Russians, and Paul's death, or the officers I was talking to would be first to die."

"Christ Almighty." He's quiet a few moments, then sighs. "What's important now is figuring out what Schultz wants from you and how to best protect you from him. I'm not afraid of him, his Russian goons, or any threats made present or future."

My smile is tired. "Are you still afraid of me?"

"No, kitten," he says tenderly, "but I'm still running

toward you. Nothing on this earth is going to keep me from you. No matter what."

I want to believe him.

I really do.

Dominic continues to hold me, his breathing deep and even. Hypnotic. *Safe.* We don't speak for a long while, but there's no more pressure in the silence. No secrets muddling the space between us. No darkness. Instead, there's quiet communion. Soft acceptance. We each carry the loads of our past, but now we carry them together.

Tears bead in my eyelashes as, finally, the truth hits of how lonely my life has been. How convinced I was of my own fallibility. My treachery and conceit. How undeserving I was of happiness or forgiveness.

The wave of grief and relief breaks free, my body quaking with hot tremors. Convulsions of purging and recovery. All the while, he holds me and murmurs comfort in my ear.

"We'll get through this together, London."

I want to believe.

42

MY MOM and I are standing in the kitchen of their house in upstate New York, the only real home we had as a family. She's singing off-key—Janis Joplin, I think—as she readies her signature blackberry pie for the oven. Sunlight from the window above the sink sparkles in her pale blonde hair, braided and wrapped in a crown around her head.

"Mom?"

She doesn't answer, doesn't turn to face me. I try to move, to walk around the island to reach her, but I have molasses-legs. Disquiet slithers through me. Something is wrong.

Daylight winks out like God flipped a switch. At the same time, the oven clangs open, revealing writhing, unnatural flames. Black and red and deepest indigo, they throw ghastly highlights over the kitchen, over my mother, who still hums Janis and lifts the pie in her hands. Reddish smoke pours from the hellish cavity, rapidly filling the room with the scent of charred flesh.

No! Mom!

Humming and smiling, she walks sedately toward the oven. The latticed pie crust oozes dark, thick liquid, which spills over her hands and stains her apron red.

I scream and scream for her, but I have no voice. Smoke chokes my airway. Every muscle in my body bunches, frozen on the burning edge of panic.

I can't save her.

I can't breathe.

I can't—

MY EYES SNAP open in the dark. A heavy hand covers my mouth, fingers gripping tight on my jaw. I suck air through my nostrils, my body instinctively bucking for freedom.

"It's me," whispers a voice in my ear. "The silent alarm downstairs just went off."

Dominic.

My relief sours as his words sink in, and fear drives its teeth into my gut. I sit up and his hand falls from my face. My vision adjusts enough for me to see his features, tight and grim. Before I can give voice to my rising panic, he speaks quietly.

"Listen very carefully. You're going down the fire escape, and then you're going to run. How's your mile looking?"

My teeth chattering with adrenaline, I whisper back, "Eight minutes."

"Make it six."

I nod, but grab his arm as he makes to stand. "You think it's—" I can't finish, but he nods anyway. My fingers slacken as he rises. Rounding the bed, he hauls me to my feet and shoves my sneakers and socks in my hands.

"You have ninety seconds before you're going out the window." He sounds so calm, but it's different than the soft control of his voice during scenes. This tone carries a different gravity—the flavor of life and death.

"Dominic," I gasp. I'm confused and frightened and my lips are numb. "Why aren't you coming—maybe it's not—maybe Charlie tripped the alarm—"

He steps close, moonlight illuminating half of his face. Dropping his forehead to mine, he whispers, "I checked the feeds from my phone. There are six armed men in the club right now. They're professionals and obviously know we're here. It's only a matter of time before they find the loft. The cops are on their way, but I can't have you here, can't worry about your safety."

"What are you going to do?" I hiss, grabbing his forearm. "Please—"

I can't lose you.

A loud boom sounds through the loft as something heavy hits the door to the loft. Dominic curses and yanks something from behind his back. There's a forbidding *snick-click* as loads the chamber of a sleek handgun.

For a blurred moment, I'm convinced I'm still dreaming. That this is a new nightmare. One of the worst I've ever had. Scratch that—*the worst.*

"Go, London," he growls, hustling me toward the window.

"My shoes—" I squeak.

"Forget the shoes." He yanks open the window, then grips my jaw in his hand. Dark eyes sear into mine. "If they wanted you dead, they wouldn't have announced themselves like this. They want to take you. I'm not going to let that happen. Go, London. Away from the street—they probably have someone out front."

They want to take you.

An image flashes in my mind—the young Russian women lying naked and cold in the morgue. A survival instinct I'd thought gone ignites like a flash fire. I scramble out the window onto the metal landing, then turn and grab Dominic's wrist.

"Come with me. Let the cops deal with them."

He shakes his head. "I need to slow them down. I'll be fine, kitten. They're on *my* turf."

Another boom is followed by the unmistakable sound of splintering wood. Dominic grabs the back of my head and kisses me hard, then pushes me backward and slams the window closed between us. I stare in open-mouthed shock as he locks it.

Go, he mouthes.

One more moment—one more look between us a thousand miles deep and wide—and I bolt to the edge of the landing, grab the ladder, and scurry to the ground. My heart gallops, white noise crowding my ears. Freezing, I look both ways, deeper down the alley, then toward the glow of the main street. Panic bulldozes my mind as the risk becomes startlingly clear. I don't know why Rudy's doing this, but I know if they catch me—if *he* catches me—I'll never know freedom again.

With a final, longing glance toward the false-safety of the light, I run into the dark.

I make it thirty feet.

A dark figure appears from the shadows and tackles me to the ground. Before I can scream, a gloved hand slaps over my nose and mouth.

"Nice to see you again, Mrs. Kirkland."

I recognize the voice—the man from the club. Terror is an afterthought, pain a distant second to rage. But no matter how hard I fight, how furiously my nails seek his face, he avoids my wrath, immobilizing me with sheer strength and weight.

Exhausted, I fall limp. Tears of fury and defeat fill my eyes, spilling as I blink up at him. A shadow-face with glinting eyes.

"That's better," murmurs my captor. "Now, before you take a nice long nap, I have another message for you. The Old Man wants you to know he's very disappointed with the direction you've chosen in life. He expected more from you. And since you owe him your life anyway, he's calling in the debt. Say goodbye to Los Angeles, Mrs. Kirkland. You'll never see it again."

There's a sharp pinch on my upper arm. My vision wavers, darkens, and my limbs grow heavy.

Static crackles and a tinny voice says, "All clear. He's been taken care of."

"Good. I've got the woman. Let's go."

No! Dominic!

A pitiful moan escapes me. Consciousness whirlpools, fading fast as I'm hoisted from the ground and thrown over a broad shoulder like so much baggage.

The last thing I hear before darkness takes me are police sirens—too far, too late.

43

I WAKE to the smell of bleach and the rhythmic *scritch-scratch* of a ballpoint pen on paper. My eyes snap open, sucking in details of my surroundings as fast as possible. A small room. Cement with no windows and a fluorescent light fixture. There's a drain in the middle of the floor, the area around it wet and dark. An empty bucket and dingy mop sit near a reinforced metal door.

My mind is slippery, disjointed, likely due to the sedative I was given. I'm still wearing my t-shirt and pajama pants, both filthy from the scuffle in the alley, damp with perspiration and clinging to my skin. I'm thirsty. My body quivers and aches. My bicep radiates tenderness from the injection site.

I'm not alone.

Moving gracelessly into a sitting position, I press my

spine to the cool wall hard enough for my bones to protest. Harder still, until I'm certain that however much this feels like a nightmare, it isn't one.

Set against the adjacent wall is a small desk and chair, their construction cheap, dark blue paint chipping. A man sits in the chair, his head bent as he writes. Nothing about him belongs here—not his proud, broad shoulders, not his thousand-dollar suit or Italian-made shoes. He knows I'm awake, of course, but has yet to acknowledge me. Games of power are his favorite.

But I've learned a thing or two about power since I last saw him. And I've learned about patience, too. Surrendering to discomfort. Awaiting change without expectation of it. He won't get what he wants from me.

So I sit, suspended amidst a dozen threads of physical and emotional pain, embraced by them and untouched. I don't think of Dominic. Of anyone or anything except not giving this man the reaction he's looking for. And I don't.

Eventually, the writing stops. The pen drops to the table. Wood creaks as the man shifts, turns the chair to face me and settles again.

"London."

"Rudy."

His features pinch, eyes surveying me with manufactured concern. "I'm sorry about your treatment. Rest assured, that man has been dealt with. He'll never hurt you again."

In another existence, I might laugh. "What are you going to do with me?"

He smiles crookedly, eyes reproachful. "Don't you want to know why you're here?"

"I don't give a shit."

A pained wince. "Language, dear."

"Fuck you."

His mask shivers and slides away, and I see the man beneath the facade. The cold, calculating monster who possesses no conscience, no accountability for his own evil. Who ruins lives for no other reason than because he can. Handsome as only the devil can be, with a silvered tongue and a rotten soul.

Reaching behind him, Rudy lifts a manila envelope from the desk. With a flick of his wrist, the folder and its contents spill onto the floor between us. Most of the 8x10 photographs land face-up. Enough for me to glean their subject.

Me.

The photograph near my left foot is grainy, a little blurred, but the central subject is unmistakable. A Saint Andrews Cross, glowing under the spotlight in Crossroad's Epicenter. It's from the night Dominic caned me. The night Charlie helped me get him back.

Dominic…

I bite my tongue until I taste blood. Until the urge to scream passes. Slowly, I take in the other photographs. Dominic and I on the beach. Dominic leading me from the alley next to the nightclub on Nate's birthday. A few shots of me bartending. Then my gaze snags on one in particular—one that makes my blood run cold.

It's the back hallway of Crossroads—empty but for Dominic and me standing close together near his office door. I remember the exact moment. A month ago, right before a shift. I'd found the gift he left for me in my locker and immediately sought him out.

"I can't accept this."

Arms crossed over his chest, Dominic smirks. "You don't even know what it is." He glances at the delicate gold chain dangling from my fingers. Attached to it is a diamond. Flawless and at least two carats, it's insanely gorgeous and makes me want to puke.

I frown up at him, anxious and borderline panicked. "I appreciate the sentiment, really… I'm just not a jewelry type of girl."

What I want to say—shout, really—is that men only give jewelry like this to girlfriends. To fiancees and wives. Not commitment-phobic submissives who can't envision a future past tomorrow.

Perceptive as always, Dominic grabs my hand, anchoring me with his touch. "This isn't that kind of jewelry. That, kitten, is your collar. The choice of whether or not you wear it is yours, but I want you to keep it. Please."

Now, staring at the photograph, I wish I'd put the necklace on. Trusted him sooner. Loved him longer. Been stronger. Braver. Less damaged. More capable of seeing and accepting the clear signs of his growing affection. The melting warmth of his eyes. The teasing curl of his mouth. The soft, tender expression that he only wore for me.

But the worst, most bitter truth revealed by the photograph is who took it. Only one person could have, since only one person walked into the hallway, coughed so we knew they were there, then apologized for interrupting and said I was needed behind the bar.

My friend.

My sassy, ball-busting, generous, funny friend, who bulldozed her way into my life and heart with unfailing encouragement and support.

Steph.

"Did you think I wouldn't keep tabs on you?" asks Rudy mildly.

Through a haze of betrayal, I search for and find

truth. "What are you blackmailing her with?" I don't disguise my anger well enough, and his lips curve in satisfaction.

"That's none of your concern." He crosses his legs, the picture of refinement in his bespoke suit. "What matters, London, is that you understand why I couldn't allow you to continue as you were. I should have come for you sooner, and I'm truly sorry for what you've had to endure. The depraved lifestyle you felt you deserved."

This time, I do laugh. "You're insane. Totally, completely nuts."

He stands and adjusts the fall of his jacket with a graceful tug. "I can see it's going to take some time for you to remember who you are." Striding to the door, he knocks twice on the metal surface, then glances back at me. He's no longer bothering to hide his disgust. "You'll have twenty-four hours to consider your choices. I'll expect a full recovery and an apology for all the worry you've caused me. Then we'll discuss the future."

My skin prickles hotly. "You're a madman," I whisper.

The door opens and I catch a glimpse of a hard-faced man. Rudy steps through but pauses before closing the door. I'm not surprised—he loves having the last word.

"Remember, dear London, there are no facts, only interpretations."

I chuckle darkly. "Blah blah, Rudy. You wanted me to embrace Nihilism? Well, asshole, I did. *To live is to suffer, to survive is to find some meaning in suffering.* I've found my meaning. Have you?"

The door slams as the last word leaves my mouth.

I sag against the wall. "Take that, motherfucker."

44

IT WAS a lot easier to act tough when I wasn't alone in what amounts to a sensory deprivation chamber. Besides the small vent in the ceiling pumping in cold air at intervals and a faint, mechanical hum from the fluorescent, there's no sound, no movement, no life.

Sitting with my knees drawn to my chest, I think about the thriller novels Paris used to devour like a kid with candy during her late teens. She was particularly fond of Stephen King. I wonder if King has ever incorporated a cell like this one into any of his novels. If not, he should. It's already messing with my head.

There might be a surveillance camera in the vent or light, watching my every move. Maybe I'm underground, a thousand tons of earth above me. Depending on how long I was out, I could be in another state. Another country. The rusted drain in the floor is an especially effective technique—combined with the lingering scent of bleach and the mop and bucket, it would be a miracle *not* to think about blood dripping from the dirty brown tails of the mop, DNA degraded and washed away with chemicals.

Point to you, Rudy.

With no watch or clock in the room, time is an elastic presence. Minutes or hours... seconds or weeks... Logically, I know I haven't been here long. Maybe twenty-four hours. I'm thirsty and hungry, but not to distraction. Which means they couldn't have taken me far. I might still be in Los Angeles.

Was Rudy here minutes ago?

Or hours?

I resist temptation for as long as I can, but the harder I try to avoid thinking about the desk, the more my gaze and thoughts are drawn to it. To the single sheet of paper on its surface, the dark blur of compact handwriting. He must have been writing for a while before I came to— words fill the sheet almost entirely.

I consider tearing the paper to shreds without reading. Or using it as toilet paper. Or leaving it to disintegrate right where it is. But in the end I'm only human, and eventually I stand and hobble-walk to the desk, favoring a cut on the bottom of my left foot—souvenir of running barefoot down the alley.

I lower myself to the chair and wait for dizziness to pass. *Is there something in the air? Did they give me more drugs?* The thoughts come and go, but leave residue behind. Like a fungus, my paranoia will only increase in time, sucking food from every fearful thought I have. I might be able to postpone being consumed by it, but it will take me in the end. Psychological warfare is Rudy's bread and butter.

Shaking with bitterness and defeat, I finally focus on the letter.

My dearest London,

I have always believed in you. When others cautioned me against your disadvantageous upbringing, your less-than-stellar academic record, my faith never wavered. I knew I could help you reach your full potential. And I did. You were perfect—every step you took exactly as I anticipated.

Alas, there were complications I did not foresee. I'll admit, my feelings were hurt when you didn't tell me about the story you were pursuing. Imagine my surprise when I received a phone call from an old friend telling me you were poking around where you didn't belong. Perhaps the fault is mine. I pushed you too hard, too fast. Forgot to teach you that the road to power is paved with patience.

You were destined for greatness. Cunning, cutthroat, sharp as a blade. You were supposed to rise with me. I would have taken you all the way to the White House. Your unavoidable demise is my greatest regret.

Another choice will soon be upon you.

Your mentor,

R

I read the letter a few more times, then crumple it in a fist and toss it to the ground. Limping back to the wall, I slide to the floor and hug my knees. It takes another few minutes, but piece by stubborn piece, my bravado disintegrates. Chunks of me fall, clashing and crashing, into that roaring void.

And the truth finds me.

Because of me, Dominic is dead. Like Paul is dead, like Felix and those young women, and like my heart and entire being and the life I didn't realize was beautiful until too late.

I should have...

Maybe if...

Too late.

WHEN THE DOOR OPENS, I don't lift my head from the ground. Don't open my eyes or move. Sometime in the last twenty-four hours—if that's how long since Rudy was last here—I've made the only choice available to me. Even if it means suffering horribly, dying here, I won't give him what he wants.

There are shuffling noises, an angry shout, and a heavy body hits the ground several feet from me. The door slams closed. My heart hammers as I open my eyes. A man rests on his side, facing away from me. Dark hair. Dark clothes.

He groans.

Without thinking, I lunge for him. "Dominic," I gasp, my hands hovering, wanting to grab and hold but afraid of hurting him. He makes a soft, small noise of pain and lifts his head, then rolls onto his back and blinks up at me.

I'm wide open. Vulnerable in my desperation. And when I see his face, my mind blanks.

Empties.

Burns to ash.

CRACK goes my sanity.

"London?" he whispers through bloody lips. "Oh my God, you're alive. *Alive.*"

He winces as he sits up, but ignores whatever pain he's in to reach for me. Arms band tightly around me, drawing me into a space that's as familiar as late nights studying in college. First dates at a pizza joint with sticky tables. Ferris Wheels and cheap champagne and marriage proposals. Walks in crisp morning air and Felix's puppy breath.

Paul finally realizes I'm stiff, unresponsive. He releases me only to frame my face with his hands. One of his eyes is swollen closed, the other tearful and locked on my face. Despite the bruises, the cracks and blood, he looks the same.

My dead husband.

45

EVERYONE HAS that one *off* relative. Mine is a second cousin on my dad's side. Edith Wilkes. Terminally awkward, colorblind, agoraphobic—we were all surprised when she showed up for Paul's funeral. After, she waited in line with everyone else to offer her condolences. When it was her turn, Paris gripped my hand so tightly it hurt, preparing me for whatever craziness was about to come out of Edith's mouth.

Edith looked me in the eye and said gravely, "Until you're broken, you don't know what you're made of." Without waiting for a response, she walked away, her frizzy blonde hair foaming in the wind. She didn't come to the wake.

Now, I have the vague wish I could have spoken longer with her. Because surely someone doesn't say something like that to a widow without personal experience in breaking.

I thought I was broken then.

I knew nothing.

"Say something, London. Are you okay? I thought you were dead. What did he do to you?"

We're sitting on opposite sides of the cell. He talks to me—I don't respond. I've never been more certain of anything than I am now that nothing is as it seems. Either my mind is truly gone, shattered, and I'm having a hallucination, or Paul's death was staged and this *ruse* is the final play in Rudy's twisted game.

Perhaps if I'd never met Dominic... if he hadn't blasted through all my darkness and brought me into the light... if I hadn't learned there is salvation in surrender, forgiveness in regret, and a future in the present... Perhaps then I would be desperate enough to believe the man in front of me.

"Why won't you look at me?" His tone is full of sorrow and confusion. "For two years, London, *two years* I've been in a windowless cell. Thinking you were dead. Losing my damned mind. Please, talk to me!"

The agony in the last words breach my numbness. I focus on a spot directly above his head. "They identified you by your teeth."

He drags in a swift breath. "I know, or I guessed. I'm missing a few."

"I saw you in the car. You were in the driver's seat when it exploded."

"I don't know who you saw, but it wasn't me. The last thing I remember is arguing with you about Felix. Then I woke up in a room just like this one with missing teeth and no idea how I got there."

Ventilation kicks on, stale air circulating between us. Slowly, I lower my gaze to his face. I don't know how I could have mistaken him for Dominic. His hair is lighter, his frame leaner, his skin pale.

"When did you find out Rudy was doing business with the Russian mob?" I ask the stranger. "Better yet, when did you sell your soul to the devil?"

Because I'm looking, I see it. His tell. The skin beneath his eyes pinches. "What? I don't know what you're talking about. I didn't know about the Russians until Rudy told me a few months ago. He's been trying to convince me to work for him, tells me about his business, the drugs and trafficking. He's batshit crazy, London. I honestly don't know why he hasn't killed me yet."

My head thuds against the wall. Hindsight is a shifty bitch, changing her story one day to the next. Casting new shadows, removing old ones.

"Just before Christmas, you started acting distant. Angrier." I'm back to staring at the wall above his head. "I chalked it up to work stress coupled with the usual holiday stress. Or my distraction with the story I was working on. I also considered that you intuitively knew I was keeping something from you. I felt guilty about that. Ashamed. But it wasn't any of those things, was it?"

"London—"

"You were so distraught when I told you about the story, that the women I interviewed were dead." I look him in the eye. "Did you know it was Rudy who had them killed? Rudy and Ivan? Or did you kill them yourself, not knowing I was connected?"

"Christ, London, you're not making sense. This is crazy! I was upset because you'd been lying for months about what you were working on, and because you were shitting on my investigation! I was angry, and scared for you, and lost my shit. I'm sorry I wasn't there for you when you needed me, but I'm here now. I need you to trust me. We have to figure out a way to get out of here!"

"How?" I snap. "How in hell do you think we can do that?"

His eyes soften, the hazel depths so achingly familiar and not. Like having déjà vu when meeting a person for the first time.

"I've had a lot of time to think about it," he says

softly, eagerly. He leans forward, almost vibrating with urgency. "He's kept us both alive for a reason. We exploit it. Agree to whatever scheme he proposes, do whatever we have to do to get out of this fucking prison. Once we're on the outside, we can escape. Go straight to the FBI. We'll take him down. Together."

He has thought about it.

It's a perfectly sensible plan.

If only...

Blinking back tears, I smile tightly. "You're forgetting one thing, Paul. I always beat you at poker. *Always.*"

There's a heavy beat of silence, broken by his sigh. "Damnit, London," he murmurs, gaze shifting to the door just as it opens.

Rudy walks in clapping.

Clap.

Clap.

"Bravo, London," he says, affectionate tone at odds with his grim expression. He glances at Paul. "You did your best, now go get cleaned up."

Paul lurches to his feet. "Rudy, please, maybe—"

"No. She's beyond our reach. And frankly, Paul, I'm disappointed that even knowing what she's been doing the last six months, you'd still want her."

Paul frowns but says nothing. He pauses at the door

and looks at me. For a moment, I see the young man I fell in love with. "I'm sorry, London. Truly."

He leaves.

Again.

Only this time, he doesn't take any part of me with him.

"Fuck you, Rudy. I told you once before, and I'll tell you again. Just.Fucking.Kill.Me."

He sighs. "Once again, you've proved yourself my life's greatest disappointment. But I won't kill you. Call me sentimental, but I care too much for you. Besides, killing you now would rob me of an asset of incredible value. Do you know how much someone like you goes for on the open market? *Millions*."

Terror ices my veins. "What?" I rasp.

Rudy smiles benignly. "Don't worry. The average life expectancy of a sex slave is relatively brief. Go easily, and you have my word that your parents, sister, and adorable niece will live out the rest of their lives in peace."

The door closes before I've fully absorbed his words. When I do, I scream.

Scream.

And scream.

NW

"Time to deliver your end of the bargain."

THIS IS IT.

Rudy is finally making good on his threat.

I'm being sold.

Either the weeks in the warehouse were a prolonged siege against my mind, or it's taken him this long to find a buyer. I wonder what Paul thinks about what's happening. If he cares that his wife will be sold to the highest bidder. Probably not, as I haven't seen him for weeks, since the day he lost his shit and almost lit the warehouse on fire.

"This is your fault."

He might be right. Somewhere along the way, I wasn't the partner he wanted. Needed. We shared a bed, a life and—I thought—a stable love. But I was too self-absorbed, too obsessed with my own glory. I missed the signs of his devolving morality, his poisoned ambition. *When did he decide that innocent lives didn't matter?*

Paul said a lot of things that day, when he burst into the warehouse drunk and carrying a can of gasoline.

"Do you know what it was like for me, leaving you? The choice I made was for us. For our future! Can't you see that?"

"There were no other options. I was being investigated. They were getting closer, London. I had to die, and your reaction had to be genuine. It was all planned. If only you'd trusted me!"

"I was going to come for you. We had passports. New identities. Rudy set everything up—a new life was waiting for us. Why did you leave me?"

"I saw the pictures, you know. Saw what that disgusting man did to you. What you LET HIM do to you. I can forgive you. You're forgiven. Please, baby, come back to me."

When my silence became too much for him, he lost all pretense of the man I'd known. Ribbons of gasoline sprayed across the floor and walls. Women screamed, fleeing with nowhere to go. A lighter clicked open and closed in his hand. He'd called me every variation of the word *whore*, bloodshot eyes full of desperate madness and colossal grief.

Paul *had* loved me. Maybe too much, past truth to blindness and deceit. Had I loved him the same? Blindly? It would explain why I never saw the monster under his skin. *Did I ever know him, or did I love who I wanted him to be?*

I'll never know the defining moment in which Rudy brought Paul's monster to light, succeeding with him where he failed with me. Was it because of our childhoods? Mine, unconventional but full of love; his, rigid, with a blurred line between love and power?

Is anything that simple?

No.

I'll never know the catalysts that made Paul who he is—or rather, revealed who he's always been. But I remember my own. The first was the day of Paul's death. Not the bomb, but after, when I looked into the eyes of evil and said, "Fuck you."

I broke that day, down to the foundation, and healed wrongly. Became a malformed woman. Puppet-like, put together with frayed thread, and an empty cavity where my heart should have been. I remember the other moments, too. Even greater, brighter catalysts. Memory-beads like stars strung together on my timeline, almost identical, yet each singular in intensity.

Dominic.

He ripped my threads. Pulled me apart, opened me up. Broke me back down to my baseline. He destroyed that puppet-woman with his tender savagery, giving me the space to put myself back together again. Like re-breaking a malformed limb, my pain only healed with more pain.

I know who I am.

They can't break me. Not Rudy. Not Paul. Not whoever buys me. *No one.*

My pain belongs to Dominic.

AFTER WEEKS IN THE WAREHOUSE, being clean is an alien sensation. My skin itches from recent scrubbing, waxing, and oiling, the process administered by silent young women with downcast eyes. They've been where I am, or haven't but know what it means. Either way, I don't ask for their stories. Let them tell their own.

Over the next hours, visitors arrive at the small motel room, entering after being searched by two armed guards. All women, all silent and unsmiling. A stylist who conditions my hair, trims it, then blowdries and curls it. An older woman, gray-haired and severe, who rips my towel off and takes my measurements with a tape and cold hands. Another, younger, with a spark still in her eyes, who gives me a manicure and pedicure and *tsks* over the state of my cracked nails. She's the only one who speaks, saying she'll be back to do my makeup tomorrow. But she doesn't look at me when she says it and leaves immediately after.

Go easily, Rudy said. Or my family will suffer. I know the threat for truth. He'll kill them all.

So I didn't fight the blindfold, the long trip in the trunk of a car. And I'm not fighting now, secluded in a dingy motel in God-knows-where, with the curtains drawn and the rooms to either side occupied by Rudy's men. Wherever this is, I have no illusions that a scream will bring help running.

The calm, quiet space inside me has taken over; my cocoon is thick and hard. Even when there's a brisk knock and a guard opens the door on a familiar face, I stay comfortably numb.

Sitting in sweatpants and a sweatshirt on the edge of one of the twin beds, I stare at my husband as he walks inside and orders the guards to leave. They obey without hesitation. The door closes, the deadbolt sliding home.

"London."

I turn away. Stare at the bathroom door. His footsteps approach and the bed dips as he sits. Close enough to touch—a million miles and a lifetime away. Of all the errant thoughts in my head, one alone threatens my cocoon. Hits me with sensory memory so hard I almost crack.

He smells the same.

Then he speaks, and I remember his betrayal.

"Please, baby, will you talk to me? I'm sorry about before, about scaring you and the other women. I would never hurt you, I was just out of my mind. I'm sorry about everything. I—"

"Save it, Paul. I don't care."

A thick pause, then he whispers, "What happened to you? Is it that man? Do you *love* him?"

My laughter takes us both by surprise. Turning on the bed, I laugh even as tears fill my eyes. I don't feel the attached emotion. No humor or sadness. But the body remembers. I search his face for something I know I won't find, am no longer sure ever existed.

"What happened to *me*? Oh, Paul, I'm sorry for whatever it was—whatever I did—that made you think I'm anything like you. Like Rudy. You're sick, and you're criminals. You deserve to spend the rest of your life behind bars."

He flinches, lips thinning. "That's rich coming from a woman who squashed lives in pursuit of fame. Do you know who had to clean up your mess? Me, London."

Horror vacates the air from my lungs. "You killed the women. Oh my God. Why? How could you do such a thing?"

Standing abruptly, he paces across the room and leans against the wall near the outdated television. Looking at him, I have the oddest sensation of seeing two people, one superimposed over the other. My distorted memory versus reality. Happy husband and hitman.

"They ID'd the wrong man," says Paul-who-used-to-be-Paul. "Sure, the photo you acquired was real. That Supreme Court Justice whose life you torched was a client. But the man they told you about? Someone far more important."

"Rudy?" I guess.

He shakes his head. "Rudy's not stupid enough to have contact with the girls."

"Reznikov."

Paul smiles grimly. "Three whores weren't worth the bullets to protect Donalds, but Reznikov was a different story. If he was implicated or arrested, it would have caused a power vacuum and set Rudy back years."

I can barely frame the words, "But why you?"

He snorts. "Do you really have to ask? Your story put you in direct opposition to New York's most powerful politician and mob boss. *That's* why I freaked out when you told me. I knew the shit was about to hit the fan. Rudy gave me a choice—kill you or them." He shrugs. "So I killed them."

Disgust coats my tongue. "What did he do to you, Paul? Did he threaten you? Blackmail you? When did you become a part of this... this... *evil?*"

He sighs, gaze lifting to the cracked paint on the ceiling. "You'd love to know, wouldn't you? My answer-seeker. Always picking, poking, taking things that don't belong to you." His eyes drop to mine. "He told me, you know. About the abortion."

47

I CLOSE MY EYES. Sink as deep as I can into myself, guarding against the poison of his words. Of course Rudy would have found out, used it as a weapon.

"You were dead." I open my eyes, knowing I owe him that much—the truth spoken eye-to-eye. "It wasn't a choice I made lightly, but you were gone and my career was over. My life blew up with that car. Rudy all but admitted to killing you—"

Paul lurches forward, dropping to his knees before the bed and grabbing my hands. Achingly familiar hazel eyes brim with feeling. Desperation. Twisted love. Shaken, I rip my hands away.

He sits back on his heels. Desperation shifts to hopelessness in his eyes. "I'm sorry for everything you went through. I know it's been difficult."

"Bullshit. You have no earthly idea what the last two years were like for me. My husband and career were stripped from me in a matter of months. I went bankrupt and had to sell the house. My reputation was torched. Rudy threatened to kill more people if I didn't leave town and never speak of what happened. *Why*, Paul?"

His hands lift, eyes beseeching and showing white. "Jesus, London. I didn't know any of that. I..." He swallows, looking away.

I snort caustically. "Because you were in a cell for two years? More bullshit."

"I was overseas," he admits, voice hollow and thick. "First Mexico, then Germany for a while, and finally France."

"Doing what?" I snap.

He shakes his head, eyes returning to me and showing me his deep shame. "Rudy gave me updates on you every few weeks. He never said... I thought moving was your choice. He promised he would tell you the truth—that I was alive and waiting for you. But it never seemed to be the right time."

His jaw works, teeth grinding, fingers clenching and unclenching. The evidence of his internal struggle shouldn't amuse me, but it does. At least in the way a condemned person might laugh at the noose. This isn't going to end well for either of us.

Paul murmurs, "It was all to keep you safe. I was always going to come back for you."

Another laugh emerges, scraping like broken glass in my throat. "For what, exactly? According to Rudy, his plan for me extended all the way to the fucking White House. What role he intended for me, I have no idea, but you can do the math. No way does that add up to you and I living it up in the South of France, selling women for profit. Which by the way, I would *never fucking do*."

"I know that. Of course I know that! We wouldn't work in that part of the business. He has other enterprises, non-violent ones. Laundering. Diamonds. We would be *free*, London. We could start the family we always talked about—"

I see red. "Shut up! Just shut up! Even if any of that were true—which it isn't—I would never go with you. You're a murderer!"

Paul frowns, head shaking. "But I did it for you. To save you. Rudy said..." He trails off, eyes going distant.

Poor, misguided Paul. His parents never taught him how to stand on his own, so cleaving to Rudy's guidance was second nature. He never stood a chance.

Dominic's voice whispers in my mind. Words spoken when I expressed bafflement over Rudy's desire for me to join him. What role I could possibly fill.

His daughter, London. His heir.

And I know, suddenly and fully, that Rudy doesn't intend for Paul to live past his usefulness, and his usefulness begins and ends with his ability to sway me. Staring at my sad, confused husband, I wonder if he knows this is his last chance. I wonder if the guards have been instructed to kill him if he leaves this room having failed. Which he will.

Can I live with his blood on my hands? I think of Felix, my sweet dog, and those three young women lying in the morgue. All the pain I've endured because of his cowardice, his moral ambiguity, his inability to recognize evil in himself and others.

Yes, I can live with it.

But I'd like a few answers first.

"You did something, didn't you? Something Rudy has proof of. That's how he trapped you."

Paul recoils to standing, gaze fluctuating wildly as he takes several steps back. "Yes. It was a mistake. A stupid mistake anyone could have made." He drags hands through his hair, clenching the strands. "Friendly fire during a raid five years ago. I killed someone. I would have owned up to it, but Rudy convinced me not to. He said it would ruin my career and yours by proxy. He buried the evidence."

Another omission, another wedge orchestrated by Rudy. "You used to want to help people," I say faintly. "Make the world a better place."

His gaze lifts, and I see it in his eyes—the realization his time is up. Only instead of the knowledge fueling a fight, he radiates defeat.

"I learned the hard way the world isn't worth saving. I'm only sorry I couldn't save you. I know it doesn't matter now, but I loved you, London."

He turns toward the door. I'm on my feet without thinking, rushing across the room to grab his arm.

"Wait! He's going to kill you, Paul! You have to know that."

Features softening, he covers my hand with his. "It's nice to know some part of you still cares."

I dig my fingernails into his arm, resisting a scream of frustration. "It's never too late to make things right. We can get out of here. We can—"

He laughs, pained and soft. "We all make choices. The day I said yes to Rudy for the first time, I ruined both of our lives, didn't I? I see that now. It's past time I paid for that choice."

"This is crazy! What the fuck is wrong with you? Don't you want to live?"

"This isn't a life. Or if it is, it's built on lies, ones I

believed and ones I told myself. I was always disposable, wasn't I? Some part of me knew it that first night I brought you to his house, but I ignored the instinct that the way he looked at you wasn't right. I ignored a lot of things. But I've had time to think."

"Five fucking minutes?" I snap.

He smiles sadly. "Maybe Rudy's fascination is for the same reason I followed you around our freshman year at NYU. The corrupt are drawn to goodness, even when they don't want to be. And no matter what you've thought of yourself, you've always been good. I'm sorry I wasn't the man I wanted to be for you."

A fist pounds on the door. "Time's up, Romeo!"

I recognize the voice. *Cinder.* He delivered me to the room earlier, then disappeared, leaving minions behind. Now he's back—which can only mean one thing.

"Don't be stupid," I hiss at Paul, who stares back at me with empty eyes. "There's a window in the bathroom—"

His fingers gently press my lips closed. "Remember none of this is your fault. Remember I loved you, and it was the great gift of my life to be loved by you in return. Do whatever you have to do to escape. I'm sorry I can't help you."

I slap his hand away. "For fuck's sake—"

A key rattles in the door. Paul shoves me back toward the bed as the deadbolt flips.

It happens fast.

Cinder appears, beady eyes finding me before shifting to Paul. He grabs Paul's arm and yanks him out of the room.

"Bring the bitch," he snarls.

Two more guards appear, closing in on me and seizing my arms. They pull me outside, across a parking lot with buckled, faded asphalt, and into the orange glow cast by a single light pole. Cinder and Paul wait there—the former standing, the latter kneeling with his head bowed.

Wherever we are, it's not Los Angeles. The air is cold and dry. Trees hug the dark skyline, blocking any hint of nearby cities or towns. Behind us, the motel is a sagging, tired beast. Single-story, with rotting siding and only a memory of paint. Long abandoned. Forgotten as surely as the many broken dolls who've passed through it.

"Closer," snaps Cinder.

When I see the gleam of a gun, I plant my heels and am dragged the rest of the way. I thrash backward, my efforts rewarded with a hard kick to the back of one knee. I collapse facing Paul, the uneven ground biting through my thin sweatpants. He lifts his head. Our eyes meet.

Cinder presses the gun to Paul's temple.

"God. Please, no."

My words are lost in the gunshot.

48

WAITING in the motel room are the same two women who washed me the first time. Their touch is gentle as they undress me and help me into the bathtub.

Using the detachable shower head and lavender-scented soap, they wash away blood and bits of my husband's brain.

It takes a while.

49

I DREAM of searching a dark house for Dominic. I have pain to give him. So much pain. But on the threshold of the final, empty room, I remember he's gone.

The grief I haven't allowed myself to feel rages like a hurricane outside thin walls. Shingles snap like twigs. Windows and doors rattle, then blow open. Lost in the storm, I sink to the floor and weep.

WHEN I WAKE, my eyes are dry and burning.

"MOVE, BLONDIE."

I slip off the backseat of the SUV, lowering one high-heel then the other to the ground. Teetering, I grab the door. A stiff breeze lifts the front of my dress but if I let go of the car, I'll fall. Gritting my teeth, I wait for dizziness to pass.

Cinder spits out a toothpick and sneers.

"Someone's going to be happy tonight. If I didn't think your pussy was poison, I'd have a taste."

His words don't affect me.

When I woke up from the dream, my heart aching like a ghost-limb, I felt some measure of peace. Odd, given the circumstances, but nevertheless real. Maybe this was what Cousin Edith really meant. At a certain point, it's impossible to break any further. And finally, you learn what you're made of.

I don't care what happens to me, only that my family stays safe. That's not to say I'm naïve about what my future holds. I've heard firsthand the horrors visited upon victims of sex trafficking. A blonde, American woman? I'll be lucky if I last the next forty-eight hours.

But I don't care about that, either. My will to live died with Paul. With his brain matter in my hair. Maybe recognizing your own powerlessness is the greatest power of all—it's certainly given me the deepest relief. If I go quietly, no more deaths will be laid at my feet. Maybe I'll meet Dominic on the other side. Maybe not.

It's a nice thought, anyway.

As Cinder walks down the dim alley to a door at the end, two guards take my arms and urge me forward. Their hold is gentle this time, probably due to fear of damaging the merchandise. The thought nearly makes me giggle.

I look up, finding the narrow strip of sky above. Darkness. No moon or stars. Only the barest hint of lights from civilization. They blindfolded me again for the drive here and kept raucous music on so I couldn't hear anything outside. It worked. I still have no idea where we are. The buildings to either side of us are old, industrial, with no distinguishing features. My only other clue is the air—cool and dry. Not cold, as most of the country is by this time of year. We might be somewhere in the Southwest. Arizona?

It doesn't matter.

Fingers snap in front of my face. "Wake up, shlyukha." Cinder chuckles, glancing at one of the guards holding me. "They gave her the good shit, yeh?"

Ah. I remember the small water bottle I was ordered to drink. *Should I be grateful to be drugged?* Probably.

I'm herded inside. Down a hallway. Cement floors, white walls, exposed lightbulbs. The lights swing wildly, oblong shadows kaleidoscoping across the ceiling—or maybe I'm the one swinging. My knees buckle but I'm quickly snatched up.

"When did she eat last?" growls Cinder, pausing a few steps ahead.

"The fuck should I know?" snaps the man to my left.

"Yesterday?" offers the one on my right.

Cinder mutters in Russian. Bad words. I giggle, swaying. A nursery rhyme pops into my head. "Little baby Cinder, jumping on the bed. He fell off and bumped his head. Or no—wait, his bumped his *face*. No one called the doctor cause the doctor was... Huh. What rhymes with face?"

One of my guards chokes on a laugh. Cinder glowers

at him. "Get her in the room. I'll tell boss we need some time."

"He's not gonna like that."

"Yeah, no shit. Just do it, or I tell him you forgot to feed her before giving her the drugs."

There are no more complaints. Cinder disappears around a corner. We follow more slowly, most of my weight supported by the men. What feels like an eternity later, I'm pushed through a door. It slams closed behind me.

"This looks familiar," I tell no one.

Same cement cell with its rusted drain. Same blue desk. I stumble forward and drop into the chair. The only reason my dress doesn't rip is that it's essentially a long strip of ivory silk with a hole for my head. With no underwear or bra, and a thin, gold belt around my waist, I might as well be naked.

The door creaks open. A throat clears. "You look lovely, London."

I don't turn. "Weren't you told I need a few minutes?"

"We don't have a few minutes. Very rich, very powerful men are waiting for you."

I spin in the chair, overcompensating and nearly landing on my ass on the ground. Rudy, dressed impeccably in a tuxedo, frowns in distaste.

I wave it off. "Whatever. You're the one who drugged me. Not to mention you killed my husband—*twice*—killed my lover, blackmailed my friend, have murdered God knows how many people, sell innocent women into slavery—"

"Enough. Get up, London."

I stand on weak knees, gripping the table for support. Rudy watches me, expression pinched. Sober, I might translate the look on his face as something like twisted affection. But now, without the barrier of sobriety or civility, I see it. The flush on his neck. His throat bobbing as he swallows. The blue eyes flickering over my chest, between my legs.

Revulsion shivers up my spine, lodges in my throat. Bile rises but I choke it down. Dominic was wrong—or his first guess was right. Rudy wasn't interested in me being his heir, after all.

I snarl at him. "Are you going to bid on me, you sick fuck?"

All pretense disappears as he steps toward me, curled fists vibrating with fury. "Wouldn't you rather it was me? I'd take care of you, London. Give you whatever you want." His gaze lowers, lifts with new heat. "Children. A family."

I've heard of the term *struck sober* before, but now I know it's real. Everything is prismatically clear, tens of smaller facts crystallizing into a larger picture. An abhorrent one.

"You killed your wife because she was infertile," I gasp out. "You freaked out when I told you Paul and I were going to start a family. That's when everything changed. When you blackmailed Paul. Started destroying our lives. Why? Because in your deranged mind, you thought I might *want* you? You were like a father to me! Not to mention you're twenty years older than me!"

"Age is nothing, London. Our minds are perfect complements. You were—*can still be*—the ideal woman for me. I only wish I'd found you before that spineless meathead did. I should have cleared the way for us a long time ago. Tell me you've never wondered..."

He reaches for me; I recoil against the wall. Sighing, he straightens his bowtie, then his shoulders. Composed, undaunted, unquestionably evil, he smiles warmly.

"Sentimentality has always been my largest defect. As such, I'm willing to offer one last time." He extends his hand. "I'll give you a life beyond your wildest dreams, London."

I pretend to consider it, watch his expression shift to hesitant relief.

"I'll take door number two, asshole."

51

DOOR NUMBER two leads to a black box with three walls, the third composed of dark, reflective glass. Rudy's grip pinches my elbow as he forces me up a few steps onto a platform lit by glaring overhead lights. The similarities—and profound differences—to Crossroad's Epicenter aren't lost on me. There, I found redemption, goodness, and peace. Despite being elevated, here I'm lower. Closer to Hell.

Cinder enters behind us and guards the door. For what purpose, I don't know—the drugs have reasserted control over my body. I'm woozy, docile. My heels are like stilts. If Rudy lets go of my arm, I'll go splat. Which actually sounds nice. The floor is stable. Likely cool to the touch, a relief against my flushed skin. But he doesn't let go. If anything, his grip grows progressively tighter, pinching nerves. My pinkie and ring fingers go numb.

"Gentlemen, welcome." Rudy speaks toward the glass, his smile serene, like he's auctioning an artifact not a person. His next words confirm just how fucked up this is. "As this item has special value to me, I wanted to personally present it to you. As you can see, the wait was worthwhile."

There's a small crackle of an intercom coming to life. "The gentleman are pleased. Turn her around for us, Schultz."

Reznikov. No mistaking his oily tenor, the accented vowels.

As Rudy puts pressure on my arm, spinning me, I wave a middle finger at the glass. "Fuck you, Ivan!" I sing loudly.

There's an eruption of voices behind the glass before the intercom snaps off.

Rudy shakes my arm. "You stupid woman. One more prank like that and there will be consequences. Do I need to remind you what those are?"

My family.

"No," I grind out.

Cinder speaks around a toothpick, "Want me to get a gag?"

The intercom crackles back on. Reznikov—sounding

about as happy as a chain-smoking asthmatic—snaps, "Bidding has commenced at four hundred thousand. Get the dress off."

The careless command makes my stomach buck with violation. Gritting my teeth, I imagine myself far, far away as Rudy tugs the belt free from my waist and lifts the silk over my head. With my back still to the glass, Cinder gets the first, unobstructed view of me. His gaze devours my exposed breasts and the apex of my thighs. Grinning at me, he licks his lips and grabs his crotch.

Swallowing an upsurge of bile, I imagine a knife in my hand. I *feel* the knife sliding deeply across his throat. The fantasy is visceral, effortless. I want to *end* him. For the pain he's caused, for murdering Paul, for his rotten soul. The fantasy helps a little, especially when my hard stare unnerves him and he looks away.

Rudy—equally if not more so deserving of a painful death—yanks me around to face the glass, his charming mask back in place. "Here we are, gentlemen. A beautiful specimen, isn't she? Perfect skin, which I happen to know heals incredibly fast. All natural breasts and face. Only two sexual partners in her life. Do I hear five hundred thousand?"

A flicker of green draws my gaze upward. Above the glass is a row of small bulbs, unnoticed until now. They flash as Rudy speaks. Six bulbs total, blaring in answer to my rising price tag.

"Seven-hundred…"

"Nine-hundred…"

"One point two million from gentleman number four. Do I hear one point three?"

I stare at the dark bulbs, riveted and unbreathing. Cold sweat breaks out on my body. *This is it.*

The intercom crackles. "Auction is closed," barks Reznikov. "Our esteemed gentleman number six has bid five million with no counteroffers."

Shock ripples through me. Rudy's fingers slacken on my arm. From the corner of my eye, I watch his mouth drop open on a silent gasp. I want to laugh at his surprise. Sob. Scream. Fight.

Now that it's too late, I want to live.

Rudy recovers from his surprise, nodding at Cinder before releasing me and stepping off the platform. He strides to the wall and picks up a mounted telephone. His voice is muffled, the hum of shock crowding my ears.

"Countdown begins," taunts Cinder behind me. "Please your master and you might live a while."

I don't respond—my only power over him, this situation. Rudy replaces the handset and nods at the glass. A light flips on inside the other room. A row of empty chairs. Two people left. A lecherous, gloating Reznikov and my buyer. Tall, with olive skin and dark hair, he stares down at the mob boss with an air of distaste.

For the barest second, a name whispers in my mind. *Dominic.* As impossible as the notion is, my heart hammers with sudden life. Stubborn, illogical heart.

The buyer shakes Reznikov's hand and slowly turns toward the glass. His eyes are light brown, and he stares at me with an odd, detached expression that chills me to my core. He doesn't look at my body, just my face. Unsmiling, he says something to Reznikov and exits the room.

Silk hits my chest. I grab the flimsy gown tossed by Rudy. "Put it on. You're being transported immediately."

"Where?" I whisper. For a moment, our history is wiped clean. I stare at him as the old London would have and regret clouds his eyes.

He looks away first, nodding to Cinder as he strides to the door. "Give her the shot."

I should have fought harder.

Cinder approaches me, a syringe in his hand. I scramble off the platform. He laughs, following. "Please, make it hard. All the more fun for me."

"Don't touch her," says a crisp voice at the door.

My buyer.

He walks into the room, snatches the syringe from Cinder's hand, and throws it on the ground. It crunches under expensive shoes. I don't know who's more surprised—me or Cinder.

"London, come here."

My head swims. Something in his voice is familiar and plucks a chord inside me. I stare at him, frozen and unblinking. Something about him...

"Who are you?" I rasp.

His shakes his head and approaches me. When he's close enough that I can see the flecks of green in his hazel eyes, he whispers, "Play along so we can get the fuck out of here, okay?"

Trembling with the beginnings of relief, I nod.

He helps me dress, which takes approximately five seconds, then bands an arm around my shoulders to guide me from the room. Cinder watches, glaring and suspicious. But five million is five million, and with the transaction confirmed, there's nothing he can do.

And what could he possibly say? That my buyer whispered something to me? That I went with him willingly? That I didn't seem afraid enough?

When we leave the room, two men flank us. Not Reznikov or Rudy's thugs, but clear-eyed career soldiers. Neither of them look at me, their gazes making steady circuits around the wide corridor.

So many questions fill my head, brim sweetly in my mouth. My heart hasn't stopped galloping. I'm afraid to hope—to trust my instinct, which tells me the man beside me is David Cross, and these men work for Titan.

A door slams. There are indistinct shouts behind us, then: "Stop them! They don't leave here alive! David, you mother-fucking traitor—mark my words, you're a dead man!"

Rudy's voice, jagged with rage.

"Looks like they found the hog-tied Russian," says one of the soldiers.

"Time to run," replies the other.

David makes a panicked, gurgling noise and lurches forward. I trip in my heels and stumble, falling hard on my knees. Without a second glance, David shakes off my hand and keeps running, disappearing around a corner. I barely have time to process shock before a soldier snatches me up, throwing me over his shoulder mid-stride.

"Fucking coward," he growls.

The other man grunts in agreement, his gun trained behind us. Two muffled pops precede a thud somewhere behind us. I lift my head and see Cinder crumpling to the ground, blood spraying from his neck.

We round a corner full tilt. Shouts fill the hallway—so many so loud they melt into one stream of chaos. Fresh air rushes over my bare limbs. Through the fall of my hair, I glimpse figures running past us, splitting like a river around our rock. As they flood back the way we came, I see bulletproof vests emblazoned with three yellow letters.

F.B.I.

Gunfire erupts inside the building. Night air surrounds me, tinged with car exhaust and filled with sounds. Running feet. Communication radios. And in the distance, sirens. A *lot* of sirens.

"Here! Over here!" The voice is familiar but thickened by a Bronx accent, which makes no sense. Not that anything makes sense right now.

"You the detective from back East?" asks the soldier, gently maneuvering me down from his shoulder.

"Yes, Josh Simmons. I'm her brother-in-law. Thank you, thank you so much."

"Sure thing. Take care of her, okay?"

"You got it."

My eyes roll back in my head as I'm swung between arms. With everything left in me, I force my eyelids to part. The man pretending to be my brother-in-law smiles down at me, turquoise eyes twinkling.

"Told you I'm good at finding things."

"Dominic?" I rasp.

Liam winks. "Bulletproof, didn't you know?"

I pass out.

52

NAPLES, NEW YORK

"WHEN ARE you going to turn that shit off?"

Paris plops down beside me on the couch, tossing her fuzzy-socked feet on the cluttered coffee table. Under her left heel is a copy of *Mindful Masturbation*, the spine creased, a rainbow of colorful Post-Its flaring from the top.

My gaze drags back to the television, where talking heads are chewing on the most sensational news story of the month. Beneath them, the bar of texts runs with highlights.

:: 6 DEAD, 18 ARRESTED IN THE LARGEST SEX-TRAF-FICKING STING IN NEW MEXICO'S HISTORY :: 36 WOMEN, 1 CHILD RECOVERED FROM ABANDONED BUILDING IN SANTA FE ::: FBI CONFIRM SENATOR RUDOLPH SCHULTZ DEAD AT SCENE OF ILLEGAL HUMAN AUCTION :: PROMINENT NEW YORK BUSINESSMAN IVAN REZNIKOV UNDER ARREST ::

Paris lays her head on my shoulder. "I'm so glad it's finally over."

I nod, staring at the screen but not really hearing or seeing the news anymore. I've watched nothing else for the past weeks. Watched as Rudy's homes in New York and D.C. were raided, learned with the rest of the nation when the FBI uncovered an encrypted computer in a safe.

Were he alive, Rudy would surely die in prison from the evidence stored on that computer. Offshore bank accounts. Dark Web sites and logins for black-market slave auctions. And audio transcriptions of every conversation he ever had with Ivan Reznikov, probably kept in case he needed leverage over the mobster. Now, there's more than enough to put Reznikov away for a long, long time—if he isn't assassinated by his own organization first.

But the most important find on Rudy's computer—at

least to me—was a digital rolodex of his clients. Names. Photographs. Sexual preferences. Transactions. Everything necessary for Rudy to maintain power in DC and New York and more than enough to implode the house of cards.

When the arrests started, Paris insisted on a party. We invited the neighbors and all our parents' wacky friends. Ordered pizza, microwaved popcorn, swigged beer like we were teenagers. Cheered like we were watching the Super Bowl as CNN recapped the upset to the power grid with clips of angry, entitled men being dragged from their homes and businesses.

That was the first night I broke down, sobbing for hours on end. Not because I was sad, or heartbroken, or hopeless about the future. The opposite, really. Because after years of wearing those goddamn cement boots of guilt and shame, they're gone.

I'm free.

Paris held me through that storm of relief and rebirth, and when I was calm she tugged me down the hall to our parents' room. We crawled into their bed like we were four again and afraid of the dark.

I slept for eighteen hours straight and haven't had a nightmare since.

"Don't you think it's weird, though?" I murmur now. "How Rudy died?"

Thanks to my *actual* police detective of a brother-in-law, we learned the details of Rudy's death. One bullet, fired point-blank into his forehead. His last sight would have been his executioner's face.

I know exactly who killed Rudy. What I don't understand is why he hasn't come for me.

Liam had no answers for me on the private flight from New Mexico to New York. For all his Irish charm, the man is a cypher. An expert at manipulation and misdirection. His favorite answer to my questions? *I can neither confirm nor deny.*

I couldn't be mad at him. Not for long, anyway. He played a large role in saving my life—not only tracking me down, but delivering the FBI to my doorstep in the nick of time. He also leased a private plane, brought me clothes, food, water, vitamins... Let me sleep on his shoulder for most of the flight home, then walked me off the plane and straight into my parents' waiting arms.

God bless that Irish prick.

"All that matters is Rudy is dead," Paris says firmly. "He's never going to hurt you or anyone else again."

I nod, thinking of Steph, her sobbing confession and apology over the phone last week. Her reckless gambler of a father owed Reznikov money—a *lot* of money—and she'd been blackmailed into helping pay back the debt.

"You need to focus on healing," continues Paris.

"Are you hungry? You're still skin and bones. Let's make brownies."

I roll my eyes. "Just admit you're the one who wants brownies."

She pats her still-flat belly. "I think this one's a boy. He's hungry all the time."

My dark thoughts evaporate. Grinning, I throw my arms around my sister. "Thank you for being here, taking the time off—"

"Bah, I just needed a vacation."

We laugh, cry a little, then make brownies.

"COME JOIN ME, kiddo. I see you lurking."

Pulling my sweater tight around me, I venture onto the covered porch where my dad sits smoking his after-dinner joint. His wild hair is more white than blond these days, his face wrinkled from sun and a lifetime of laughter and more recently, worry for me.

He lifts the corner of the heavy blanket on his lap. I slip beneath the warmth, tucking my feet under me on the bench, and curl into his side. Patchouli and marijuana wrap around me—the scents so familiar. Infinitely calming and safe.

"Daddy." I sigh, dropping my head against his wool-clad shoulder. "What am I going to do?"

"What do you *want* to do? You want to wait around here for some knight in shining armor to rescue you from yourself?" He snorts. "That doesn't sound like the London I know."

"But—"

"No buts," he says with gruff affection. "God only knows how it happened, but our kids are go-getters. Go on and get, would you?"

The screen door creaks; my mom steps onto the porch. "You have a phone call, London. Christ, it's cold out here. Jimmy, you want your hot toddy out here or inside?"

Leaving my parents to their negotiations, I head to the kitchen. The ancient, wall-mounted phone waits, receiver dangling from its curly cord and swaying against the wall. Rolling my eyes at my mom's refusal to step into the twenty-first century, I grab the phone.

"Hello?"

"I swore I wouldn't interfere, but I can't take it anymore."

I blink. "Liam?"

"Your lovesick idiot is sitting in a hotel room in Syracuse trying to convince himself he doesn't deserve you."

My vision sparkles; my shoulder thuds against the

wall. Hand to my chest, I press against the pressure and pain there. "W-what?"

"It's ridiculous. He's also drinking himself half-to-death. I've told him a thousand times what a selfish asshole he is, but he's stuck on the idea he failed you."

"He didn't," I whisper.

"I know. But if our Dominic has an Achilles heel, it's his savior complex." He pauses. "Got a question?"

"For fuck's sake, Liam! What hotel?"

Liam chuckles and tells me the name, then sobers. "There's something else, too. Another reason for my call. My contact at the FBI says they've ID'd a body found in the woods by that motel. As insane as it sounds, it's, um —I'm not sure how to say this..."

"It's okay. I know who it is. Paul Kirkland."

Thankfully, the words emerge with minimal pain. The sad fact is, I grieved my husband—and everything that wasn't or might have been—two years ago. The Paul I met recently was a stranger with a familiar face. More than that, we were strangers to each other.

"So, erm..." He clears his throat. "I've got nothing to add."

I laugh shortly. "Liam? Thank you. For finding me, alerting the authorities. For being a good friend to Dominic—"

"All right, that's enough, yeah yeah, you're welcome.

And I had help with the heavy lifting. Just go save our boy from himself, okay?"

"Okay."

Smiling, I replace the receiver.

"Was that the Irishman?" asks Paris.

I turn, finding her leaning against the fridge with a pint of ice-cream and a spoon. "Yes. Liam."

"Next time you talk to him, tell him Josh wants a word."

My smile stretches. "Will do. He told me where Dominic is."

"Good." She pauses, eyes narrowed and thoughtful. "Are you ever gonna tell mom and dad about what happened with Paul? Or contact Paul's parents?"

I shake my head. "There's been enough pain, don't you think?"

She pops the spoon in her mouth and speaks around it, "Amen to that. Go get some sleep so you can go get your man."

"So bossy."

She grins. "What are big sisters for?"

53

THE BEAUTY of brokenness is it exists simultaneously with an opportunity to rebuild. To create newness, fight for happiness. To ultimately choose love over fear—which despite best intentions is easier said than done.

The first time I broke, I didn't bother rebuilding. Didn't want to or consider myself worthy or care to fight. Not until Dominic channeled and transformed my pain into something beautiful was I able to conceive of life after the past. He freed me from my darkness.

Time to return the favor.

I'm up before dawn and out of the house by 6:30, headed south on the 390 in my dad's ancient Bronco. As much as I want to drive straight to Syracuse and yell sense into Dominic, I woke up knowing I needed to make a detour first. Partly for him, but mostly for me.

Five-and-a-half hours later, I hand over my purse at the security checkpoint in the headquarters of Titan Securities in Fairfax, Virginia. When I'm cleared, I approach the sleek chrome counter. A polished older woman with a headset asks if I have an appointment.

"No, but I'd like to see David Cross, please."

Her lips quirk downward. "Mr. Cross has no available appointments today." She says it in a way that clearly implies *or tomorrow, or ever.*

Too bad for her, I was born stubborn. "I understand he's a busy man, but will you call him and tell him London Limerick is here to see him?"

"I'm sorry, ma'am, but—"

"It's all right, June," says a woman behind me. "I'll take care of this. Ms. Limerick?"

I immediately know who it is. Who it *has* to be. Why else would the cool female voice drip with contempt thinly veiled by politeness? Who else would recognize my name and be compelled to *take care of it.*

Ashley Cross is beautiful—perfectly manicured, highlighted, and dressed—but I expected as much. None of that means anything, because with one look I see the ugliness inside her.

She doesn't offer a hand. *Shocking.*

"I can see you know who I am, Ms. Limerick."

I nod. "Yes, hello. Is your husband available? I'd like a few words."

Ashley smiles cooly. "Absolutely not."

I frown. "I'm sorry? I'd like to thank him—"

"What about the word '*No*' do you not understand?" She sniffs delicately. "You must be a terrible submissive."

Calm radiates through me. Two steps forward brings me nearly nose-to-nose with Ashley. She doesn't back down, but bullies rarely do. Not until someone makes them. She's an inch taller, but I'm a thousand times the woman she is.

"Take me to David, or I talk to the press today." Comprehension flashes in her eyes, followed by fear. "Clearly you've heard about your husband's less-than-courageous performance in New Mexico."

"*Shut up,*" she snarls.

"Mrs. Cross, is everything all right?" calls June.

She glares over my shoulder. "Tell David he has a VIP visitor coming up right now. Quit staring and do what I say."

June snatches up a phone.

I FOLLOW Ashley's clicking stilettos and swaying blonde hair into a private elevator. The doors close behind us; she inserts a key, punches the top floor, and we begin to rise. Standing on opposite sides of the compartment, we watch the ticking lights over the doors and ignore each other. The silence is a blessing; I have nothing to say to her. Nothing positive, anyway, and I've had enough negativity to last me a lifetime.

Halfway up, my luck runs out.

"You almost got Dominic killed, you know. He spent four days in the ICU after those men attacked him. The family was distraught."

I bite my tongue on asking why she cares—and why she's lying. After blowing up his phone every day for a week, Liam finally told me what happened to Dominic. Three bullets hit the tactical vest he slapped on after I went down the fire escape, and the final bullet grazed his bicep. He spent a total of three hours in the hospital and six at the police precinct explaining why the loft was full of bullet holes.

Liam was baffled by the lack of bodies. I wasn't. Leaders make hard choices, weigh odds and risks, and *good* leaders choose the option with the lowest body count. But I also know Dominic is beating himself up for the choice to let those men go. Even though he couldn't have known I'd been captured, and might not have been able to stop all six men *and* find me before I was drugged and driven away.

What if are small words with crippling power. All too well, I understand the pain they bring to the heart and mind. The only cure I've found for regret is acceptance and, eventually, forgiveness. I'm not quite at the second one yet. Maybe someday. Maybe never. But I can give both to Dominic, at least until he can give them to himself.

Meeting Ashley's frigid stare, I concede to the part of her statement that's true. "I did put his life in danger, but I never wanted to involve him or anyone else."

Her eyes—a darker green than mine—narrow accusingly. "Then why did you?"

I wonder what bothers her more—that Dominic put himself at risk for me, or that she doesn't have control over his life anymore. Or maybe, just maybe, she carries her own demons of regret. The thought triggers a modicum of empathy. Enough to keep me from sinking to her level.

"Because he insisted on loving me and supporting me through it," I answer honestly. "Because he's a brave, humble, generous man who asked me to trust him. Because I love him, Ashley. *All* parts of him."

Her lip curls. "Then you're as sick as he is."

I shrug. "If that's what you think, I feel sorry for you."

In my unflinching gaze, I let her see what I won't say —we both know who landed the better brother.

As long as he lets me back in.

I shove the thought away. One problem at a time.

The elevator dings as it stops, the doors opening on a penthouse full of sprawling offices. With a sniff, Ashley strides out. I follow a few feet behind, looking around and trying to imagine Dominic here in a suit and tie with a phone at his ear. Maybe when we first met, but I can't envision it now.

We finally reach the corner office. The biggest, of course. David—a slimmer, oilier version of his brother— stands from behind his desk with an expression of forced welcome. He's handsome, I'll give him that, but he lacks the raw masculinity and magnetism of his brother. A used-car salesmen to Dominic's tycoon.

"London, what an unexpected surprise. Darling, would you get us some coffee? Or, London, would you rather something else? Tea? A cocktail?"

As he's rambling, Ashley leaves the office and slams the door behind her. David and I stare at each other for a beat. His neck turns red, then his face.

"I apologize for my wife. It's been a trying few months with... everything."

I walk toward the massive desk he's hiding behind, taking a seat in one of two club chairs. "Honestly, David,

I don't give a shit about Ashley. I'm here because I want to know why you were at the auction."

He smooths his tie and sits, avoiding my gaze. "I'm not sure what you mean. Dominic is my brother—of course I wanted to help him."

I shake my head. "Knowing your history, that's doubtful but also beside the point. Rudolph Schultz kept tabs on me for months before he had me kidnapped. He knew exactly who Dominic was to me. Why on earth would he allow you—his *brother*—to be one of the bidders?"

David stiffens. "How should I know? My brother and I had a very public falling out and it was common knowledge we hadn't spoken in years. I worked hard to convince Schultz of my interest, played up the bitter-sibling angle. I can only assume he was willing to take the risk based on my performance, and of course, the promise of my bank account."

I smile benignly. In my former career, my colleagues knew this expression well. It meant I was about to spring my trap.

"Is that the story you shipped the FBI to keep them off your back? Because we both know it's bullshit."

David glances at the office door. "I think we're done here."

Still relaxed and smiling, I tap my chin thoughtfully.

"You know what I think, David? I think it was in your best interests to make sure Schultz didn't leave that auction alive, and that's why you helped Dominic. Because you knew it was your only way to stay out of a prison cell."

He scoffs. "I don't know what you're talking about."

"Don't you? Your name was on Rudy's computer, wasn't it?"

He jabs a button on his desk. "Security to my office. Now."

I stand, laying my palms flat on his desk. In another life, I'd never have the balls to do this. But I'm changed. I know what I'm made of now. And I don't give a shit how powerful this man thinks he is—I have more.

"Don't you want to know how I figured it out?"

He doesn't say anything, fingers clenched on the desk, brow furrowed in disdain.

"I spent a lot of time with Rudy Schultz. Despite the vileness he hid from me, I knew him, knew every nuance of his personality and voice. And that's how I know he knew you. The way he said your name at the end. *How he called you a traitor.*"

"Bullshit."

I shrug. "Sure, my opinion wouldn't hold up in court, but you know what will? Proof you had someone at Titan hack into Rudy's computer and delete evidence of your involvement in the sex-trafficking ring. How confident are you that your guy didn't leave any trace?"

His pale face tells me I've hit the nail on the head. A fist slams the intercom button so hard the panel beneath it cracks. "Security, if you're not here in ten seconds, you're fired!"

I lift my hands placatingly and back toward the door. "I'm leaving. Just one more thing—I have a few contacts left in mainstream media. If I ever see you darken Dominic's doorstep asking for his help, or hear even a whisper of you or your darling wife badmouthing him, I'll point the F.B.I. in your direction. And don't think I've forgotten what happened in that warehouse, how you dumped me to save yourself. I have a lot of experience with smear campaigns, David. Let's see how long you stay at Titan's helm after I'm done with you."

He stands, jaw rigid and lips pinched white. There's dark, violent rage in his eyes. "Are you sure you want to threaten me, Ms. Limerick?"

He doesn't scare me in the least.

My smile is slight and saccharine. "Is that what I'm doing?"

A voice behind me says, "Sounded more like a promise, little brother."

The world pauses. Restarts.

I spin on my heels.

Dominic.

He stands in the doorway flanked by two men. I recognize them immediately as the soldiers who saved my life. The taller one—who carried me out of the warehouse on his shoulders—winks at me, then turns his attention to David.

"This woman bothering you?"

The other soldier discreetly rolls his eyes.

David blusters, "Took you long enough! Escort her from the premises immediately. Why the fuck are *you* here, Dominic? Is this.. is she here because of you?"

"Nope. London does whatever she wants. I merely watch in awe." Dominic's gaze shifts to me, full of warmth and pride. "Any chance I can get a ride back to New York?"

Blinking back tears, I nod.

54

DOMINIC and I don't speak much as he follows me to the Bronco. The space between us is crowded, thick with too many words, the absence of words, the electricity before a lightning strike.

He settles in the passenger seat without asking. Like it's the most natural thing in the world for us to be here, now. Like I haven't not seen his face in months, like an ocean of pain hasn't drifted between us, secrets kept and confessions unmade. So close, so far away, he watches me as I put the car in gear and head back to New York.

A thousand times, I open my mouth and close it, lightning on my tongue seeking air. I want our world to crack with it.

I want to understand.

Eventually, what comes out is, "How do those men stand working for your brother?"

His gaze shifts from the passing scenery. Not to my face but to the dash, where there's a smorgasbord of jam-band stickers. Most are faded with age and peeling—Phish, Grateful Dead, Rolling Stones...

"I'd like to think it's partly out of loyalty to me," he says at length, "but more likely it's because being personal security to my brother pays extremely well."

His voice. His *voice.* It thickens the air in my lungs, drips down my spine and finally curls, feline-like, around my heart.

The truth hits me—he's *here.* Safe. Alive. And I'm never letting him out of my sight again.

"Eyes on the road, kitten." Humor. Darkness.

"*Dominic.*" My whisper is *need* and *longing* wrapped in half-healed grief.

"I know. I'd touch you if I didn't think you'd crash the car."

I sniffle-laugh, my fingers twitching on the wheel. "Still the arrogant ass I know and love."

I expect laughter, or a quip, or anything besides the silence that greets me. When I glance across at him, he's staring out the window. Furrowed brow. Tight lips.

Seconds from freaking out, I remember Liam's words: *He's stuck on the idea he failed you.*

The storm of fear and uncertainty passes. He's here, and he's mine. I'll help him get past whatever's holding him back. Just like he saved me, I'll save him.

"Want to meet my parents?" I ask lightly.

Silence reigns for another few moments, but I can sense his barriers shifting, melting.

"I'd love to," he says.

NO WORDS WOULD HAVE PREPARED Dominic for the full impact of my family, so I didn't bother with any. I merely led him onto the porch, waited for the front door to swing open, and stood back, grinning, as he was engulfed in a three-way Limerick sandwich. Paris, at least, had the manners to hug him briefly. My parents didn't let him go for a good five minutes, and then only to drag him to the living room.

An hour later, we're finally left alone. The coffee table is littered with random appetizers and drinks no one touched but that Paris kept bringing out like clockwork every fifteen minutes. Dominic hasn't moved from his position in the center of the couch. He looks a bit shellshocked and... lighter.

"Want to go for a walk?"

He jumps to his feet. "Fresh air sounds great."

I chuckle, leading him into the foyer for our discarded coats. "Told you they were a riot."

Dominic smiles in agreement, eyes sparkling. Without asking, I reach up and pull a thick beanie onto his head. His lips part in surprise, gaze scanning my features. Like he finally sees me. Finally believes this is real.

"You're okay." His voice cracks.

Eyes stinging with tears, I trace his jaw with my fingertips. "Fine, thanks to you."

He swallows, the spark in his eyes dimming, barriers going up. I tap the end of his nose, then wrap one of my dad's scarves around his neck. He watches me unmoving. Barely breathing. So beautiful. So afraid.

It's hard, but I don't smile.

"Come on."

I grab his hand and tug him outside. The late afternoon sky is a washed-out denim, the air frigid. A line of clouds sits to the north.

"Supposed to snow later tonight," I remark as we head down the front walk to the street.

"Is that right?" Teasing tone.

"Yep. Might be snowed-in tomorrow."

"Hmm."

"How's the club doing?"

"No clue."

"When are you heading back to L.A.?"

His fingers twitch in mine. "That depends."

Glancing at him, I bite my lip on another smile. "On what?"

Dominic tugs me to a stop. His eyes—hesitant, conflicted—scan my face.

"London, I... *Fuck.* I don't know how to do this."

"It's okay." I step forward, nestling my head beneath his chin. When he doesn't move, I grab his arms and pull them around me. "Hug, please."

A pained laugh warms the top of my head. "There's something you need to know, but I'm terrified it will change everything. That you won't want to be with me anymore."

"Do you have a secret family?"

"*What?* No."

"Another submissive?"

He growls. "Kitten—"

"Then we're good." I lift my head, find his eyes. "I'll start. I'm still mad at you for that stunt at the club, mainly because I thought they'd killed you."

"I shouldn't have left you," he rasps. "Once again, I made the wrong call—"

I grab his coat and give him a shake. "Oh, shut up,

Dominic. You're human. You did what you thought was right. And you *made* it right in the end."

"I killed Shultz." The words come fast, breathy.

Careful to convey only acceptance, I nod. "I know."

"I wanted to kill them all."

My heavy exhale fogs the air between us. "I know. It's okay. Thank you, Dominic. Thank you for ridding the world of that evil man."

Finally... *finally*... his hands cup my face. They're warm from being in his pockets—searing against my cold cheeks.

"Do you mean that?"

"One-hundred percent."

"What you went through,"—he swallows hard—"I want you to know I'm here, and I'll listen if you want to talk about it. Whatever you need, it's yours."

I think of the body buried outside that shit-hole motel. Of the broken dolls in that warehouse outside Santa Fe, and the women who tended to me before the auction. And I think of the three young women whose lives ended because they dared to tell the truth.

I'm going to tell their story.

My story.

And I don't give a shit if there's an award at the end of it.

I look up at Dominic. "I love you, and I'm going to

tell you everything. But right now, I'm only going to say I missed you more than you'll ever know, and I'm dying for you to kiss me."

Tears well in his eyes. "I love you, London."

I grin. "I know. Now kiss me. *Sir.*"

He does.

EPILOGUE
(SOME YEARS LATER)

Dominic

"AGAIN."

"Sir, we have to get back—"

"Did I say you could speak?"

My palm meets her ass in a deeply rewarding *crack*. Her low moan is the sweetest music. Poetry lives in the bloom of red, the way she wiggles unconsciously, hips jerking up for more. She doesn't have much leeway, roped face-down and spread-eagle to my desk. But that doesn't stop her from trying. Beautiful woman.

I stroke myself base to tip, prolonging my agony and hers, then step between her spread legs to tease her with penetration. She mewls, pushing back despite the pinching of the rope on her wrists. Panting with pain and pleasure. Needing what I can give her. Soaking my tip and the edge of the desk.

"Please, sir."

Hot satisfaction pulses down my spine, makes my balls throb with urgency. "Again," I growl as I push an inch inside. I want nothing more than to drive inside her, thrust into her body. Own her pleasure, her pain, her heart and soul. Just as she owns all of me.

But even sweeter?

Making her wait for it.

Bending over her, I use both hands to stroke her crown, then toss her thick hair to one side. My fingers claim her neck, her shoulders, her arms with firm, possessive sweeps. I press a kiss to the back of her neck, lick a path down her spine. Tease her tight rim with my thumb until she's poised on the edge, then reach beneath her and pinch her clit. And when she's gone—trembling, soaring—I thrust inside.

She explodes, pulling me into her storm, her waves breaking fast and furious on my cock. *Ah, fuck.* If I didn't have the patience of a saint, I'd come from the sheer wonder of her submission. Her absolute trust. The unequaled gift of her transparency.

She is my redemption.

A fist pounds on my office door, followed by a shout. "You're missing my fecking wedding shower!"

London snort-laughs, which feels... interesting. Ignoring the irritating Irishman, I swirl my hips lazily, relishing in her answering gasp. My eyes lift to the wall over the desk, where a series of tasteful black-and-white nudes hang. Nate was the artist, but the ropes on her body? Mine. The stripes on her shoulders? *Mine.* The soft, loving curl of her lips?

All fucking mine.

Liam kicks the door. "Come *on.* We're about to open presents!"

"He's so whipped," whispers London.

I smack her ass, then smooth the sting. She trembles, laughing silently. I grunt at the resulting, vice-like effect and speed up my strokes.

"Unless *you* want to be whipped, kitten, you'll tell the happy groom we'll be right out."

I punctuate my words with hard thrusts. She whimpers, her back flushing with humiliation and helpless desire. Anchoring her hips with my hands, I increase my pace to punishing.

"We're—sorry—Be—right—there!"

"Assholes!" yells Liam. But he's laughing as he walks away.

When I'm sure he's gone, I grab London's hair and

pull her toward me as far as the ropes allow. She chants my name as my thrusts become vicious. Not until her walls seize around me again, until I hear her sweet cry of release, do I allow my orgasm to overtake me.

Wrecked and replete, I collapse onto her back. My lips find her neck and I nip lightly at the salty, damp skin.

"Thank you, sir."

"You're very welcome. Thank *you*."

She sighs happily, fingers wiggling above her head where her wrists are tied together. The diamond on her ring finger glitters. The same diamond one she wore around her neck for years—through her healing and mine, through testifying at Reznikov's trial, through the long months in which she wrote her true-crime novel. Then, through the insanity of her success afterward, and through our joint-venture founding *Road to Hope*, a nonprofit to help law enforcement rescue and rehabilitate victims of sex-trafficking.

She's more than I ever dreamed of. More than I thought I deserved.

"I love you," I whisper.

"I know."

Smug kitten.

I pinch her hip. She laughs.

STAY CONNECTED

www.lmhalloran.com
lm@lmhalloran.com

ACKNOWLEDGMENTS

As always, thank *you*. When I was a little girl, my favorite daydream was imagining life as a published author. You've made my longest, biggest dream come true. Thanks for taking a chance on me.

Massive shout out to my incredible beta readers. You guys rock my world. I can't tell you how much I appreciated your early feedback and enthusiasm for this story.

Rachel C., thank you for recognizing my need to explore as a writer and for your honesty, integrity, and support as I wander forward on this journey.

Celinka, Marika, Katy, Steph—with all the insanity and drama that goes on, I'm so grateful to have a growing tribe of women who focus on positivity and lifting each other up.

To all the bloggers, editors, proofreaders, designers, and readers who work tirelessly for us Indies... you amaze me daily.

This book... *whew*. Not gonna lie, this one was as much of a challenge (*caning! yikes!*) as it was fun and at times emotional. I've never directly grappled with sadism/masochism, a topic I believe shouldn't be dealt with lightly. There's a fine line between dramatization and damaging fabrication. In my research and through interviewing people who are/have been in the BDSM community, I was hugely impressed with how important consent is to the lifestyle. I wanted to be extremely clear about the pillars of Safe, Sane, and Consensual. And I hope I was.

And finally, as always, to my incredible husband—your confidence and encouragement carry me through the worst doubts and lift me higher even on the best of days. I love you.

ALSO BY L.M. HALLORAN

FORBIDDEN ROMANCE

The Dark Before Light

The Fall Before Flight

The Muse

ROCKSTAR ROMANCE

Breaking Giants

Breaking Silence

A PERFECT SONG DUET

First Verse

Last Chorus

SMALL TOWN ROMANCE

Room for Us

Time for Us

DARK ROMANTIC SUSPENSE

Double Vision

Perfect Vision

The Golden Hour

ILLUSIONS DUET

Art of Sin

Sin of Love

BILLIONAIRE ROMANCE

The Reluctant Socialite

The Reluctant Heiress

• • •

URBAN FANTASY
AS LAURA HALL

THE ASCENSION SERIES

Ascension

Reckoning

Unraveling

Rebirth

Tribulation

Revelation

ABOUT THE AUTHOR

When not writing or reading, the author can be found chasing her daughter. Some of her favorite things are puzzles, podcasts, and small dogs that resemble Ewoks.

Home is the Pacific Northwest.

lmhalloran.com

facebook.com/lmhalloran

instagram.com/lm.halloran

tiktok.com/@lmhalloran

pinterest.com/lmhalloranauthor

bookbub.com/authors/l-m-halloran

amazon.com/author/lmhalloran